BY HOPE UNITED

*Margaret Allan titles from
Severn House Large Print*

By Faith Divided
Yesterday's News

BY HOPE UNITED

Margaret Allan

Severn House Large Print
London & New York

This first large print edition published in Great Britain 2004 by
SEVERN HOUSE LARGE PRINT BOOKS LTD of
9-15 High Street, Sutton, Surrey, SM1 1DF.
First world regular print edition published 2003 by
Severn House Publishers, London and New York.
This first large print edition published in the USA 2004 by
SEVERN HOUSE PUBLISHERS INC., of
595 Madison Avenue, New York, NY 10022.

British Library Cataloguing in Publication Data

Allan, Margaret, 1922 -
  By hope united - Large print ed.
  1. Women clergy - England - Yorkshire - Fiction
  2. Large type books
  I.   Title
  823.9'14 [F]

  ISBN 0-7278-7360-1

Except where actual historical events and characters are being described
for the storyline of this novel, all situations in this publication are
fictitious and any resemblance to living persons is purely coincidental.

Printed and bound in Great Britain by
MPG Books Ltd, Bodmin, Cornwall.

*This book is dedicated to the doctors
and nurses at Harrogate District Hospital and
110 King's Road.
Also to the army of friends who gave us
such wonderful support and kindness during
2002.*

One

It was a wonderful day for so early in the year. The sky was so incredibly blue that the long streamers of white left behind by the commuter planes on their way to and from the airport a dozen miles away stood out starkly. Andrea and Bill climbed up from the village via the Monks' Steps, with Lucky pulling on his lead in his eagerness to reach the moor.

'Dave's sheep are all down in the fields close to the farmhouse ready for lambing, so you can give Lucky his freedom,' Andrea said when they reached Abbot's Moor.

They watched as the young red setter bounded away, startling a brace of pheasants, whose raucous cries shattered the still, frosty air. The dog paused momentarily, ears pricked, then wagged his tail and moved on to explore an interesting scent at the base of a huge, oddly shaped rock. Bill took Andrea's hand, holding it tightly as he cast about in his mind for the words he must say to her before they went back to the village far below. It was not going to be easy.

'Isn't it a marvellous morning? It's hard to believe we're still only in February.' Andrea turned her glowing face towards Bill, pushing back a thick strand of silky black hair from her face as she did so.

Bill felt the breath catch in his throat as his eyes absorbed the beauty of her face and figure. Yet it was the loveliness of her spirit and the warmth of her personality which had made him fall in love with her. He ached with an intensity which was hard to control to make Andrea his own, to love and cherish her in public as well as in private. The problem was that Andrea had made it clear she was not ready for that yet. She certainly would not be ready for what he had to say to her this morning, but he would still have to say it.

'I hope it's like this when Mum and Dad come down for Easter,' she said as he was assembling in his mind the words she would not be expecting to hear.

His hold on her hand tightened. 'I need to talk to you about that. I need to do it right now.'

There was a frown creasing the ivory skin above her brilliant blue eyes as her footsteps slowed to a standstill. 'That sounds a bit ominous, Bill. Is there a problem about their visit? I thought we had it all worked out.'

Bill sighed, and rubbed one rusty eyebrow

as he had a habit of doing when perplexed. 'Yes, we did seem to have it all worked out, until I heard from my American agent this morning. It seems they need me over there to do some more work on the book illustrations, and since I'm going over to do that, Miriam's set up some lectures and demos that she thinks will enhance the sales of the book when it comes out.'

'When? When will you have to go?'

Here was the crunch. No good putting it off. 'Quite soon. The middle of March.'

Andrea drew in her breath sharply. 'How long will you be away?'

'Three to four weeks.'

'So you won't be here when—'

'No, I won't be here when your parents come. I'm so sorry, darling.'

Andrea swallowed. 'I suppose the trip will be worth a lot of money to you?'

He nodded. 'To *us*. That's what I wanted to talk to you about. I'd like to make it our wedding trip. Our honeymoon,' he added.

Andrea's eyes widened with dismay, then sparkled with glints of anger. 'You know I can't do that,' she said.

'I don't see why not. You must have some time off due to you. Weren't you talking about having some days off before Easter?'

'When my parents came. To take them out and about a bit.'

'I'd like you to take that time to come to

America with me.'

'I can't! It's too soon.' Her voice was decisive.

'It only means bringing our marriage forward a few months.'

'As I said, it's too soon,' she insisted.

'Why, when we love each other? You do love me, Andrea, don't you?'

'You know I do.' Her voice softened, became warm again as she said that.

'Then why is it too soon for us to be together?'

Andrea hesitated. Bill might not see this her way. 'I mean it could be too soon for the church members. They might not understand.'

In his frustration Bill used the sort of words he did not often utter these days. 'What the hell has it got to do with the church members?'

'I haven't been here long enough yet for them to know what sort of person I really am. Some of them, mostly the older ones, will be shocked at the idea of me marrying again only eight months after Ian died. I could lose their respect.'

'They might be prepared to understand if they knew about—' he began.

'I don't want them to know! I don't want anyone here to know, except you,' she broke in.

'If you won't marry me yet, please come

with me to America, Andrea. At least for part of the time,' he begged. 'We need to have time together away from here.'

Andrea sighed. 'I would really love to do that, Bill, but in a village as small as Nyddbeck if the manse is seen to be empty at the same time as you are away the gossips could have a field day. That wouldn't do my reputation any good.'

Bill shook his head in disbelief. 'This is the year 2000. We are not living with Victorian ideas now,' he argued.

'I can't afford to lose the respect of my church members, or of anyone else in this community. You *must* try to understand that, Bill. Otherwise...'

Bill swallowed his disappointment silently. 'We'll talk about it later, when you've had more time to think about it,' was all he said.

They walked on to catch up with his dog, but their hands were no longer joined. There was space between them and the brightness of the day was suddenly spoiled for both of them.

Of course he should have been expecting Andrea's arguments against going to America with him either before or after their marriage, Bill told himself later in the day as he set up his easel close to the ancient bridge which gave the village of Nyddbeck its name. Concern for the villagers, and for the people who were part of Andrea's other church in the market town of Nyddford, was always going to be Andrea's priority. She had come here to serve those people, and serve them she would, no matter what the cost to her own personal life.

He had known when he asked her to marry him a few weeks ago that it would always be so. What he had not admitted then was his own impatience to be openly sharing her life. He did not want to have to keep his feelings for her a secret; he wanted the whole village to know that he loved Andrea Cameron. He wanted the whole of Nidderdale to know it. He wanted the world to know it, and he wanted Andrea to go to America with him for at least part of his working trip. So far, he had lost the argument, but he would try to talk Andrea round later. In the meantime he must discipline his turbulent thoughts and give all his concentration to starting work on the watercolour he had promised to paint for Andrea to give her parents for their wedding anniversary at Easter.

As she drove out of Nyddbeck and put the car into low gear ready for the long haul up Abbot's Hill, Andrea lifted her eyes for a few seconds to the cross which stood partway up the hill. As she dropped her gaze again to the road ahead, her thoughts went back to Good Friday, when they had walked from

Nyddbeck Church with the large plain wooden cross. They had anchored it securely in the place where all who passed that way would see it and be reminded of what it stood for. The Easter cross on Abbot's Hill was a tradition in this particular Yorkshire dale.

Ben Harper had carried the cross on one of his sturdy shoulders. Dorothy had wanted Ben to hand over this task to one of the younger men in the village, but Ben would not hear of it. 'It's always been done by the most senior male Elder from Nyddbeck Church,' he had pointed out. 'I'm proud to do it, so please don't fuss, my dear.'

Dorothy had been right to worry though, because before the villagers went back to the cross on the hill early on Easter Sunday morning to cover it with the daffodils, jonquils and primroses, which symbolized Easter joy, Ben had suffered a heart attack and was under intensive care in the District Hospital.

Andrea had devoted much of her early-morning prayer time today to ask for Ben's speedy recovery, and that Dorothy should be given the strength to cope with this acute anxiety. It was only a few months since Dorothy's own health had been causing much concern but she had managed to get well in time for her marriage to Ben on New Year's Eve. Since then, they had been so happy together. Now their long-awaited happiness seemed already to be in jeopardy. Because Ben was so ill his son had been informed and was now on his way from America. Dorothy had wanted to drive to the airport to meet Matt Harper today, but she had been persuaded to allow Andrea to do so instead.

As she left the flower-covered cross behind and gathered speed when she reached the wider, straighter road which cut across the acres of moorland known as Abbot's Moor, Andrea was unable to banish her own anxiety about Ben, and about whether they had done the right thing in sending for his son. Matt and his father had been at odds with one another for some years and Dorothy had doubted the wisdom of asking Matt to come back.

On the way across the moor, Andrea drove past Abbot's Fold Farm, where Dorothy Harper had lived during the years of her first marriage to Jacob Bramley. As she slowed down at the road junction which led to the farm, Andrea received a salute on a car horn, and a quick wave, from her friend Julie Craven, who was renting Jacob's Cottage from Dorothy's farmer son David. Julie would be on her way to work at the Health Centre in Nyddford, Andrea guessed. Was she making any progress in her efforts to get closer to David now that she was living in the farm's holiday cottage? It was not the sort of thing you could ask about without sounding intrusive, even though Julie had become quite a close friend during the last few months.

Her friends had been such a blessing to her during her first long desolate weeks here; people like Dorothy and Julie, like Ben Harper and Bill Wyndham. Especially Bill Wyndham. The sight of a huddle of sheep suddenly deciding that the grazing was better on the opposite side of the moorland road brought Andrea's vehicle to a halt. The sheep probably belonged to David Bramley, and the tractor trundling across the moor in the direction of the sheep probably belonged to David too. The dog sitting up front with the driver was probably Tyke. As the thoughts crowded into her mind, the man in the driving seat recognized her car and raised his hand to give her a wave. Tyke barked a friendly greeting.

Andrea smiled as she recalled that only a few months ago David Bramley would not have taken the trouble to acknowledge her. In fact he would most likely have gone out of his way to be rude to her because he resented her presence in Nyddbeck. Now the grin he gave her, as she slowed down the tractor and sent Tyke to round up the straying animals, showed he was glad to see her.

'You're out early this morning, Andrea,' he called.

'I'm on my way to the airport to meet Matt Harper in,' she replied as Tyke moved his parcel of sheep tidily to a safer place.

'I offered to do that, but Ma said I ought to stay here as lambing time is so near. Thanks for helping out,' David said.

'I'm glad to do anything I can to help Dorothy and Ben at such a time,' she told him.

Now David was frowning. He didn't look anything like as handsome when he frowned. Andrea held her breath and waited for what was to come.

'They don't deserve this.' His voice was curt. 'After such a short time together.'

'I know.' Andrea was tempted to say that many people didn't deserve what came to them, but stopped herself in time. David's temperament was volatile. With farming in such a hopeless state and his mother's partner critically ill, the less one said to antagonize him the better.

'Ben's such a good guy. One of the best.' David shook his head, totally at a loss to understand why such things should happen. 'Why? Why him?'

'I don't know, Dave. I wish I did,' was all Andrea could say before she left him and drove on towards the airport.

Once there, she found herself with almost

16

an hour to wait before Matt Harper's flight was due to arrive, so she sought out a relatively quiet place to sit and read through some of the more complicated items which the post had brought to her that morning. It was not easy though to concentrate on the minutes, agendas or reports with all the hustle and bustle going on around her. It was almost impossible to push to the back of her mind her anxiety about what Ben Harper's reaction would be when his son turned up at the hospital. Because Ben had said they were not to send for Matt. He had gone further than that and declared that if Matt went to see him he would have nothing to say to him.

'It was all said years ago, when he decided to take the job in America instead of staying on in the family business with me. So there's nothing more to be said.' These were Ben's final words on the subject.

Dorothy's eyes had met Andrea's as she heard them. Andrea had been shocked by the despair she had seen in them but she had made no comment. Ben was so desperately ill that the family doctor had advised that his only son should be informed. So Dorothy had telephoned Matt and asked him to return to Yorkshire as soon as possible.

It was going to be difficult meeting Matt Harper for the first time this morning and trying to explain, after he had left his job in America and crossed the Atlantic at short notice, that his father was not yet ready to talk to him. Andrea was hoping her heartfelt prayers would help her to handle the situation correctly, and maybe bring the two men back into the close relationship they must once have had.

Because she did not normally wear her collar of office unless engaged in official church duties, Andrea was wearing a bright-blue sweater with her black ski pants and her long, dark hair was hanging loose about her shoulders. So the man whose black eyes were searching the waiting crowd for a man wearing a dark suit and a clerical collar failed to identify her.

Andrea, never having met Matt Harper or seen a photograph of him, was equally un-sure which of the several youngish men who had not so far been claimed by friends or family members could be Ben's son. She had just made up her mind that the smart-suited late-twenties guy who looked a real whizz-kid must be the person she was looking for when a stunning girl who was obviously late for the arrivals dashed up to him and flung her arms about his neck. Soon they had all gone except for the burly, black-haired man who was becoming more and more impatient as he paced back and forth, consulting his watch from time to time. Perhaps this man, who looked rather older than she had anticipated, was Ben Harper's son? He had to be. She took a few swift steps in his direction and spoke to him.

'Are you Matt Harper?'

His frown deepened. 'Yes. Is there a message for me? Someone was supposed to meet me in.'

'They did! I've been here for ages. Only I had no idea what you looked like,' she told him.

He was looking bewildered now. 'Dorothy Bramley told me when she rang that I'd be met by the minister from the church at Nyddford.'

Andrea laughed. 'You were! I am! The minister for Nyddford with Nyddbeck, I mean. My name is Andrea Cameron.' She held out her hand to him.

He took it, hesitantly at first, then his features relaxed and as he smiled at her she began to see the likeness to Ben because it was the same wide grin which instantly brought lightness to the rather stern set of mouth and chin.

'They didn't have ministers like you when I was last in North Yorkshire, Miss Cameron,' he told her, relinquishing her hand with reluctance. His eyes were warm with admiration for Andrea's brilliant blue eyes and creamy skin. When they moved down to take in her slim, shapely figure she moved slightly further away from him.

'It's Mrs Cameron,' she corrected him, 'and it's Dorothy Harper now, not Dorothy Bramley. Perhaps you were not aware of that?'

Plainly, he was startled to hear it. 'No, I certainly was not.' The frown was back to mar his high forehead. 'When did it happen? The marriage I mean.'

'Last New Year's Eve. I married them at Nyddbeck Church.'

'Why?'

The question, and the way it was voiced, took Andrea by surprise. So much so that she took her time about answering. Matt Harper did not sound pleased to hear of his father's marriage to Dorothy, so she must be careful how she handled this. Perhaps a lighthearted touch would help?

'Because that's what I do, marry people if they ask me to.' She smiled as she told him that.

'That wasn't what I meant, and I'm sure you know it wasn't.' His eyes were challenging now but she did not flinch from what had to be said.

'If you meant, why did your father marry Dorothy, I can tell you it was because he loves her. He's loved her for a long time. Perhaps you didn't know that?' Her eyebrows, dark and finely arched, rose as she stared back at him.

'There was no need for him to marry again. He had a housekeeper to run his home even before my mother died.' Matt Harper sounded really put out.

'Perhaps he wanted more than that? Maybe he was lonely, especially after you went to live in America and he didn't have your visits to look forward to?'

'He didn't want my company, even when I was still living in England. When we met, we always seemed to end up arguing.'

'That happens sometimes when father and son are very much alike. It wouldn't mean that your father didn't care about you,' she said quietly.

'There's been very little evidence during the last few years, since Mother died, that Dad gave a toss for me. So I learned to get on with my life without him.'

'Yet you came back as soon as you heard about his illness.' They were walking out into the fresh air of the car park as Andrea voiced that thought.

'I saw it as my duty to come; as what my mother would have wanted me to do. I didn't come for his sake.'

Andrea heard that with a sense of shock. Of course family members ended up at odds with one another over a wide variety of issues but often these were put aside at times of crisis. In the case of Ben's son, this was possibly not going to happen. She sighed deeply as she opened the door of her car and slipped into the driving seat. Matt was not yet aware that his father did not want to see him. How would he react when he did know that? Poor Dorothy was going to find herself caught up in a family feud that would put enormous strain on her. What could she herself do to help in such circumstances? It was difficult to think of anything right now.

'I expect your father will still be glad to see you,' she said in the moment before the car engine sprung to life.

'I wouldn't be too sure about that!' Ben's son spoke so dismissively that Andrea knew it was time to move the conversation on to a safer subject, such as the beauty of the Yorkshire landscape on this early spring day.

Matt Harper kept his gaze glued to the scenery as they left behind the flat land which encompassed the airfield and drove towards the distant craggy hills, through sprawling villages of grey stone dwellings gathered around square-towered churches. Beyond the buildings were large sloping fields surrounded by silvery-grey drystone walls. The sight of these walls had an un-expected effect on Matt. He found himself remembering a time from his childhood when on an expedition to gather conkers which had fallen from the horse chestnut trees one September morning he had found part of a drystone wall which had collapsed sufficiently to allow his father's sheep to escape into the road.

Even at that young age, no more than nine or ten years old, Matt had known how hazardous that could be both for the sheep and for passing motorists. So he had forgotten all about his intention of gathering conkers ready for the playground battles next day and started trying to repair the wall. Having first driven the sheep back into the field, he had been hauling the rough, lichen-covered boulders back into place with a great deal of difficulty when his father had come in search of him.

Clearly, as though it had happened yesterday, Matt was able to recall his father's words. Ben had looked down at his son and scratched his head as he spoke what was in his mind. 'Why the heck didn't you use the phone box to ring your mother and tell her where you were? She's going spare, just about off her rocker, because you didn't come home for your dinner.'

'I didn't have any money for the phone, Dad,' had been his excuse. He was not going to admit he had forgotten all about his dinner in his determination to mend the broken wall.

'Why didn't you come home then and tell us?'

Matt had been puzzled by all this fuss, just

because he was late for his dinner. Not until much later had he remembered the local boy who had gone missing and not yet been found. It was all very simple to him. 'I didn't want the sheep to get out into the road again. They could have been killed, couldn't they, Dad?'

'Aye, you're right there. Well done, lad! We'll make a farmer of you, one day.'

His dad had put an arm about him, well pleased by his thought for the animals. Dad had been a fit young man in those days; no older than he himself was at this time. Now his father was an old man, over sixty and gravely ill after a heart attack. While they had been driving from the airport, his dad could have died without knowing that to be with him quickly Matt had left behind the interview scheduled for today which would have given him an executive-level promotion.

That memory of his father, glowing with pride as he praised his young son for putting the safety of the sheep first above his own needs, seemed to haunt Matt during the journey to Nyddford. What had caused his father's heart attack? Had it been brought on by the present appalling state of the British farming industry? Matt had learned plenty about that from American newspapers and radio stations and had known periods of acute disquiet as he wondered

24

how his father was coping with a situation which seemed to be going from bad to worse. He had known how right he had been himself to leave it all behind and go to work for a huge American company marketing animal feeds. There had been no future for him in Nyddford with the family farming and transport business once he and his father had become so much at odds with each other.

'Not far now.' The voice of the girl who occupied the driving seat brought his wandering thoughts to an abrupt halt. 'The abbey ruins are just ahead of us.'

Had she been talking to him all the way from the airport, while his mind had been so deep in thoughts of the past? If so, she must think him very rude for not answering her.

'I didn't realize we were so close. My thoughts were all over the place. Sorry if I've not been paying attention to what you were saying.'

Andrea smiled. 'I haven't been saying anything. I guessed you'd need some space to get your mind under control before you meet Dorothy.'

'Yes.' He turned his head to take another look at Andrea Cameron. Her eyes were firmly fixed on the road ahead. They were very beautiful eyes, deep blue and serene, set beneath finely arched dark brows. Her skin was ivory, with a pale rose flush on the high cheekbones. Her nose was long and slender, her chin set at a determined angle. 'I'm not looking forward to that. To meeting my father's wife, I mean.'

'Why not? Dorothy is a lovely woman!'

Andrea Cameron was annoyed with him for his prejudice, he guessed then. She was a lovely woman herself. How had she come to take on the life of a rural church minister when she could probably have followed a much more rewarding and higher paid career? Matt pulled his mind away from that subject with some difficulty.

'Marriage to her hasn't done my father much good, has it?' He knew as he uttered the words that he had spoken without sufficient thought. His swift glance into Andrea Cameron's face confirmed that she was annoyed with him.

'Marriage to Dorothy has done Ben a great deal of good. He's happier now than he's been for many years. If you don't believe me, ask him! Though he certainly won't thank you for doubting it enough to *have* to ask.'

Her voice was crisp. She was holding her anger in check, but only just. He would need to be more careful about what he said next.

'I meant to say that getting married at his time of life was probably a mistake.'

26

Matt turned his head again a moment after he had spoken, and knew he had made another blunder. An even worse one than before. It was there to be seen in the way Andrea's chin lifted and her mouth tightened. He could not see the expression in her eyes but he guessed there would be distaste darkening their brilliant blue.

'Your father may be very ill, but he's not senile,' was her response. 'He certainly isn't losing his marbles, if that's what you are implying.'

'I'm not suggesting that,' Matt broke in hastily. 'I was only thinking that in this day and age he didn't need to marry her. Most people don't, do they? They just move in together and share a home for as long as they feel like sharing.'

In the silence that followed he found himself holding his breath as he waited for Andrea's reply. At the top of Abbot's Hill, where the road branched to the right for Nyddford, she slowed the car right down to allow another vehicle to precede them but instead of gathering speed immediately, as Matt expected her to, she turned into a parking bay which provided a wide view of the pale-green and silvery-grey dale and switched off the engine.

'There's something you need to know before you meet Dorothy Harper,' she began quietly. 'Your father *chose* to marry

27

Dorothy because he loved her, and has loved her for a very long time. The reason he did not ask her to go and live with him, for as long as they felt like it, was because he has too much respect for her to think of her in those terms. He would not have asked her to live with him outside of marriage when they were young, because times were very different then. His ways are obviously not your ways, but I hope you'll be able to treat Dorothy with the same respect as your father has done.'

'I can hardly do anything else, since I'll be staying in Ford House for the time being.'

'She'll want to make you welcome for Ben's sake.' Andrea switched on the engine as she spoke, eager now to complete the journey to Ford House.

Dorothy was looking out for their arrival and came down the short flight of steps to greet them. She was dressed in a rose-pink sweater and a navy skirt. Her grey eyes were anxious.

'Will you stay and have coffee, Andrea?' she asked.

Andrea glanced at her watch. 'Thanks, Dorothy, but I really don't have time. I have a meeting with the architect in ten minutes.' She gave the older woman a quick hug, then turned her gaze to Ben's son. 'I hope there's soon better news of your father. He'll be glad to know you are here.'

'I wish I could be as sure of that as you seem to be,' was Matt's morose reply before he reached for his suitcase and strode into the house.

Dorothy sighed. 'It's not going to be easy explaining to him that Ben won't see him. Say a prayer for me please, Andrea,' she begged.

'You know I will, Dorothy. Try not to worry. Things *will* work out for the best. Now I must go and meet the architect and find out just how bad the news is about the condition of Nyddford Church roof.'

'And I'd better go back to my angry young stepson. Perhaps he'll mellow with the years, as his father has done?'

Andrea laughed softly as she slipped into the driving seat. 'That might depend on whether he finds someone like you to share his life with.'

With those words Andrea drove away to meet another man she was not looking forward to meeting.

Two

As she drove back to Nyddbeck later in the day Andrea felt weighed down by the problems which seemed to be crowding in on her. Her head ached so much that she longed to close her eyes and go to sleep just to shut out the pain, but there would not be time for even a quiet half hour with all that she had to do. As so often was the case, a cup of coffee and a sandwich on the hoof would have to suffice. All she could hope for was that there would not be too many messages on her answerphone when she reached Nyddbeck manse. Maybe there would be a message from Bill? If there was, she knew that her tiredness and depression would soon be banished.

Just to think of Bill, as she reached the foot of Abbot's Hill and turned into Beck Lane, made her heart beat faster. Only Bill was not here in the village waiting to welcome her home. Bill was far away, thousands of miles away on the other side of the Atlantic. He had only gone there last week, and would not be back until his project of illustrating a series of books about Yorkshire villages written by an American author had been completed and all his speaking engagements and demonstrations done. So he would be away from Nyddbeck for another three weeks.

How was she going to cope with all the problems that at present appeared to be multiplying in and around Nyddbeck and Nyddford without Bill to lean on? Why had he been taken away from her just when she needed him most? Just when she had become so accustomed to talking things over with him and listening to what he had to say. Bill had hoped she would change her mind and go with him on his American trip, and she had been so tempted to do that. It would have been so wonderful for them to be together in a place where her work did not always have to come first.

She had spent much time fighting this temptation, and praying about it. In the end the vow taken in one of her churches before the people she had come here to serve had won, and she had decided that the good opinion of those people must come first with her. None of those people were aware of what only Bill and she knew about her first marriage. If they had known about that, they might have understood about her and Bill, but she did not want them to know. That part of her life was over, if not yet forgotten, and in the process of being healed by her own strong faith and Bill Wyndham's love for her. Bill was thousands of miles away from her now. Had he come to terms yet with the hurt her decision not to go with him had caused?

As she reached the end of Church Lane, where Bill's home and studio were situated, the sight of her little church, standing on raised ground just above the triangular village green, reminded her of how she was going to cope while Bill was away. She was going to cope in the way she had coped before Bill came into her life, by living for her faith and her service to the people of Nyddford with Nyddbeck. But she was still going to miss Bill's presence here in the village, so close to her own home.

She was going to miss sitting quietly beside Bill while he was painting a picture of one of the Yorkshire Dales villages, or the ruined abbey up on Abbot's Moor, or here in the heart of Nyddbeck where the shining water flowed beneath an ancient packhorse bridge. She was going to miss having Bill cook supper for her, or join her for supper in the manse. She was going to miss sharing his long walks with Lucky...

As soon as she switched off the car engine, she heard Lucky's bark welcoming her home. Poor Lucky must be quite desperate to get out of the house to satisfy his bodily needs, and to chase off some of his boundless energy. Food and drink would have to be postponed until after she had taken him for a walk. Fatigue and lack of food made her hands tremble as she searched for her front-door key, while from inside the manse the barking reached a crescendo.

'I'm coming, Lucky,' she called. Then, as she dropped her keys, she saw the flowers, the dainty basket which held delicate stems of freesias among a bed of ferns and spray carnations. Their perfume enveloped her as she carried them into the hall, guessing who had ordered them to be sent to her via Interflora even before she read the card that was tied to the handle of the basket with satin ribbon. The card was small and held only a few words, but they were the right words. Words which brought a swift rush of emotion to her.

'I miss you so much.'

Then the emotion was banished as Bill's dog hurled himself ecstatically at her, lashing her with his madly waving tail while he leapt up to put both long slender fore-paws on her shoulders so he could manage to lick her cheeks.

'Get down, Lucky! Lie down!' Andrea ordered, choking on her laughter. 'Just because Bill told you to look after me it doesn't mean you have to lick me to death!'

The young red setter surveyed her with laughing eyes, then walked towards the door. Andrea grabbed his lead from the hall table and allowed him to pull her out of the manse garden and in the direction of the riverside footpath which was his favourite walk. As they left the house she heard the telephone begin to ring. Whoever wanted to speak to her would have to leave a message on the answerphone. Right now, Lucky's needs must come first!

Dorothy Harper replaced her telephone with a sigh. She had hoped so much that Andrea would be at home when she returned from her visit to the hospital because she needed to share with her friend and minister the despair she had experienced as she sat at her husband's bedside that day. When, full of doubt and apprehension, she had hesitantly asked Ben if he would like his son to visit him Ben had uttered the single word 'No!' and turned his head away from her. It had been on the tip of her tongue to tell him Matt was already at Ford House, but he looked so terribly frail and ill that she had been afraid to do that.

Instead she had cut short her visit and spent a few quiet minutes in the hospital chapel trying to pull herself together spiritually and strengthen her flagging courage before she went back to Ford House to face Ben's son again. What was she going to do about Ben's son? How was she going to tell him, after his speedy response to her phone call about his father's illness, that Ben refused to see him? It was certain to increase his unspoken hostility towards her. She had known that Ben and his son had not been communicating with one another for some years, but she had hoped Ben's sudden serious illness would bring about their reconciliation. How wrong she had been!

Dorothy had also hoped that Matt Harper would have been pleased that his father had her there in his home to care for him. The reverse appeared to be the case. Matt spoke to her only when strictly necessary and everything about his attitude showed plainly the resentment he felt towards her. Did he resent her presence in Ford House because he could not bear to see anyone taking his mother's place, even though his mother had been dead for many years? Or did he just dislike her for the person she was?

From where she sat, at the large mahogany desk in the small room at Ford House which Ben used as a study, Dorothy could see the framed photograph of herself and Ben which had been taken on their wedding day three months ago. She picked it up and held it close to her, seeking comfort from it. Ben had looked so different today from the man in the wedding photo: the man who looked so much younger than his sixty-five years, and so very proud and happy. Would he ever look like that again? Or were their days of shared joy already gone for ever?

This last thought sent such a shiver down her spine that she forced herself to her feet, lifted her head, straightened her shoulders and told herself she'd feel better when she had made herself a cup of tea. Hospitals always had a depressing effect on her. So she'd have some tea then take Ben's labrador, Goldie, for a walk. She was on her way to the kitchen to set the kettle to boil when it occurred to her that she hadn't seen Goldie since she came back from visiting Ben. A little knot of worry about the absence of the dog pushed away the greater worry about Ben as she looked around in the conservatory, in the utility room, in the front porch and finally in the bedrooms for the animal.

Usually when she came back from the hospital, or from shopping or church, Goldie was there with a welcome for her. Not today though. Today there was neither sight nor sound of the golden labrador. She must look in the garden, though if Goldie had managed to get out there he would have heard the car and come bounding to the garage to welcome her. It was perplexing. When Dorothy had made a thorough search of the extensive flower garden and the vegetable garden, looked into the greenhouse and the garden shed and still found no sign of the dog a new thought came to trouble her. Had Ben's son left one of the doors open and allowed Goldie to wander off on his own? That was when she realized that Matt was nowhere to be seen.

Matt must have gone out while she was at the hospital. Perhaps *he* had gone to the hospital? If he had, and if he suddenly appeared at Ben's bedside, what effect would that have on her beloved Ben? Fear clutched at Dorothy's heart and sent her hurrying back to the house, where she found the kettle steaming away on the Aga but no sign of either her stepson or the dog. She was attempting to hold the mug of hot liquid still enough to drink from it when she heard the outer door into the back hall open, followed by the sound of Goldie barking. A moment later the dog came bounding into the kitchen, followed by Matt.

'Oh, I'm so glad to see you!' she began, slopping the coffee over on to her hand as Goldie barged into her.

Matt looked startled, and in that moment amazingly like Ben. 'Why, is Dad worse?'

'No. They said his condition was unchanged.' Dorothy mopped up the spilled liquid, then asked Matt if he would like some tea or coffee.

'I'd like to know why you were so relieved to see me, first. Then I'd like some coffee.'

Ben's son was very direct, and again in that respect reminded her of his father. No wonder they had been at odds with each other. They were too alike to be able to avoid flare-ups at times, Dorothy realized in the moment before she answered Matt's question.

'It was because of Goldie. When I got back from the hospital and he wasn't here I got into a bit of a panic because I knew if anything had happened to him Ben would be more upset than ever.'

'Didn't it occur to you that I might have taken him out for a walk?'

Dorothy shook her head, feeling foolish now. 'No. I never gave it a thought. I was just so worried that we might have lost him. He's such a dear old dog that to lose him would have been the last straw.' She turned away so that Matt would not be able to see the moisture that had rushed to her eyes. A moment later she was in control of herself again and busy making him a mug of coffee.

'I suppose I ought to have left you a note to say I'd taken Goldie out,' Matt admitted rather grudgingly. 'I just didn't think you'd be so upset.'

'Wouldn't you be upset if you thought something might have happened to him?' Dorothy spoke more sharply than she had intended. 'I mean, with your father being so ill...'

Matt stared down into the mug she had just handed to him. 'I would have been upset for my own sake; because Goldie was my mother's dog. I bought him to keep her company when she became too ill to be able to go out much.'

'Oh, I didn't know that.' Obviously Matt had been very close to his mother, so perhaps that was why he resented her own presence in his old home. At a loss to know what to say to him next, she busied herself preparing Goldie's evening meal.

'When can I go in to see my father, now that I'm here?' Matt asked into the silence which had lasted for too long.

This was the question Dorothy had been dreading, and she was not sure how to answer it. Yet it would have to be answered at once.

'You were going to warn Dad I was here before I went in to see him, weren't you?' Matt reminded her.

Dorothy swallowed, then took a deep breath to relieve the tension that was making her feel slightly dizzy. 'Yes.' She felt for the edge of the table and sat down in one of the Windsor chairs.

'Well? What did he say?'

Dear God, how was she going to answer that? There was only one way. 'He said no.'

She heard the swift intake of Matt's breath, followed by another long moment of silence.

'Bloody hell!' was his explosive comment. 'To think I missed out on my chance of a move up in the company to come dashing over here at once, then the awkward old sod refuses to see me!'

Goldie, alarmed by the violence in Matt's voice, gave vent to a low rumble of protest.

Dorothy, angered by the way Matt had described his father, voiced her own disapproval. 'He's a very sick man, so he won't be acting like a very reasonable man at the moment. You should remember that.'

'How long have you been married to him? Three months? Maybe not long enough to know what an awkward cuss he can be if he doesn't get his own way every time. You'll find that out for yourself in time, if he survives.'

'I've known your father for a lot longer than three months,' she told him very quietly. 'I knew him when I was a young girl, before I married Jacob Bramley. I also know a lot about the behaviour of sick men. My first husband was ill for a long time before he died, and I looked after him at home for most of the time. I'm quite prepared to look after Ben at home, once he's well enough to leave hospital.'

Suddenly Matt's fury seemed to evaporate. He gave a great sigh, then flopped down into the chair on the other side of the table

from Dorothy and looked at her in bewilderment with the dark eyes which were
so much like Ben's. 'What am I going to do
if Dad goes on refusing to see me while I'm
here?'

Dorothy smiled, feeling her own hurt feelings disperse when she recognized the
genuine concern in her stepson's voice.
'You're going to need patience for a few
days, Matt, until Ben comes to his senses.
He's going to have to do that quite soon
because there are problems to do with his
business which he could be glad to have
your help with.'

Matt shook his head. 'He won't allow me
to help there. That's how we came to fall out
with each other in the first place, because
my ideas were so different from his. So
much better than his, only he wouldn't see
it that way.'

'He'll have to see it now. The doctor says
he won't be able to work the way he used to
before the heart attack for quite some time.'

'Who's looking after the business now,
while Dad's in hospital?'

'On the transport side, his foreman, Tom
Bellamy. My son David is doing what he can
to help with the farming side. Ben cut down
on the farming when prices at the auction
fell so badly. He just kept enough stock so
that the buildings were not empty. He said
he couldn't face living on a farm without

41

any animals around him,' Dorothy explained.

'That's what I missed the most when I
took the job in America, working with
animals. While I'm here, I'll take over the
farm and give your son a break. I expect he's
got plenty to do on his own farm, if he's still
in farming.' There was a question in Matt's
eyes as he spoke.

'He is, but he's having a struggle to keep
going. Prices at the auction marts are so
bad, for sheep in particular, that it's almost
impossible to cover costs. It's been touch
and go at Abbot's Fold Farm a couple of
times during the last two years. In fact all
that's kept us going has been renting out the
cottage Jacob built for our retirement, and
doing bed and breakfasts in the farmhouse
sometimes. The money David's wife earned
with her nursing used to help the farm, until
she was killed,' Dorothy finished sadly.

'Your son's wife was *killed*?'

'Yes. Jill was killed one stormy night when
she was going out to visit a patient. A big
tree fell on her car and crushed it.'

'Did she work at the Nyddford Health
Centre?' Matt wanted to know.

'Yes. Jill was a lovely girl, and I was very
fond of her,' Dorothy added.

'My mother was fond of her too. She used
to come here to give her injections. How
awful it must have been for you and your

son,' Matt said quietly.

'David took it very badly. He's still not really over it. He blames himself for what happened.'

'Why should he do that?'

'Because they needed the money that Jill could earn with her nursing so badly once the farm got into difficulties. I've tried and tried to convince David that Jill went back to nursing because she loved it, and believed it was wrong to waste her skills by staying at home once the children went to school, but he still has black moods when he blames himself for the accident.'

'Your life must have been hard in recent years?' Matt sounded concerned about that.

'Yes. David has needed a lot of help in the house, and with the children.' Dorothy paused, then went on. 'Your father wanted me to marry him the year before last. We made plans for our wedding then, but after Jill died we had to postpone them because I was afraid to leave David on his own.'

'Are the children very young then? How does he manage now you are living here?' Matt asked.

'They aren't quite *so* young now. Carla is almost sixteen and Jack's eleven.'

'Not so much of a problem now, I suppose, if they're at senior school...'

'It isn't easy for children of that age to cope with losing their mother so suddenly, especially when their father isn't able to give them sufficient time.'

'But you decided to go ahead and get married anyway?'

Dorothy was unsure how to take that, whether Ben's son was criticizing her, or his father. Or both of them. 'I had been unwell for some time, and Ben wanted to look after me. So he persuaded David to accept help from Mrs Grainger a couple of times a week after we were married and I came to live here.'

'A very convenient arrangement,' was Matt's comment before he went out of the kitchen and up to his room, leaving Dorothy perplexed about exactly what he meant by that remark.

Once upstairs, in the room he had inhabited as a boy, Matt stood at the window looking out over the view he had known for most of his life. There was the flower garden which had been his mother's joy even when she could no longer work in it, then the vegetable plot and the large greenhouse. Beyond that were the few fields where the sheep grazed, enclosed by drystone walls. To the left of the house were the sturdy grey stone farm buildings which now housed the transport vehicles and the farm machinery which his father hired out to other farmers.

Matt sighed as he looked back with regret to the days when it had been his intention to stay here in Nyddford and take over Harper Farm Transport when his father retired. It hadn't worked out like that though because there had been too many clashes over the way Harper Transport was being run. Ben Harper was unwilling to give way to his son's ideas in that direction. So Matt had turned his back on the family business and accepted the offer made to him by his girlfriend's father of a job in his American company.

He had met Susanna while at university, and taken a long vacation with her family while awaiting his degree results. His father had not been pleased with him for staying away from home so long at the busiest time of year for the hiring of farm machinery. This had led to a major clash of wills, with Matt insisting he had earned a long break and his father declaring that he owed some time to the business which had helped to pay for his education. Susanna, eager to keep him with her on her side of the Atlantic, had persuaded her father to offer Matt employment in his own much larger company.

Matt had felt certain that once his father heard he had been offered that position he would ask him to stay in Yorkshire with the family firm and become a partner sooner or later. Instead Ben had blown his top, let fly with some very unpalatable home truths about Matt's ability to work hard enough to make a partnership worthwhile, and then told him to go, adding, 'Don't bother to come back when this marvellous American job falls apart for you because I won't want to know!'

So Matt had gone, and the job had not fallen apart but proved to be a success. His partnership with Susanna had not worked out so well. She had been too possessive, using her position as her father's daughter to try to keep Matt with her instead of allowing him to travel as extensively as his job required. He had begun to feel stifled by her possessiveness, and more and more certain that he had made a mistake in ever becoming involved with her. The interview he had missed because of Ben's critical illness would have provided him with the opportunity to live far enough away from Susanna to be able to decide whether he really wanted to marry her and start a family, as she wanted, or if it was time to break free of their relationship. But because of his father's illness he would now have the time and space to rethink his entire life and, hopefully, to make sense of it while he was back home in the place where he had grown up.

Back home! Yes, that's where he was. Back home in the place which had changed so little while he had been away. Ford House was the same spacious, comfortable, rather beautiful family home he had sometimes been homesick for in the luxurious purpose-built apartment he shared with Susanna. Nyddford was probably the same busy market town where he had spent his schooldays. He would find out about that while he was helping with the farming side of his father's business, and waiting for his father to allow him to visit him.

Right now was the time to do that. He was not used to being kept hanging about while other people made decisions about his life. That was not the American way. While his father was out of action he would take a good look at what changes needed to be made, and set about making them while he had the opportunity.

'What's going to happen if Gran's new husband dies, Dad? Will she come back here to live with us then?' Carla wanted to know as she cleared the used dishes from the supper table in the kitchen of Abbot's Fold Farm.

David Bramley spun round to face his daughter as he was on his way to the door that led into the back hall. There was a thunderous scowl marring his long, narrow Dalesman's face as he spoke sharply in reply. Watching him, Carla wished she had not asked the question.

'We'll talk about that when it happens. If it

happens. Right now, all I'm interested in is when you are going to finish clearing the table and washing up.'

'I'm being as quick as I can. Why can't our Jack do it for a change?' Resentment was spoiling the loveliness of Carla's young face.

'Because I need Jack to shut up the chickens while I look at the ewes again. You've got nothing else to do with your time.'

'I've got my homework to do. I didn't finish it last night.'

'Why not?'

'Dad, if Gran's new husband dies does that mean I won't get the new bike he promised me for my birthday?' Jack broke in.

David sighed, choking back the impatient words that were about to burst from his mouth. He was far too ready to snap at his children. Even though he was aware of that, he was so often unable to stop himself from speaking in anger when he ought to be more patient with them. Of course young Jack was worrying about whether or not he'd get the new bike Ben Harper had promised him. The lad had outgrown the bike he was at present using, and there had been few treats for the children on their birthdays or at Christmas since the farm had been facing hard times.

'Don't be worrying about that, son. I

expect Ben, Mr Harper, will get better,' he managed to say quietly.

'He must be very ill if they're saying prayers for him in the church,' Carla put in. 'Gran says they are, and in the church at Nyddford as well.'

David frowned when he heard his daughter utter those words, but did not comment.

'I wouldn't mind if Gran did come back to live with us, would you, Dad? She was good to us, wasn't she?' Jack's voice was eager. There was a strong bond between him and his grandmother which had deepened after his mother's untimely death.

'Yes, but we've got Mrs Grainger coming to help us twice a week,' David reminded his son.

'It's not like having Gran here all the time,' the boy pointed out.

'Julie is good to us. She makes us cakes, and dinners sometimes,' Carla said as she started to pile dishes into the sink ready for washing.

Yes, Julie had certainly been very good to them since she'd come to live in Jacob's Cottage. She brought pies and puddings over to share with them. Or invited them to the cottage for a meal when she was not on duty at the Health Centre. She was good to David in other ways too, ways that his children did not know about. So good that he found himself wondering at times whether he was falling in love with her. Being in love with Julie would make a big difference to all their lives. It would probably mean him marrying her, and maybe having other children with her.

David was not sure he was ready for that. Yet he could not go on indefinitely finding comfort in being with Julie in Jacob's Cottage while his children were at school. It would not be fair to her, if she wished to marry and have children. If Ben died and his mother came back to the farm to live, as she might expect to do, those times alone in Jacob's Cottage with Julie would not be possible, would they?

He pushed that disturbing thought away from him, called Jack to go with him, and went out to take another look at the ewes which were now so close to dropping their lambs.

Three

Carla watched from the kitchen window as her father walked across the farmyard, with Jack and Tyke following. They were on their way to take another look at the sheep to make sure the animals were all safely in the enclosures closest to the farmhouse now that lambing time was almost here. Her dad would be on the alert all the time then, and staying up all night once the lambs began to arrive. It would not be as easy then for her to slip out while she was supposed to be doing her homework and go down to the village to meet Josh.

Things would be even more difficult if Ben Harper died and Gran came back to live at Abbot's Fold. If that happened, Gran would be here all the time and would be sure to ask where she was going. It just wasn't fair that Mr Harper should have a bad heart attack when he had only been married to her gran for three months. Gran had been so happy in her new life at Ford House – Carla was able to sense that when

51

Julie took her and Jack there for supper sometimes.

Dad seemed not to have been nagging on at her as much since Gran went to live in Ford House and Julie came to live in Jacob's Cottage, but since Mr Harper became seriously ill he was getting really bad tempered again when she forgot to do the washing-up or get the vegetables ready for dinner. Carla had noticed it again today when their Jack kept on about what would happen if Mr Harper died. She was really, really worried about it, and just didn't know how to handle it.

Things here at home had been so absolutely awful for most of last year that she had thought about running away to London so she could get a job there and do as she liked. It was only meeting Josh Bolton that had made her decide to stay. Why didn't Dad get married again to Julie? Or at least ask Julie to move in with them. There wouldn't be as much pressure on *her* then to do things around the house, and she would be able to go down to the village to meet Josh whenever she wanted. Dad and Jack were well away from the farmhouse now, moving upwards to where most of the sheep were gathered in the shelter provided by the drystone walling. So she would make the most of her chance to dash down the Monks' Steps to Nyddbeck, where Josh

52

would be waiting for her at the Mill House...

It was late when Andrea put her car into the garage at the manse for the last time that day. So late that many of the lights in the cottages that were strung out along Beck Lane had already been switched off and the only illumination came from the Victorian lamp standards which were set close to the bridge, at the entrance to the church, and at the place where Church Lane joined with Beck Lane on the edge of the village green. Weariness enveloped her, so that even the act of closing the garage door seemed like too much of an effort.

All she longed for now was sleep, the sort of deep dreamless sleep that would shut out all the problems that were weighing so heavily upon her. Things like the report the architect had warned her about at their meeting today, the poor condition of the Nyddford Church roof. Things like Ben Harper's critical illness. Things like Dorothy Harper's worry about how she was going to cope with Ben's son while he was waiting to visit his father. Things like Bill having to be away in America for so much longer than he had planned.

Before sleep though there was Lucky to walk again. There was the answerphone to check too. Since she was almost asleep on her feet, it was almost certain to hold something else that would add to her worries. Already Lucky was on the other side of the front door signalling his gladness to hear her return. Oh Bill, if only you were waiting for me on the other side of that door all my tiredness would vanish. This last thought brought an ache to her throat.

Bill's flowers were there even though the man himself was thousands of miles away. They were there filling the hall with their fragrance. Bill's dog was there too, young, excitable and very bored with his own company because he was used to being with Bill all day either in the studio in Church Lane or out on a painting session or a long hike. Andrea sighed as she slipped the lead about his neck.

'We're not going far, Lucky, so you'd better do what you have to do quickly before I fall asleep on my feet,' she told him before she let him drag her at speed across the bridge and over to the green. From there Lucky halted only for long enough to water the grass before heading for Church Lane and his own home. His home and Bill's.

'It's no good going this way, Lucky,' Andrea warned him. 'Your master's not here.'

In spite of her words Lucky insisted on dragging her as far as the large detached stone house which was Bill's home and studio. Once there, he stared at the shuttered windows which were all in darkness, then gave vent to a melancholy howl that made Andrea shudder. There was something weird about being here with Bill's dog when Bill was away. Something quite scary. Lucky seemed to sense it too as he whined again. This mournful attitude in the usually boisterous young dog was unnerving. Andrea bent to give him a comforting stroke on the top of his silky head. The owl that was so often to be heard from the great oak tree close to the beck flew low over their heads, startling both of them.

'Home, Lucky!' she ordered, shivering in the chill of the night air.

Lucky wasted no time in sniffing out exciting smells on Nyddbeck Green, as was his usual custom. Instead, he pelted back across the bridge so fast that Andrea had to let go of his lead and allow him to race ahead of her. He had developed into a strong, energetic animal during the three months since she had found him shut inside the church one day, abandoned by the owners who had tired of him all too quickly. The dog had become special to her because on the day Bill had taken Lucky into his own home Bill had also invited her into Beckside to share his meal on her return from a traumatic journey which had left her feeling shattered in mind and body. She had shared with Bill that night all the feelings of shock and anguish that her discovery of Ian's secret life had brought to her.

Bill had been so wonderful in the way he had just listened while she poured out all the pain and disillusion she had experienced shortly after her arrival in Nyddbeck. She had been able to cry on his shoulder after telling him of the decision she had come to after having her faith tested to the limit by what she had found out about Ian. It had been such a relief to unburden herself of all those griefs which had previously been known only to herself and her God. Such an enormous lifting of the burden she had been forced to live with. She had not wanted to leave Bill that night. Yet Bill, loving her as he did, had not taken advantage of her state of mind by persuading her to stay.

'Thanks, Lord, for bringing Bill into my life,' she whispered as she let herself into the manse and buried her face in the flowers Bill had sent.

As she raised her head again and thought of making a milky drink to take to bed, she noticed that the answerphone was blinking. The temptation was strong to let it go on blinking until early the next morning. It could just be someone wanting to book an appointment for her next parish surgery, or needing to change the time or place of a meeting. It could also be an emergency though. Someone in trouble who needed the help she was here to give. With that thought uppermost in her mind, she pushed the appropriate button and listened as Dorothy Harper spoke in a breathless, distressed voice.

'I'm just leaving for the hospital, Andrea. They rang to say Ben's condition has deteriorated and I should go at once.'

That was all Andrea needed to hear before she grabbed the jacket she had only just discarded and thrust her arms back into it. Instantly, Lucky was on his feet and ready to go with her.

'Sorry, Lucky, not this time,' she said before she left him giving a grumble of disappointment.

As she drove the ten miles to the District Hospital on the far side of Harrogate, there were many prayers drifting in and out of her mind: silent prayers for Ben, who might not survive the night. Ben, who had been such a tower of strength to her when in her first few months as minister of Nyddford with Nyddbeck she crossed swords so many times with David Bramley while trying to help his family. Ben, who had admitted to her one night that he was jealous of the friendship which had grown between Dorothy and Bill Wyndham during the months when Bill had been renting Jacob's Cottage. Ben, who had loved Dorothy for so many years and waited so long to marry her. Surely their happiness was not to end so soon?

Her next prayers were for Dorothy, an Elder at Nyddbeck Church who had become such a dear friend. There was no doubt in Andrea's mind that Dorothy's faith would see her through even the darkest of times, as it had done already during her first husband's final long illness and the tragic sudden death of the daughter-in-law she had loved. Her prayers were that Dorothy's own health would not fail because of the severe strain she was enduring so bravely, and that Ben's son would behave kindly to her. That might be a vain hope, she knew, but no prayers were ever wasted. All were important.

Finally, as she reached the outskirts of Harrogate, she prayed that there would soon be a reconciliation for Ben and his son. There must be, or Matt Harper would carry with him for the rest of his life a burden of bitterness which could sour any new relationships he made. Perhaps his bitterness had already done that? It was certainly possible because even on their short acquaintance she had gained an impression of Matt as being a man rather at odds with himself in spite of his good looks and his successful career.

'Dear Lord, please help me to help them all in whatever way You decide is best.

Please let me get it right,' were her heartfelt prayers as she turned her car into the almost empty visitors' car park at the District Hospital.

She did not need to read the directions which pointed to the Intensive Care Unit. The way was already very familiar to her. There was that eerie air of peace and emptiness all about her as she traversed the corridors that would bring her to the place where Ben was only just hanging on to life. The way was familiar to her because there had been other members of her country parishes who had been transferred to this hospital from the smaller hospital at Nyddford. Before she entered the unit she put a hand into her pocket to find the slim white collar of office which would allow her to join the family members when they needed her most, and slipped it inside the neck of her shirt.

There were tears sliding slowly and silently down Dorothy's face as Andrea put a gentle hand on her shoulder. The older woman looked up into her eyes and whispered an almost inaudible word of thanks. Matt Harper, sitting on the other side of his father's bed, acknowledged her presence with a brief nod before staring down again at the man who lay so still and grey-faced amid the array of wires which connected him to the apparatus that was monitoring his progress. Andrea found herself staring at that monitor as she continued to pray, keeping her arm about Dorothy's shoulders. It was a long night, a seemingly endless night for the three people gathered about the bed of Ben Harper, but dawn came at last to bring pale colour to the sky. The nurse who had been constantly checking Ben's condition throughout the night sent them away then to the small waiting room close to the unit.

'Doctor will come and have a word with you soon, and I'll ask someone to bring you some tea. Then you'll probably be glad to go home and get some sleep,' she told them.

'I'd rather stay here,' Dorothy insisted.

'You need to get some rest or you'll not be fit to take care of your husband when he comes home,' the nurse said then, with a smile.

Dorothy's face lit up with the hope her words brought. 'Do you really think?' she began.

'I think he's turned the corner, but Doctor will tell you more. He's here now.'

The doctor spoke to Dorothy and Matt with guarded optimism about Ben's condition. 'You'll need to make him slow down and take life easier when he's allowed home,' he went on. 'He may have had such a fright that he'll be willing to do that, but if he isn't it'll be up to you to see that he behaves himself.' He paused, then addressed himself to Matt. 'I see from his notes that he's still running his own business. Will you be able to take on more of the responsibility there from him?'

Watching Matt's face as the doctor spoke, Andrea saw doubt, followed by indignation, chase each other across his features. 'I hope you're not putting the blame for what's happened to my father on my shoulders?' he challenged. 'There have been other factors in his life which I certainly have not been responsible for.'

Was he referring to his father's marriage to Dorothy? If so, he had no right to do that.

The doctor smiled. 'I'm not in the business of allocating blame for what has already happened to your father, Mr Harper,' he said quietly. 'I'm only involved with the business of trying to make him well again, and you could have a part to play in that.'

'If he'll let me! He wouldn't even agree to see me after I'd crossed the Atlantic to get to him,' Matt burst out so vehemently that Dorothy put out a hand to calm him down.

The doctor smiled again. 'He'll have plenty of time to think again about that during the next few days. Just have patience. In the meantime I suggest you all go home and get some sleep, as I'm about to do.'

Andrea parted company with Dorothy

and Matt out in the car park, where the birds were already greeting the new day with their song. She was close to exhaustion now, and close to tears too as she looked from Dorothy's weary face to Matt's set features.

'Will you be all right, Dorothy?' she asked. 'Or would you like me to come back and stay with you for a while?'

Matt Harper spoke before Dorothy could say anything. 'That won't be necessary, Mrs Cameron, thank you. I can cope with everything. You'll be ready to get back to your home. Your husband will be glad to see you back, I guess, since you've been away all night.'

Andrea opened her mouth to reply, but found herself bereft of words. Matt had made it sound as though she had been out all night partying while the man in her life had been obliged to put up with her absence as best he could. Nothing could be further from the truth, and she would tell him so! Ben's son really was a pain; she had had enough of him for one day.

Dorothy hurriedly put Matt in the picture before she could do so herself. 'Andrea's husband was killed in an accident last summer, just after she came here,' she told him while Andrea was still struggling to find the right words.

'Oh!' Plainly Matt Harper was taken

aback. 'How terrible for you, Mrs Cameron. I'm very sorry,' he went on. 'Would you like to come back to Ford House for some breakfast? I'm quite good at cooking bacon and eggs,' he added.

'Yes, do come back with us, Andrea,' Dorothy urged.

'Thanks, but I'm not hungry.' Andrea knew she sounded ungracious but she was past caring about anything now except getting back to the manse and her bed.

'When did you last eat?' Dorothy wanted to know.

Andrea brushed her friend's concern aside impatiently. 'I can't remember. It's not important anyway.'

'But it is! You know you have a habit of letting everything else take priority over your meals, Andrea. So if you can't remember when you last ate it must have been a long time ago. You really ought to let us give you some breakfast, my dear.'

'Yes,' Matt chipped in. 'As I said earlier, I'm a dab hand at cooking bacon and eggs. Why not let me prove it to you—?'

That was as far as he got. Andrea was feeling quite faint now and afraid that she might flake out if she didn't take the weight off her feet and get into her car at once.

'I can do without food, and I can certainly do without all this fuss,' she snapped as she turned away from Dorothy and Matt, opened the door of her car with unsteady fingers, and dropped into the front seat with a sigh of exasperation. As she switched on the engine she turned her head and caught a glimpse of the hurt on Dorothy's face, and the astonishment on Matt's features. A moment later she was moving away from the pair of them so carelessly that she caught the nearside wing of her vehicle on a bollard as she attempted to escape through the car park exit at an awkward angle.

'Damn!' she said aloud. 'Damn! Damn! Damn! That's all I need.'

Her hands were shaking as she began to back out from under the raised arm of the traffic barrier. As she did so she saw through the mirror that Matt was striding towards her. He was so close that she was forced to stop. She wound down the window as he spoke to her.

'Are you sure you're fit to drive?' he asked.

Normally, Andrea was not a woman driver who had an attitude, but this had been a long day and a very distressing one for her. So she spoke what was in her mind without thinking. Spoke it in a way she was not accustomed to speaking.

'Are you sure *you* are behaving towards Dorothy as your father would wish?'

She did not wait to hear his reply. Instead, with a grinding of gears that sent a shudder through her, she left Matt and Dorothy, and the hospital, behind and turned into the main road that would lead her home to Nyddbeck.

Julie Craven heard the formal message that came from Andrea's answerphone, then replaced the receiver. It was the second time she had tried to make contact with Andrea that evening. So Andrea must be at a meeting which was running later than usual. Or she could be at the District Hospital in Harrogate visiting Ben Harper, who was recovering slowly from his heart attack. Julie could guess how much Andrea would be missing Bill now that his visit to America had been extended, and wanted to arrange for her to have supper at Jacob's Cottage one evening while Bill was away. It would be a chance for her to repay the friendship Andrea had given to her so generously during the last few months.

Those first months in the area had been traumatic for Andrea after she had been widowed on the day of her induction as minister of the two churches, yet she had found time to give comfort and friendship to Julie, who had still been recovering from the sudden death of her friend Jill Bramley. Andrea had been through a terrible time with Dave when he'd rejected all her efforts to help his mother and his two motherless children. Much as she adored Dave, Julie

65

had been furious with him for his refusal to accept help from either her or Andrea during the period when his mother became ill through overwork.

She was feeling quite annoyed with Dave again now, and had wanted to talk about that to Andrea, whose advice might have helped her calm down. The problem was that gradually, and maybe without him realizing it, Dave was slipping back into the black mood which had been ruining the lives of his children, and his mother, a few months ago. Of course times were very bad for British farmers, with prices at an all-time low and crippling regulations being imposed to make things even worse, but it wouldn't help if Dave allowed himself to become aggressive again with those around him. At least he owned his farm, the beautiful farmhouse, and all the acres of land surrounding it, rather than being a tenant-farmer with rent to pay.

Dave also owned this lovely grey stone cottage which had such superb views of Abbot's Moor, the abbey ruins and the distant craggy hills. It had been built for his parents to live in on their retirement. Jacob Bramley had not lived to enjoy the home called Jacob's Cottage. Dave's mother had moved back into the farmhouse to look after her son and his children until her marriage to Ben Harper. The cottage had been let to holidaymakers then.

It had been Dorothy Bramley's idea that Julie should live in Jacob's Cottage while she was looking around to buy a small place of her own within easy travelling distance of the Health Centre at Nyddford, where she worked. Julie loved living there but she knew this could not continue because there were holiday bookings for the cottage which would bring in more than twice the rent she was paying, and Dave needed that money to keep the farm going.

She knew she ought to have been looking round for somewhere else to live long before now. Yet as the months since she had moved into Jacob's Cottage slipped by so happily with Dave coming out of his long grieving for Jill and spending more and more time here with her when his children were at school, she had begun to hope that he was falling in love with her and would ask her to move into the farmhouse with him. Only it didn't seem to be happening. Maybe it never would happen. That last thought gave her a jolt.

Perhaps she had been wrong all along in thinking that once she was living here, right opposite his farmhouse, Dave would find it easy to go back to the relationship they had shared before he met and married her friend Jill? It had seemed to her sometimes, lately, that Dave *was* falling in love with her because he came more and more often to the cottage to make love to her while they were alone at Abbot's Fold. Or invited her to share a meal with him and his children which they cooked together in the farmhouse. She had loved Dave for so many years, even through the years when he had been married to Jill. During those years she had tried to fall in love with someone else, one of the men who invited her out from time to time or one of the guys she worked alongside, but it had not happened. It never would happen now, she knew. It had to be Dave for her, or no one.

When she'd moved into Jacob's Cottage in the first week of January and Dave brought her the plant which was blooming so healthily on the living room windowsill, she had, without thinking, reached up to kiss him and been excited by his response. His response had made her aware that he was ready to start living, and loving again, and she had determined to make him love her. All these weeks later, in early April, she knew Dave enjoyed making love to her. She had her doubts though about whether he was ready for the sort of commitment she wanted from him.

Already she was thirty-six, and her biological clock was ticking relentlessly on. If she were to have a child of her own it must be soon, and if Dave was not prepared to commit himself to them adding a child of their own to his Carla and Jack, whom she already loved, then she would leave here very soon. There were those holiday lettings of Jacob's Cottage booked for May, and there was that tiny house she had heard of close to the Health Centre in Nyddford. Perhaps it was time she took a look at that house? Perhaps it was time she made a move away from this rented cottage where it was so easy for Dave to come and share love-making with her whenever he felt like it without taking their relationship any further and asking her to marry him? Or at least to move into the farmhouse and share his home.

She would take a look at the little house in Nyddford tomorrow. It was time for her to move on, with or without Dave.

Four

Yawning her way across the kitchen floor in the direction of the electric kettle, Andrea almost fell over Lucky, who was on his way back from giving the postman a boisterous greeting.

'Oh, I'm sorry you didn't get your late walk last night, Lucky,' she said as she bent to caress his silky auburn head. 'You must be desperate to go out now.'

Lucky barked his agreement, so Andrea ignored her own longing for a cup of tea and opened the door that led from the kitchen into the back garden and watched him dash away. Then she went to sort through the pile of envelopes which the postman had brought, moving through them impatiently in her search for something which might have come from Bill. Yes, there was an air-mail from Bill! She would read it while she was drinking her tea, then she'd have to get a move on and take Lucky for a proper walk before she did anything else.

The lanky red setter was back in the kitchen eager for his breakfast by the time she was gulping down the hot liquid and skimming through Bill's letter. Bill's description of his days spent completing drawings for the American author's book, and embarking on a hectic lecture tour, brought him vividly to life. It also brought to her a deep physical longing for Bill.

This longing for him convinced her that she ought to have gone with him to America as he had begged her to do. Bill had not really understood how she felt about that, she felt sure. 'Why should it matter, in this day and age, that we've gone away together, darling?' he had argued. 'We're both free, and we'll be getting married before the year ends, won't we?'

His puzzled expression had indicated plainly to her that he was quite unable to believe that some members of her church would be ready to criticize her for something which in his view had nothing at all to do with them. Had Bill been right, and she wrong about that?

'Some of them must know by now that we're close friends,' he had pointed out.

'Close friends, yes! Us going away together on holiday would look like something very different to them,' had been her own argument against the idea.

'It won't be a holiday for me. It's a working trip for which I'll be well paid, and the break would do you good after all the hours

71

you put in here and in Nyddford. I don't want to go to America without you. I just can't bear the thought of being away from you.'

The expression on Bill's face as he told her that was almost her undoing. She was so much in love with him that it would have been easy for her to push aside her doubts and go with him so that they could be truly together in a way they could not be when they were under the scrutiny of her flock here in Nyddbeck. It was then though that she had unwittingly recalled how much she had once been in love with Ian. This thought was so bleak that Andrea wished it had not come into her mind just when she was so tempted to forget the past and enjoy the present.

'The time will soon pass,' she had said quickly, before she could change her mind. 'I'll be so busy, and so will you. We'll be going away together in June when I take you up to Scotland to meet my parents. Please try to understand, Bill. Gossip of the wrong sort could do so much harm to my work here, just when people are getting used to me and beginning to trust me. I'm not prepared to risk that.'

Now, as she re-read Bill's letter, Andrea knew that though she had been right to put her work first because she had been here to give her support to Ben and Dorothy

Harper when they needed it most, she still must suffer this aching longing to have Bill back in the village again where she could see him almost every day. The extra time Bill was staying on in America for was already seeming endless to her, in spite of her busy life. Her hasty scan of the rest of her post confirmed that there was no shortage of things for her to do. There were agendas for meetings and little notes asking her to visit people who were not too well, plus an ominous estimate for the urgent work that required to be carried out on the roof of Emmanuel Church at Nyddford. This sent her spirits into free fall as she carried the letters through to her study to be dealt with later in the day. The airmail from Bill she tucked into the pocket of her dressing gown to be enjoyed again later.

Julie Craven parked as close as she could get to the tiny terraced house situated on the north side of Nyddford and opened out the paperwork about the property supplied by the agent. According to these documents, the house was in good structural condition but needed some updating. Probably that was why the price was within her means. It was certainly conveniently situated for her work at Nyddford Health Centre. Much more so than Jacob's Cottage, which was a five-mile drive away.

She hadn't gone to live in Jacob's Cottage because it was convenient for her job though. The reason she had moved in there when Dorothy Bramley offered it to her was because living in Jacob's Cottage would place her for some weeks right under Dave Bramley's nose and give her the chance to help him recover from Jill's death. Dave had not objected to her moving into the cottage which Dorothy had handed over to him soon after her own marriage to Ben Harper. He seemed to welcome her presence there.

Nothing had ever been said outright, but Julie had guessed that Dorothy was perhaps hoping she would use her time there to help Dave, and maybe become part of his life. Dave so much needed her in his life. He needed her to care for him and his children; needed her to bring love and warmth to him again. As Dave began to spend more time with her, her hopes had been raised that he would ask her to marry him or at least move in with him. He hadn't done that, so she must put distance between them. If this tiny house proved to be suitable for her needs, and her available cash, she would come to a decision quickly. Distancing herself from Dave Bramley and his children would hurt her less if she did it swiftly, she decided.

An hour later her decision had been made. The house was so neat and compact that it would be ideal for a woman on her own.

There were only four rooms to be kept clean and tidy, so she would not need to spend much of her precious free time on doing housework. The living room was an attractive shape, with a large bay window and a stone fireplace, the kitchen was long and narrow, not large enough to provide for large-scale entertaining but sufficient for her sort of cooking. Two small bedrooms and a shower room were on the floor above. It was all clean and needed only a change of colour from the bright-green walls to a paler shade downstairs and from the vivid pink upstairs to something more restful. A final inspection of the rooms and the small paved back garden, where she planned to have container plants, convinced Julie that if the owners accepted her offer this little house would do for her.

She had locked the front door and was walking down the short path to the front gate when the strident noise of a car horn startled her. Surely her own vehicle was not blocking someone's exit? A moment later she gave a sigh of relief as she recognized Dave's face, grinning at her through the open window of his Land Rover. She responded with a smile and a wave.

'I thought it was your day off today?' he called out to her.

'It is.'

'Oh!' He glanced back at the house she

had just left, and saw the For Sale sign set close to the gate. 'Don't tell me you've been visiting there? The place is empty.'

'That's what brought me here. It's for sale, and I'm going to make an offer for it,' she added recklessly.

Dave's thick eyebrows shot up almost as far as the strand of black hair which had a habit of straying down to his forehead.

'Why the hell are you doing that?' he shouted above the hooting being made by an impatient driver who was waiting to get past his Land Rover.

Julie bit back her reply and slid into the seat of her own vehicle, leaving Dave to take the unsociable comments of the man in the van whose way he was obstructing in the narrow cobbled street. Why shouldn't Dave do a bit of waiting and wondering, as she had got used to doing during the last few months? It wouldn't do him any harm. She was still smiling at the thought as she drove away in the direction of the street where Nyddford's one and only property agent had his premises.

When she returned to Jacob's Cottage a couple of hours later, having put in her offer for the house and done some shopping at the supermarket on the edge of Nyddford, she hardly had time to close the cottage door before Dave was there hammering impatiently enough with the horse-shoe knocker to make her smile with satisfaction. Of course, he would be anxious to know more about what she was planning to do, and how it would affect him. She did not rush to let him in but spent a couple of minutes in her bedroom first brushing her hair and applying lipstick and perfume. Her smile deepened when she heard him bashing on the cottage door again as she went through the hall to open it.

'Hi! Are you coming in, or are you just wanting to give me the latest news about Ben?' she asked him calmly.

'I'm just wanting to know what's going on.' Dave stepped over the threshold as he spoke. The scowl that drew his black eyebrows close above his long slender nose reflected his dour mood.

Julie came straight to the point. 'I suppose you mean, why you saw me looking at a house that's for sale in Nyddford?'

'That's exactly what I mean. You never mentioned to me that you were thinking of buying a house there.' His voice was sharp, his eyes accusing.

'I thought you would have realized by now that I'll need somewhere else to live in less than a month from now when the people who've booked this cottage for their holiday arrive.' Her own brown eyes, usually so warm with the special regard she had for Dave, were challenging him now.

His frown deepened. 'There's plenty of time for us to come to some arrangement before then,' he hedged.

Julie was really mad with him now. 'Not for me, Dave! I need to know what's going to happen in the near future, and I can't wait any longer to find out,' she snapped.

'We've got plenty of rooms in the farmhouse. You could always move in there when you have to leave here. It won't be any problem.'

He spoke as though he was offering a home to a stray animal, she thought. Her anger against him built up inside her until it was ready to boil over. She clenched her hands as she fought to appear cool and to speak reasonably.

'It could be a problem for me, Dave, and one I'm not prepared to take on board. So I've been looking out for somewhere else to live. Somewhere permanent. I think I've found it today. In fact I've put in an offer for the house in Nyddford.' She managed to deal with the wobble in her voice before she went on: 'I've asked for an early completion, so I probably won't need that room in your house.'

Dave's face registered his disbelief for a long, long moment. During that time Julie listened to the thud of her own heart beating rapidly as she waited for him to say the words she was longing to hear. Words that would prove he loved her and was not just making use of her time and her emotion because she was there on his doorstep. Then the tension was broken for both of them as the two collies began to bark in unison to warn their owner that outsiders were approaching the farm. A motorbike could be heard traversing the lane that led to Abbot's Fold. Carla was home from visiting her grandmother at Ford House, and Josh Bolton was with her.

Instantly, Dave was out of Jacob's Cottage and striding to the farm gate to meet them. Julie moved to the window which over-looked the farmyard and watched as they met. She did not need to wonder what was being said. The words came clearly to her through the open door. Her heart sank as she heard them. Dave was back to his old ways, it seemed. Back to the harsh unreasonable treatment of his teenage daughter which had caused her, and his mother, so much worry last year. His attitude then had resulted in Carla hanging around Bill Wyndham too often when he was living in Jacob's Cottage, simply because Bill showed a kindly interest in her.

'You should have been back home long before this! What about the supper? You haven't even started making it yet, have you?' Dave spoke harshly to his daughter. Carla would be mortified that her father should speak to her like that when her boyfriend was around, Julie guessed.

'It won't take me long to do the vegetables. Gran gave me a steak and kidney pie for us to heat up. There's enough for Josh too,' Carla said hurriedly. 'Josh can stay, can't he, Dad?' There was pleading in her voice, but Dave ignored it.

'If I'd known you were going to your gran's to beg food from her I'd have made sure you didn't go in the first place. Don't you think she has enough to do, having Ben's son to look after in between the journeys she has to make to the hospital?' he snapped.

'I didn't ask Gran for the pie!' Carla broke in fiercely. 'She said she made it when she was baking one for her and Matt.'

Josh Bolton must be feeling very uncomfortable by now, Julie thought. He would hate being dragged into this family row, and it could get worse. Carla would be ready to blow her top by now. At sixteen years of age, her temperament was volatile. She was so like her mother had been when she and Jill first met as trainee nurses.

'I don't like you riding pillion on that bike either. I told you before...' Dave was really losing it now and Julie knew he would regret it later.

'It's perfectly safe! Josh is a good rider—' Carla protested loudly.

Dave did not allow her to go on. 'He hasn't lived here long enough yet to be used to our roads.'

'He's been here three months. I'm not afraid to ride with him.'

'Don't you think our family has suffered enough from traffic accidents? I shouldn't have to remind you of that, but you seem to have forgotten.'

'I haven't! You know I haven't! How can I forget when you keep trying to spoil all our lives because of what happened to Mum?'

Julie knew there were tears threatening to engulf Carla now. Her heart ached for the girl, and for Dave too. She had thought, very recently, that Dave was coming to terms at last with what had happened to Jill. Now she guessed she had been mistaken. Maybe Dave would never come to terms with the loss of Jill? Or allow his children to do so. She watched as Josh Bolton, Carla's young American boyfriend, put his arm about her as she began to weep.

Dave opened his mouth to deny the truth of what his daughter had just accused him of, but could not manage to get the words out. The huge burden of anger and bitterness that was still inside him was about to explode in an avalanche of fury when he heard the stifled sob that Carla let go. His own eyes began to burn then and his fury became fear that he would break down and weep in front of Carla and her American lad. It must not happen! Not here, anyway. The only place he would allow it to happen was up on the high moorland above the farm; that place which had shared so much of his grief and despair.

Turning his back on the two young people, he strode away. His usually straight shoulders were hunched as he stumbled on. The first difficult tears were sliding down his weathered cheeks as he made for the track that ran up steeply from behind one of the farm buildings to Abbot's Moor. On his way he encountered Jack, coming back from a visit to his schoolfriend who lived on another moorland farm a mile or so away. His eleven-year-old son greeted him before they met, his rosy cheeks breaking into the wide smile he had inherited from his mother.

'Were you coming to tell me tea's ready, Dad?'

Lost still in his misery, Dave scowled at the boy who, except for Jill's easy smile, was so much like him in looks, though not in temperament. 'No! It's not ready. You'd better go and see to the chickens till your sister gets round to making it.'

The smile on the boy's face was snuffed out instantly. He hesitated, about to say something else, then turned away from his father and ran down to the farmyard.

Dave groaned out loud as he watched him go. Oh God! I've done it again! Why can't I keep my bloody awful temper under control? Why? Why? My kids don't deserve this. It's not their fault, it's mine. All mine! What the hell am I going to do about it?

His anguished words were shut inside his head, tormenting him with the knowledge of his own failure to cope with his family after Jill's death. He knew he had humiliated Carla, who would find it hard to forgive him for speaking to her like that when Josh was with her. At sixteen, Carla was already difficult enough to deal with. She ought to have had her mother to guide her, but Jill had died when she was only fourteen. His own mother had done her best when she was living with them in the farmhouse for the year or so before she married Ben Harper. His mother would have been very upset if she had heard him losing his rag with the children this afternoon.

A new thought came to him then, an equally unwelcome one. What had Julie Craven thought when she witnessed the scene in the farmyard and overheard what he had said to Carla and Josh? Julie was already going off him, he suspected. So his exhibition of foul temper would only have made things worse. Why was Julie going off him now, when only a couple of weeks ago they had been so close? Was it because of his moodiness? Or had she met someone else? There had to be a reason for her making her mind up so suddenly to buy a house in Nyddford. The reason had to be either his own difficult moods, which he seemed unable to control, or another man.

Julie must meet plenty of other men in her work at Nyddford Health Centre, doctors, male nurses, physios and the like, as well as the people who went there for advice and treatment. If she was planning on buying a house close to the health centre it could only be because she had met someone there, but why hadn't she told him instead of going to look at properties without saying anything to him?

Dear God, what a fool he had been to allow himself to become so fond of her that it hurt to even think of her with anyone else. It was not as if Julie had ever given him a clue during those months since she had moved into Jacob's Cottage that she was spending time with someone else. She had kept it a secret from him, and just gone on making him welcome in the cottage for coffee, and for talks about his problems with his farm or with the children. Sometimes those talks had led to love-making that always seemed to be good for both of them. Had the love-making only happened because Julie was sorry for him?

That last thought was so repugnant to

Dave that he jammed the heel of his boot viciously against the weirdly shaped outcrop of rock that he came to lean on when his black moods drove him to seek solitude. The pain of that impact brought sweat to his brow. He slid to the springy turf that in a few months' time would change from brown and bronze to a brilliant purple, dropped his head on to his knees and allowed the darkness of his despair to engulf him.

Five

Julie felt a lump in her throat as she watched Dave stride away from Carla and Josh. There was something about the way his shoulders were hunched as he stared down at the hard surface of the yard rather than glancing around to make sure all was well with animals and buildings that indicated the strength of his anger. Perhaps also the depth of his regret that he had vented that anger on his daughter and hurt her so much.

Was it her fault that Dave had lost his temper with Carla and told her off in front of Josh? It looked as if Carla was crying now. Josh had his arm about her and was pulling her head into his shoulder. Julie wondered then if she ought to go across to them and see if she could help. No, that might look like interference to the girl and make things worse. So even though she was fond of Carla, Julie turned her back on the scene, closed the cottage door and went into the kitchen to put away her shopping. In a month or so from now she would be away from Abbot's Moor and living in the little house in Nyddford. Dave Bramley and his black moods would no longer be on her doorstep then to bewilder and hurt her.

In her study at Nyddbeck manse Andrea flexed her aching shoulders and looked away from the computer screen, at which she had been staring for too long. It was good to look instead out of the window at the back garden, where daffodils were in bloom beneath the gold of the forsythia bush. There were things that needed to be done out there in the garden, things Bill had told her to leave until he came back from his American trip. Beyond the garden she could see over the drystone wall long straight lines of new pale green shoots showing through the rich dark earth of Dave's huge field.

How was Dave coping with all the extra work that helping out with the farming side of Ben Harper's business would be placing on his shoulders? Because of pressure of work in her two parishes she had not got round yet to answering the message left on her answerphone a few days ago by Julie, so she had no idea whether Dave was managing to cope with Harper's Farm while Ben was in hospital. She must reply to that message now before it got buried again beneath the rest of her workload. It was a relief to stand up and straighten her back after working for hours on her sermon for next Sunday. She went at once to the phone in the hall and tapped out the Jacob's Cottage number.

'Hi Julie! Sorry I haven't answered your message earlier,' she began. 'Things have been a bit hectic here.'

'Aren't they always?' Julie laughed. 'At least if you are kept busy you won't be missing Bill quite as much.'

'Not true! I'm missing him even more than I expected to. There are so many things I wish I could talk to him about,' Andrea answered with a sigh.

'Anything my ears could help with? We could meet either at your place or mine,' Julie suggested, adding, 'I've got lots to tell you.'

'Have you something exciting to share?' Andrea wanted to know. She could hardly wait to hear whether Dave had got round at last to talking about marriage to her friend.

Julie hesitated. 'Not what you might be expecting to hear. Or hoping to hear. It's something quite different I need to talk about. Something I'd hoped would not be happening.'

Andrea frowned. 'I don't like the sound of that. Do you want to talk about it now?'

There was a moment or so of silence before Julie answered. 'No! I don't think I can do that just yet. It's too soon. I'll find it easier when I've come to terms with it and feel calmer.'

'I still don't like the sound of it,' Andrea said thoughtfully. 'We must meet very soon. Why not come to supper tonight, if you're not sharing a meal with Dave?'

'I'm certainly not doing that.'

Julie's response came too quickly, and there was something in her voice that brought unease to Andrea. 'Come and share with me then. Make it fairly late, about nine, because I have to spend an hour or so with the Youth Drama Group at Nyddford.'

'Are you sure you won't be too tired by then?'

Julie's voice sounded rough, almost as if she had a sore throat. Or had been crying, perhaps?

'I'm quite sure. I'll have some pasta ready, so you'd better be hungry. I certainly will be.' Andrea laughed as she tried to lift what she was now certain was a gloomy mood for Julie.

'I'll be with you then, but I'll bring the food. Lasagna, it's already prepared and in my freezer. Thanks a lot for making time for me, Andrea.'

Julie rang off, leaving Andrea wondering whether the lasagna was already prepared because she had been expecting Dave to share it with her. Things seemed to have been going so much better for the family at

Abbot's Fold Farm since Julie had moved into Jacob's Cottage. Because Dave's children got on well with her, Julie found it easy to help them, and Dave. It was looking quite likely that Julie would become part of that family before long. Dave's mother had been doing the same sort of wishful thinking, Andrea knew. At least until Ben's heart attack pushed all other thoughts out of her mind. However, it was wasting time to speculate on what had made Julie sound so depressed. That precious time would be much better spent on saying a prayer for Julie and Dave. So Andrea shared her concern about her friends with her Lord.

Then Lucky, newly awakened from his sleep close to the radiator, came to lick her hand and lash her with his long plumed tail while he looked hopefully towards the place where his lead hung on a hook beside the front door. Andrea glanced at her watch as she spoke to him.

'Yes, it's time you had a decent walk, Lucky, and I need one too to chase my worries away.' With luck, if they didn't meet anyone who wanted to talk on their way through the village, they could walk as far as Abbot's Moor and make up for the short walks Lucky, and she, had been forced to limit themselves to during the last couple of days. It would be wonderful up there on this dry bright day. She slipped on a warm bright-red fleece and clipped the lead on to the red setter's collar before they left the manse and made their way over the bridge. Nyddbeck was quiet at this time of day. There was no one about to delay them. Lucky made a brief stop to water the grass on the village green then began to pull strongly on his lead, dragging Andrea past the entrance to her church and along Church Lane in the direction of Bill's home.

'It's no good, Lucky, Bill's not there,' she warned him but she knew her words fell on deaf ears. Lucky lived always in hope that if he went to Beckside he would find his beloved master. When they reached the closed gates of the house the dog gave them a puzzled stare and whined his disappointment so sadly that Andrea bent to give him a hug before moving him on towards the Monks' Steps.

'I miss him too, Lucky, and he'll be missing us,' she told him softly.

Soon they were at the top of the long flight of shallow steps which had been there ever since the days when the monks from the abbey had come down to minister to the people of Nyddbeck. There was a stiff breeze moving fluffy white clouds about in the great canopy of blue sky overhead. The air was like good wine, so crisp and invigorating that Andrea's mental fatigue was banished as she followed one of the sheep tracks that dissected the moor. As for Lucky, he lifted his long, elegant nose from time to time to take in the scent of small moorland creatures and the pheasants which were so abundant at this time of the year. He made a sudden lunge for one of these splendidly plumaged birds, and almost took Andrea off her feet as she tried to restrain him.

'Behave yourself, Lucky!' she ordered breathlessly.

Lucky responded with a crescendo of joyful barks. It was as she made her way back to the steps which would lead her to the village that she caught sight of someone sitting slouched against the great piece of dark rock that from this angle resembled an animal head. She frowned. From this distance it was not possible to recognize the man, but since Lucky was already bounding in that direction and taking her with him she could only hang on to the lead and follow. It was, she discovered then, Dave Bramley. Her frown deepened when Dave did not look up at the sound of the dog's bark but kept his head down on his knees.

What was Dave doing, alone up here without either his collie or his tractor? He could not be inspecting the sheep from Abbot's Fold because Andrea knew that this close to lambing time the ewes would be in the paddock closest to the farm buildings where Dave would be able to keep an eye on them. Was Dave feeling ill? Or was he upset? Had there been bad news from the hospital about Ben? If so surely Julie would have told her when they had spoken just before she left the manse.

Or was this a special day that brought sadness to Dave? The anniversary of his marriage to Jill, or her birthday? Perhaps even the anniversary of Jill's death? Such questions crowded Andrea's mind, and brought her a dilemma. Ought she to try to find out what was wrong? Should she take the risk of intruding on Dave's solitude? Or would it be best to pretend she had not seen him; just go away and leave him to deal with whatever was troubling him as best he could?

'Tell me what to do, Lord, please,' she prayed silently as her restraining hand on Lucky's collar warned him that this was a time to lie down and be quiet.

The light was beginning to change the colours in the sky from blue to grey, with tinges of soft pink and violet showing beyond the distant dark hills. Still Andrea waited, close enough to Dave for him to be aware of her but not near enough for him to feel threatened by her presence. Then the silence all about them was broken by the sound made by a skein of wild geese chattering as they flew overhead in perfect formation. They were moving from the river where they spent their days to the dam far below where they would spend the night. As the beating of their great wings died away Andrea knew what she had to do.

'Is it anything I can help with, Dave?' she asked quietly.

At first she thought he was not going to answer her. Then he got to his feet reluctantly and shuddered as though chilled to the bone from sitting too long in this exposed place.

'It's nothing anyone can help with. I wish to God they could.' The words came so slowly that they seemed to be dragged out of him against his will.

'Surely nothing can be as bad as that? So bad that you can't even tell me about it, I mean. Is it a bad memory troubling you, Dave? Or some problem on the farm? If it is, it might be better shared with someone—'

That was as far as Andrea got before he broke in, and when he did, it was the old Dave back again. The man who had made her life more difficult than ever just after she took up her work in Nyddbeck and was having to come to terms at the same time with being widowed.

'It's every bloody thing that's wrong, and nothing you can say will make it any better. So don't bother wasting your time trying.

94

Keep your energies for those who are daft enough to believe in the same things as you do. Though God alone knows how you can still manage to do that.'

Andrea sighed. 'Oh Dave, you should know by now that I'm not just here for those who are able to believe as I do. That I'm here for anyone who needs my help, and that includes you.'

Now it was Dave who let go of a huge sigh. 'I know you do your best, Andrea, but how can I make sense of what's happened in my life? Of losing Jill, and being left with two children I can't cope with and a farm that's a disaster area. Then just as my mother marries a great guy like Ben and I see her happy again, he goes and has a massive heart attack. Where's the justice in that? How can you explain that away to me?'

Andrea bit her lip. Her heart ached for Dave and his family, but there were no easy answers she could give him or anyone else in these circumstances. She had travelled these same dark tunnels of hopelessness herself after the death of her only child, and later when Ian was killed, but she had always been supported by her faith. Dave Bramley had no such faith.

'I can't explain it to you, Dave,' she began slowly, carefully. 'All I know is that during my very worst times I was always helped by knowing how many people were praying for me. Their prayers were like a thin crack of light coming through an almost closed door. A light that grew stronger as I came to terms with what had happened.'

Dave moved impatiently, embarrassed perhaps by what she had said and not knowing how to respond to it. As he remained silent, scuffing the dead heather beneath one foot, she sought in her mind for the next set of words. They had to be the right words.

'Have you ever talked about this to Julie? I know she was Jill's best friend, and that you get on well together. Now she's living so near to you it might help for you to talk to her, to share your worries with her...' Andrea's voice tailed off as she gave him time to consider what she had just suggested.

'Julie's already had more than enough of my problems, it seems,' Dave broke in fiercely then. 'She's had enough of my company as well.'

Andrea frowned. 'What do you mean, Dave? I'm not with you on this one.'

'I mean she's got someone else!'

Andrea was too startled to say anything at first. All she could do was stand and stare at Dave with her blue eyes wide and unbelieving. Then Dave amended what he had just said, hot colour rushing up into his cheeks as he did so.

'I mean she's moving out of Jacob's

Cottage soon.'

She must be very careful what she said next, Andrea knew. 'I suppose there'll be holiday bookings starting any time now, so she'll have to move out. Perhaps she'd like to come and stay with me in the manse? I've got room there for her.'

'We've got spare rooms in the farmhouse! Two of them. I've already told her she can have one of those, but she's turned it down.'

This didn't make sense to Andrea, until she recalled how strange Julie had sounded when they had spoken on the phone an hour or so ago. Though if Dave had made his offer of the room in the same way he had spoken of it just now, she was not surprised Julie had turned it down.

'That doesn't have to mean she's not interested in you any more,' she began carefully. 'Or that you are not still friends.'

'That can't be true!' Dave burst out so explosively that Lucky got to his feet and growled. 'She wouldn't be buying a house in Nyddford if it was.'

Andrea was astonished to hear that. She found it hard to believe. 'Are you sure you haven't got this wrong, Dave? Julie didn't say anything about it to me when I rang her this afternoon.'

'I haven't got it wrong! I saw her looking at the place today when I was driving out of Nyddford, and she told me less than an hour ago that she had put in an offer for it.'

Andrea took a deep breath, then let it go on a sigh. Obviously things had gone quite disastrously wrong for Julie and Dave, but why? They seemed to be so good for each other, and they needed one another. Dave's children needed them both, but Dave was a proud man and a very stubborn one. Pig-headed at times, as people would say here in Yorkshire! So what had gone wrong between them? Was that what Julie wanted to talk to her about tonight?

'Julie's coming to supper with me tonight. Perhaps she'll tell me about it then.' Andrea knew it was time for her to go. There was nothing more she could say that would help Dave. Perhaps she had already said too much? It seemed like it when Dave spoke again.

'Now I know she's had enough of me and my problems! We usually eat together while Carla and Jack are at your church drama group.'

'I'm sorry, Dave. I didn't know that,' she told him un easily.

'At least it's you, and not this other guy she's meeting,' he said morosely.

'I don't know where you got that idea from.'

'Why else would she want to go and live in Nyddford when she could have one of the rooms in my farmhouse?'

98

Andrea bit her lip, and wondered just how Dave had voiced his offer of that room in his home. 'I don't know, Dave. You'll need to ask Julie that yourself, won't you?'

Immediately his body straightened and he prepared to depart. His chin was up and his eyes were indignant. 'I certainly will not! She can do as she damn well likes.' He shook his head as though bewildered by this obviously unexpected situation and took a couple of steps along the sheep track that would lead him back to his farm. Then, while Andrea was still staring after him and wondering what it was all about, he turned round and flung his final comment in her direction.

'You won't be surprised at her turning her back on me, will you?'

'What on earth do you mean?' Andrea was amazed to hear him say that.

'Not much of a catch for a girl like her, am I? A farmer struggling to make ends meet, working all sorts of unsociable hours, and with a couple of out-of-control kids thrown in. She'd be throwing herself away on a guy like me when she could have a doctor or a soldier or an accountant, wouldn't she?'

Andrea began to lose patience with him then. She knew she must keep a tight control on herself, because this was the old Dave who had caused so many problems for her last year. The man who had so often lost his temper with her, or with his children. The man who found it so easy to snub Julie Craven. The man who had no idea, it seemed, of just how long Julie had been in love with him.

'If you really think so badly of yourself, Dave, how can you expect anyone else to see you differently,' she challenged him.

It didn't work. In fact her words seemed to make things worse. 'I knew you'd agree with Julie. You were bound to. People like you and Julie have no place in your lives for men like me. You go for the successful guys, the ones who've got it made, don't you? The guys like Bill Wyndham.'

Andrea was stunned to hear him say that. Angry words came speeding into her mind; words that jostled one another to force their way out of her mouth. Then she looked again at Dave and saw the utter misery reflected not just in his eyes but in the way his shoulders were hunched as the icy chill of despair settled over his whole body.

'You're so tired that you are not thinking straight, Dave,' she said gently. 'I expect you've been doing too much, with looking after Ben's farm as well as your own. Perhaps you can ease off a bit now that Matt's arrived? Let him take over some of what you've been doing. I'm sure he'll be glad to help.'

'What makes you think that? Matt Harper's used to a different way of life now; going to work in a good suit and never getting his hands dirty. He's only come here to look after his own interests, to be on the spot ready to take over the business when his father dies.' Dave's voice was derisive.

Andrea shook her head in disbelief. 'I think you are wrong about that, Dave, but you've convinced me that I'm wasting my time in trying to cheer you up. So I'll leave you and get back to the manse.'

She did not wait to hear what his reaction would be to that piece of information. The moor was no place to linger now that it was growing dusk because there were many outcrops of limestone rock waiting to trip a careless walker. It was also distinctly chilly now the sun had gone down.

'Let's go, Lucky,' she said with forced cheerfulness as she turned her back on the man who owned this part of the moor and walked away.

Six

When Andrea answered Julie's ring on her doorbell late that evening she saw at once, in spite of her friend's skilled application of eye make-up, that the other girl had been crying.

'Hi Julie! It's good to see you.' She put a restraining hand on Lucky's collar as he dashed forward to add his own welcome. 'Don't let this crazy animal get his paws on you. He's just been over the wall after a squirrel, so his feet will be messy.'

Julie forced a laugh. 'I don't mind. Anything he leaves on this skirt will blend in with the rest, the mud from Tyke's paws and Brack's paws. At least they don't show on this jazzy fabric. You know, I really adore these dogs. I think I'll change my mind about having a cat and get myself a lovely big dog instead. Perhaps a rescued dog, like Lucky.'

So what Dave had said must be true. If Julie was already seriously considering taking on a dog it could only be because she was moving away from Abbot's Fold, where the two collies belonging to Dave Bramley were in charge. Andrea's concern for her deepened.

'Do you need to talk first? Or shall we do that after we've eaten?' she asked as Julie straightened up from making a fuss of Lucky and slipped off the bright-green fleece which she wore over her cream sweater.

'Oh, we'd better eat first before I start to unload all my woes on to your shoulders. Otherwise you might lose your appetite.' Julie forced a laugh as she said the words.

'I doubt it! I'm absolutely starving after my walk on the moor with Lucky, and then doing battle with the Youth Drama Group,' Andrea confessed.

Julie shook her head. 'You're a glutton for punishment to take that on, Andrea. Why don't you hand it over to one of the professional youth leaders from Nyddford Youth Centre?'

Andrea shrugged her slender shoulders. 'It's not as easy as that. I wish it were. They just don't have the funding these days to provide enough trained youth workers for all the places where they are needed. Because the Emmanuel Drama Group mostly consists of church members' children, I'm afraid it has no chance of getting a professional leader at present. So it's up to me to keep it going. I really would hate to see it fold, because the kids who turn up on drama nights are so enthusiastic. They seem to really enjoy taking part in the short dramatic pieces we've started using during the family services at Nyddford. In fact I'd like to try putting one into the next family service at Nyddbeck, if I can manage it.'

As she listened, Julie felt a growing concern about the weariness which was plain to see on Andrea's face. The colour brought to her friend's cheeks by the bracing moorland walk had disappeared now and there were little lines of exhaustion marring the paper-white porcelain complexion. Andrea was working too hard, and there was no Bill here now to encourage her to ease off and relax when she had the chance.

'If you can't get professional help with your youth club, isn't it possible to get volunteers from your own church members?' Julie suggested.

Andrea placed the dish of the lasagna Julie had brought with her into the microwave while she considered this. 'I don't know. I did tentatively suggest at the last church meeting that I'd welcome some help, but most of the people there that night were in the older age groups, so I was not too surprised that there were no takers.' She rubbed her eyes, confirming Julie's suspicions that she had, as usual, packed too much into her long working day.

'It might be worth trying again, because there could be older people who have experience in amateur dramatics. I mean, some of the people who've moved into the area on retirement may have been in drama groups where they used to live and work. I was in a drama group myself when I was doing my training at Leeds.' Julie stopped then, suddenly aware of the eager light that came into Andrea's tired eyes.

'You could be just the person I need! Young, lively, experienced. Good with teenagers too—'

'Don't go on!' Julie broke in. 'I ought to know better than to give someone like you that sort of info. I must need my head examining!'

Andrea laughed. 'If you'll give it a try, I'll pick you up next week and every week until you've made your mind up about taking it on. What do you say?'

The silence was lengthening when the microwave bleeped. 'I wouldn't need the lift for long. Only until I move to Nyddford,' Julie said.

Andrea drew in a deep breath and held it while she made up her mind whether to comment on this statement. It would probably be best if she did not mention her meeting up on the moor with Dave. It would certainly be wiser if they ate first. She would be better able to concentrate on Julie's problems when she did not feel quite so faint from lack of food. If Bill were here he would be cross with her for skipping lunch, and tea...

'Shall we eat before we talk about what you've just said? I have a feeling once we start on that subject it'll be a long session, and I don't want to flake out on you in the middle of it.'

'Yes, we'd better eat first. You've got into bad habits again just because Bill isn't here to keep an eye on you, haven't you, Andrea?' As she spoke, Julie was lifting the dish from the micro and placing it in the centre of the kitchen table alongside a bowl of salad and a basket of bread rolls. 'I'll serve, then I'll know you get plenty,' she said sternly. 'You are not to say a word until your plate is clean. Understood?'

Andrea laughed as she poured apple juice into two tall crystal glasses. 'Yes, Sister! Certainly, Sister! I bet you terrify your patients when you start giving them orders?'

Then Julie laughed too. 'Only the young guys, and not for long!'

There was silence as they ate, except for the exaggerated sighs which came at intervals from Lucky, who had been banished from under the table by Andrea and now reclined in his bed with a woeful expression.

'This is gorgeous, Julie. You really are a

super cook. I never seem to get the same flavour into my food as you do. How do you manage it?' Andrea asked when her plate was almost empty.

'Perhaps I have more time to spend on my cooking than you do. You're always in a rush to get to a meeting or a service. Or to go and visit someone, aren't you?'

Andrea had to agree with that. 'I've certainly had a lot of that to do lately, what with all the people who fell and broke arms or legs during those heavy March frosts. Then Ben Harper and Dorothy having such a bad time since Easter,' she added with a sigh.

'How are they doing now? Are things any easier for them now Ben's son is here?' Julie wanted to know.

Andrea shrugged. 'It's hard to tell, because Dorothy is a very loyal person and Matt is a man with an attitude. Though I can understand him being a bit put out, having come over from America at short notice only to find his father refuses to see him. I wish I could do something about that.'

'Such as?' Julie prompted.

'Talking sense into the pair of them. Because the way they are behaving is putting an enormous strain on poor Dorothy.'

Julie frowned. 'That isn't good for her at all. I think I'll drop in to see her tomorrow after I've finished my stint at the Health

Centre.'

'I'm sure she'll be pleased to see you. She's very fond of you. In fact I think she's been cherishing hopes of you and Dave getting together permanently,' Andrea said with a smile.

'Then she's about to be disappointed. I'm buying a house in Nyddford.' Julie spoke harshly, as though it hurt to be sharing that news with Andrea.

Andrea bit her lip. She must be very careful of what she said next. Julie must not know that her news was no surprise because Dave had already told her about the proposed move to Nyddford. Their friendship, or their love affair, was obviously in a very fragile state indeed if Julie was really intending to move to Nyddford. So she took her time about asking the question she knew Julie would be expecting from her.

'I didn't know you were thinking of doing that,' she began carefully.

'I'm not *thinking* of doing it, I actually *am* doing it!' Julie broke in vehemently.

'Why?'

'Because there are holiday bookings for Jacob's Cottage starting very soon, so I have to move out. It seemed a good idea to find somewhere to live in Nyddford close to the Health Centre. Somewhere permanent.'

'It won't be easy to do, will it?'

'I've already done it. That's what I'm

trying to tell you, Andrea. I've found a small house, a nice little house, and made an offer for it which has been accepted.'

So it was true, what Dave had told her up there on the moor this afternoon. Andrea felt a wave of disappointment engulf her.

'What on earth did you do that for?' she asked, forgetting her usual caution in choosing the right words with which to deal with other people's personal problems. Immediately then she realized her mistake and rushed to put it right.

'I'm so sorry, Julie! I shouldn't have spoken like that. It was because you are my friend, and I'm deeply concerned that you could be making a terrible mistake with this move. You've been so good for Dave, and for Carla and Jack.'

'Not good enough for Dave to make sure I stay there.' There was a wobble in Julie's voice as she spoke the words.

'Does he know what you are intending to do?' Of course he knew – that was what had put him into such a black mood that he'd gone up on the moor this afternoon to brood instead of doing something to stop Julie from leaving. Something like asking Julie to marry him. Didn't he realize how lucky he was to have someone like Julie so much in love with him that she would willingly take on his children, his farmhouse and all his problems?

'Yes! He knows but he doesn't care.' Julie's voice was muffled as she attempted to hold back the tears that threatened to overflow. 'I'm sure you are mistaken about that.'

'I'm not! All he did when I told him I was leaving the cottage was offer me a room in his farmhouse. As if I were no more important to him than a lodger! A bed-and-breakfast booking, except that I'd have to cook my own breakfast.'

Those final few words, which brought a hint of a smile to Andrea, which she swiftly stifled, were all that were needed to unleash a torrent of weeping as Julie pushed aside her plate and let her head fall forward as she gave way to her despair. Immediately, Andrea was on her feet to put her arms about the other woman. She felt her own eyes begin to sting as she tried to bring comfort to Julie.

Lord, please help me to say the right things; to help Julie, and Dave, she prayed silently while she kept her arm about Julie's shaking shoulders.

Lucky came to her aid then, lifting his head from his paws to stare with puzzled eyes at the weeping girl. Julie was one of Lucky's favourite people and even though he was a very young dog he was already sensitive to atmosphere. So he lifted his beautiful red-gold head and howled. Then he got to his feet and came to place his mouth on Julie's knee, whimpering softly as he licked at the tears which fell on his silky fur. So it was that Julie became aware of him and put a hand out to stroke him.

'Oh Lucky, now I've upset *you*.' She gulped as she bent to put her arms about the dog. 'You really are a darling. I'll be far better off sharing my life with someone like you than with that damned, stupid, pig-headed David Bramley.' She scrubbed the moisture from her eyes and gave Andrea a watery grin. 'Sorry about that, Andrea.'

'It's nothing I haven't heard before. At least you'll feel better for getting it off your chest,' Andrea told her with a chuckle. 'Even Dave's mother has been known to describe him as pig-headed. I love that expression. It seems to belong to Yorkshire, though it could be used to describe men from other places. Are you sure you are ready to give up on Dave? Are you certain that you haven't misunderstood him?'

'I'm quite certain that all he did was offer me one of the spare bedrooms in the farm-house. He said it wouldn't be any problem.' Julie gave a mirthless laugh as she shared that with Andrea.

Andrea hesitated. 'What did you say to that? Or would you rather not tell me?'

'I said it *would* be a problem for me, and not one that I was prepared to take on board. I was prepared to tell him why not,

111

only I didn't get the chance.' Julie sniffed back another tear.

'Why not?'

'Because while Dave was still standing there looking flabbergasted, Carla arrived home on the back of Josh Bolton's motorbike. So Dave left me and went storming over to them, blasting off about having forbidden Carla to ride on motorbikes. Then he put his head down and almost ran up the hillside away from them, leaving Carla in tears and me watching it all from Jacob's Cottage and wondering whether to go and try to comfort Carla or if she would think I was interfering.'

'So what did you do?'

'I saw that Josh had put his arms about her, and I guessed she'd rather be comforted by Josh than by me. So I went back into the cottage and started putting things into one of my suitcases, ready for the move. It seemed the only thing to do.' Julie ended the sentence with a defiant note in her voice.

'Don't you think that maybe Dave was caught on the hop when you told him you were buying a house in Nyddford?' Andrea suggested thoughtfully.

Julie frowned. 'What do you mean? I'm not with you, Andrea.'

'I mean that perhaps he had got so used to your being there whenever he needed someone to talk to that he'd never even thought about what would happen when you had to move out. Maybe not realized just how much he would miss you.'

'He knew there were bookings coming up for the cottage. What did he think I was going to do then? Where did he think I was going to live?'

Andrea smiled. 'You said he offered you a room in his farmhouse...'

Now Julie scowled at the memory. 'It was the way he offered it! So – so offhand. As if that was all he had to do to make me stay!'

'He probably didn't realize he was coming over like that. I mean, Dave's rather lost confidence in himself since the farming industry started to go downhill. Perhaps he thinks he hasn't got much to offer you, Julie? Certainly not as much as he would like to be able to give you.'

Julie didn't seem to agree with that. 'He knows I understand about his problems. We've talked them over often enough while I've been living in Jacob's Cottage.'

'Talking them over in a general sort of way isn't the same as asking you to become personally involved with them though, is it?'

Julie took a long moment to think about that. 'He must know that I care enough about him to be willing to share his bad times. I can't believe he doesn't know that.'

'Perhaps you just need to be there, close to

him, for a little longer?' Andrea suggested.

'You're surely not advising me to move into one of his empty rooms, Andrea?' Julie sounded very shocked at the idea of Andrea advising that.

Andrea laughed softly. 'No. I'm only saying don't move out of the cottage until the very last minute. Have patience with Dave for just a little longer. Think about it!'

Julie shook her head slowly. 'The trouble is that time isn't on my side, Andrea. I'll be thirty-seven soon and I'd really like to have a child, Dave's child, before I'm too old.'

Andrea digested that in silence.

'You do understand about that, don't you?'

'Yes, of course I do.' Andrea's voice was wistful. The desire to have a child before it was too late was something she understood only too well. It was what she wanted herself. Not a child who would replace her own wee Andrew, who had died six years ago at the age of three. She wanted a child who would have Bill for a father. Bill also wanted children. He had told her so on the night before he left for America, when he had begged her for the last time to fly out there to join him for a few days.

'We could marry very quietly out there,' he'd said, 'and keep our marriage a secret for the time being until you are ready to release the news. I know I said I'd be waiting for you when you are ready to take me as your husband, but I don't think I realized then just how hard the waiting would be. I want to settle down with you here in this village; to be part of your life and for you to be part of mine. I want us to have children who'll grow up here in this lovely place. I'm tired of having to hide my love for you, Andrea. I've had enough of pretending that we are no more than friends. Please come out and join me, even if it's only for a few days.'

'But you'll be working. That's why you are going, isn't it, Bill?' Even as she'd said the words, there had been a fierce longing inside Andrea to do as he asked.

'I won't be working all the time. There'll be evenings, and nights,' he had added softly as they were parting company in the porch of Beckside after a shared supper.

So nearly had Andrea agreed. Maybe she would have done if her mobile phone had not broken into the moment and forced them apart. The call had sent her to a remote farmhouse where a woman had given birth and wanted her premature child to be baptized. There was no time to be lost. She would not see Bill again until he came back from America. This was the life she had chosen, but it had been so hard to say goodbye to Bill before she drove through the starlit landscape to carry out this sad service for those who needed her most.

'You're dreaming, Andrea.' Julie Craven's voice broke into her wandering thoughts. 'Did what I said upset you? Bring back memories of your own little boy, I mean. If it did, I'm so sorry.'

Andrea shook her head, and managed a smile. 'It was Bill I was thinking about,' she confessed. 'I was remembering how, when he was trying to persuade me to go and have a few days in America with him, I got this call on my mobile that sent me right across the moor to baptize a premature baby who was about to die.'

'That must be the worst part of your work,' Julie murmured.

'Yes, but in this case the wee fellow took a turn for the better. He's in hospital, but improving.'

'Do you regret not going with Bill? I suppose you must. Though I don't think I should have asked you that!'

Andrea smiled. 'Since we're friends, you'll know the answer to your question, though I am really glad that I've been here for Dorothy when she's needed me.'

'She's so grateful for the support you've given her. Each time I've phoned her, she's told me that. I've promised to call in and see her when I finish at the Health Centre tomorrow. I would have done so earlier but she's been spending most of her time at the hospital.'

'You'll probably meet Ben's son then.'

Julie pulled a face. 'I don't much like the sound of him. I think Dorothy's having problems with him. He's already wanting to make a lot of changes in the business before he's even spoken to Ben about them.'

'He can't talk to Ben about them if Ben won't allow him to visit,' Andrea felt bound to point out in fairness to Matt.

'No, of course he can't. I wonder what will happen when Ben's allowed home?' Julie mused. 'They'll surely have to speak to one another when they are living in the same house, won't they?'

'If they don't, life will be unbearable for Dorothy. So we've got to hope they both come to their senses before then. Dorothy says they are both stubborn as mules and simply can't, or won't, see one another's point of view. Ben's never forgiven Matt for taking the job in America, and Matt's never forgiven his father for letting him go. Ben thought the job would fall apart; Matt made sure it didn't. In fact he was in line for a promotion interview when Ben had his heart attack but he let it go to come over here. Only to find his dad refused to see him. Matt was furious,' Andrea concluded.

'What is he really like?' Julie wanted to know.

Andrea frowned. 'He's good-looking, well-spoken, well dressed too. In fact I think he's the sort of son Ben would be proud of, if only he could forget about their past differences.'

'I wonder how long he'll stay, now that Ben's out of danger? Will he be able to stay for long enough to go on helping out with the farming side of the business until the lambing is over at Abbot's Fold? Dave was helping with Ben's animals until Matt arrived, but he needs to be at his own farm now. He's already tired out, and lambing means being out with the ewes during the night as well as in the daytime.' Julie's voice was full of her concern for Dave.

'If you move out of the cottage too soon, you won't be on the spot to keep an eye on Dave, to give him a meal, or make him a hot drink, will you, Julie?'

Julie did not answer. Instead she got to her feet and began to clear the dishes from the table. Then she began to wash them.

'I thought I'd leave those until morning,' Andrea protested.

'You'll have that hound to walk in the morning, so you don't want the washing-up as well,' Julie said as Lucky, knowing instinctively that it was time for his late-night treat, went to stand close to where the biscuit tin lived. 'I'll let you get to bed then. You look as if you could do with some rest. I thought you were going to take some time off when your parents came down?'

'I couldn't do that after all, because Dorothy and Ben, both being Elders, were going to take on some of the work while Mum and Dad were here. Ben's illness put a stop to that.'

'Don't work too hard, Andrea, or you'll be ill,' Julie warned as she slipped on her fleece ready to leave.

Andrea patted back a yawn as she laughed. 'If it's advice time, don't leave that cottage until you have to, Julie.'

Again, Julie did not answer.

Seven

Julie was so determined to keep her promise about going to visit Dorothy Harper as soon as possible that when her work at Nyddford Health Centre was finished the next day she went to Ford House, stopping on the way to take another look at the little house which would soon become her permanent home. As she lingered by the gate, taking in the brightness of the crocuses flowering in a low container beneath the bay window and admiring the brass furnishings on the immaculate white front door, she vowed that she would move into the place just as soon as she was able.

Even with the memory of Andrea's words of advice still so fresh in her mind, she knew that she would not remain in Jacob's Cottage for a day longer than she had to. Because she had been cut to the quick by what had happened there earlier that day. When, as she was having her breakfast in the living room, she had seen Dave striding across the farmyard in the direction of the cottage, her heart had given a huge lurch and she had got to her feet so swiftly that she knocked over the milk jug. She felt sure that Dave must have had time now to recover from the shock the news of her impending move had given him, and to consider what it would mean to him. So he was coming to talk to her before she left for Nyddford. Andrea had been right: he had just needed time to realize how much he would miss her.

She was out in the hall even before the clatter of the door knocker could sound, eager, excited, warm with anticipation of what would surely happen now. Her hands were unsteady as she flung open the door and looked up into Dave's face. What she saw there dashed her hopes instantly. Yet she could be wrong. She had to be wrong.

'Hi! Dave! Have you time to come in for a coffee?' Her smile had wavered as she waited for him to refuse. Because she knew in advance that he was about to do just that.

Dave had shaken his head. 'I only came to bring you this.' He held out a long envelope which bore the logo of Nyddford's only estate agent. 'I found it inside the open flap of one of the big envelopes that came through my own letterbox. I knew it would be important to you, so I brought it over at once. I was going to put it through the door for you, if you hadn't seen me coming.'

'Thanks, Dave. Thanks a lot.' Julie had

deliberately allowed her fingers to touch Dave's as she reached out for the letter. There were a few seconds then when she thought that was all it needed, just a momentary contact to remind him of how close they had been until a day or two ago, and how wonderful it would be if they could be that close again. Hope died swiftly when Dave almost snatched his hand away and took a couple of steps backward. Yet patience and persistence were a part of Julie Craven's personality, so she tried again.

'Are you sure you won't have a quick coffee? The kettle's still hot,' she began.

'I'm quite sure, thanks, and I know you'll have plenty to do if you're moving out at the end of the month.' The words were curt; the expression on Dave's face was stern, unrelenting. Tyke, standing at his master's heel, had caught the enticing aroma of fresh toast and moved towards the open front door, certain of his welcome, his white-tipped tail waving happily.

'Lie down, Tyke! Lie down!' Instantly, Dave's words had stopped the collie and he had dropped to the concrete surface of the yard, placing his head on his outstretched paws.

Julie had stared into Dave's set face, noting the straight line of his mouth, the coldness of the dark-grey eyes and the heaviness of the frown above them. Was this the same man who had spent so much of his limited spare time with her, talking about the problems of getting young Jack into bed at night and out of it in the morning in time for school; about trying to stop Carla from spending too much time with Josh Bolton, who would be going back to America in a few months, and about how his mother would cope with life if Ben did not recover from his illness?

Was this the man who, when his children were out at the Youth Club or the Church Drama Group, came to share a meal with her, and after the meal often shared love? Was that all she had been to Dave since she moved into Jacob's Cottage: someone to ease the worries from his mind; and bring pleasure to his body? She had been a fool to think he loved her and would ask her to share his life. Obviously, he still loved Jill. Maybe he always would. Since the thought brought such an unbearable ache to her heart Julie had shut the door of the cottage in his face and went to throw the remains of her breakfast in the rubbish bin.

When she moved into this dear little house she would no longer be forced to see Dave Bramley as he went about his work on the farm. She would share her time then, when she was not working, with a nice big friendly dog. Dogs were faithful. They did not make use of you and then turn their back on you.

So from now on she would share her love, all of her love, with a dog.

Dave's dog lay close to him, only a yard or so away, as he prepared the big hay shed where the new-born lambs and their mothers would be sheltered if late snows, known as 'lambing snows', descended on the dale. Tyke watched every move made by his master, alert and ready to obey his command instantly. Only his master seemed to have forgotten he was there as he moved the bales, and moved them back again, then went to stand at the open door staring across the farmyard at the place where Tyke so often went in search of toast, biscuits or other tasty snacks. Tyke was always uneasy when his master was in this mood because it meant that his mind was not concentrating on the important work that they did together. The work that Tyke had been born to do; the work that he loved. It was time to remind his master of that.

'I'm a right bloody fool, Tyke,' Dave said when he felt the strong black mouth of his collie give his right knee a hearty nudge. He put a firm hand on the dog's head and kept it there, finding comfort from the communion with this faithful creature who seemed to know what his thoughts were before he knew them himself. 'I must be the biggest bloody fool in Yorkshire. I've had her to myself for all these weeks, just thinking that there was plenty of time, that I didn't need to rush into saying anything till I'd got the lambing over with, and now I've left it too late. While I've been putting in extra hours helping out with the animals at Ben Harper's place Julie's got tired of waiting and found someone else. Oh God, why can't I get anything right these days?'

Tyke licked his hand a couple of times, and began to send grumbles up from his strong white-ruffed neck. Dave spoke again. 'Who the hell is this guy? Has he been coming here while I've been away at Harper's place? Is he going to share this house she's buying in Nyddford? Is that why she's in such a rush to get away from here, so they can move in together? Why else would she want to move out in such a hurry?'

Tyke licked his hand again and leaned closer into his knee.

'There was no need for her to go as soon as the holiday bookings start. I told her there was no problem about that because she could have one of the spare rooms. What did she mean about it being a problem to her? Did she think I might make a nuisance of myself if we were living in the same house every night?' Dave's bewildered stare moved from Jacob's Cottage to the beautiful silvery-grey stone of his farmhouse. 'Of course, she could have been right about that. I've found it hard enough to keep away from her while she's been living in the cottage, until this last couple of weeks when I've been too damned tired to stay awake at night. Maybe she thought I was getting tired of *her* because I wasn't always in a rush to make love, so she's found someone who's not dead on his feet by nine o'clock every night. Someone with a damn sight more to offer her than the life of a farmer's wife.'

As this last thought hit him he kicked out with his left foot at a protruding piece of stone with a degree of force that made him wince. Tyke yelped and moved away from him, to survey him from a distance with reproachful eyes.

'I've blown it, Tyke! Let her go when I should have begged her to stay. Now I can't even be civil to her because I'm so bloody jealous of this other guy. If I'd gone in for the coffee she offered me this morning I might have found out who he is, only I was too stupid to see that.' He let go of an enormous sigh, then called his dog to him.

'Come here, Tyke! Good lad! There's always work for us to do. Never any short-age of that. Not much else to look forward to though now she's going, is there?'

Julie bought flowers from one of the shops in Nyddford Market Place. Carnations, apricot with dark-red frilly edges, and with

126

a beautiful scent. She knew Dorothy was fond of carnations, and she was very fond of Dorothy. They had met soon after Dave married Jill and their friendship had continued after Jill's death, even though for the year or so after the accident their only contact had been by telephone. At that time Dave did not make her welcome at the farm where his mother was looking after him and his children. Julie pushed that memory away from her as she lifted the carnations from the passenger seat after driving up to the front door of Ford House.

She rang the doorbell, then glanced about her as she waited. The garden was missing the loving attention of Ben Harper. Ben would be so eager to get back to his home and his garden. Where was Dorothy though? When Julie telephoned that morning, Dorothy had said she would be back from visiting Ben at the District Hospital by this time. Julie frowned as she pressed the bell for a second time.

'Hi! You must be Julie?'

Julie spun round to face the speaker. He had come from the back of the house and taken her by surprise because the chunky shoes he wore made no sound as he moved along the path to come to a stop at the foot of the steps.

'Yes, I'm Julie Craven. I came to see Dorothy.' Her eyes took in the burly build of the man, the open-necked shirt of checked fabric, the jeans that were so obviously new yet already had gathered earth stains on the knees and grass on the hems. Above the casual gear were straight shoulders, a square face that looked vaguely familiar, and eyes which were assessing her with a good deal of interest.

'She said you were coming to see her on your way home from the Health Centre. Are you a bit early, or is she rather late?' The voice was quite pleasant, with its intriguing mixture of local accent overlaid with the faintest transatlantic twang.

'I'm not early, because I stopped to buy the flowers. Is she not back yet from the hospital?'

'Have you rung the bell?'

'Yes. Twice, as a matter of fact.'

'Could she be slightly deaf?' he speculated.

Julie shook her head. 'No.'

'So she can't be in the house?'

'If she had been, she would have opened the door by now. Especially with Goldie making all that racket.'

'I'd better let him out, it's probably time he had some fresh air and exercise. Will you come in and wait, Julie? Or do you have to be somewhere else in a hurry?'

'I don't have anywhere else to go right now. So I'll wait, if only to make sure that all is well with Ben.'

'Have you any reason to think it might not be? Were you thinking he could have had a relapse?'

The question was asked calmly, but the man's eyes were sharp with anxiety as he moved up the four wide stone steps until he was on the same level as Julie.

'I don't have the latest information about him, only what Dorothy gave me this morning,' she told him as he opened the beautifully carved oak door with keys taken from the ring which sat on his right hip. 'She seemed to be pleased with his progress then.'

'Come in, Julie. Go straight through to the sitting room while I let that wretched dog out.'

Julie did so, thinking how delightful the spacious room was, then wondering again why Dorothy was not back yet. It was unlike her to be late for any appointment, whether it be a business or medical one, or an informal meeting such as this with a friend. She made her way into the wide bay window which gave a view of the curving drive, from where she would see the car as soon as it appeared. It was too soon to start worrying about her friend, but not too soon to be wondering what had happened to delay her.

'I should have introduced myself before now. Though you've probably guessed who

I am,' Matt said as he came into the room.

'Yes. You have to be Ben's son, Matt.'

He was frowning now. 'Have to be? Why? I could be the gardener...'

'You're so much like Ben.'

'In what way? I don't see it myself.'

He didn't sound too pleased about the likeness to his father, yet it was undeniable.

'The same shape of face, the same eyes, and eyebrows...'

He scowled at her. The eyebrows, thick and black, lifted rapidly in the way Julie had seen Ben's eyebrows lift. Then: 'Would you like some tea? I'm sure you would if you've just finished work for the day.'

'I can wait until Dorothy arrives. You look as if you were working at something yourself?'

'I'm helping with the animals while I'm here. It helps to fill in the time.'

'While you're waiting to go to the hospital? I don't suppose you are used to having time on your hands during the day?' Julie said.

'I'm not! When I think what I could have been doing back home; where I'd have been by now, I think I must have been crazy to come dashing over here as I did.'

Julie knew what he meant; knew that Matt was angry and hurt that having come all this way his father still would not meet him – though she was not going to become involved in discussing that situation with him.

It was up to father and son to resolve their differences. It would be advisable to change the subject, she decided.

'You said "back home". Does that mean you've settled permanently in America?'

He hesitated for a second too long. 'I thought I had, until this happened. Now I'm not so sure. The promotion I was in line for just when my father became critically ill would have been the deciding factor. Now I don't know whether I'll ever get that chance again.'

'Wouldn't the company make allowances for you having to make this trip at short notice?' Julie asked. She was feeling a stir of sympathy for him now. It must have been bitterly disappointing for him to sacrifice his chance of a good promotion, only to find when he reached Ford House that his father refused to see him.

Matt shrugged his heavy shoulders. 'I don't think so. There's very little sentiment in business, Julie, especially in the States.'

'Was this promotion terribly important to you?' She asked the question not out of any real interest but rather to fill in the waiting time that was now beginning to drag, perhaps for both of them.

Matt took his time about answering. 'Yes, it was. Because it would have given me the opportunity to move away from where I was living.'

Julie's curiosity was aroused. 'Couldn't you do that anyway?'

'No.' His answer was decisive.

'Why not?'

'I would have needed a very good reason for making such a move. The promotion would have supplied that reason.'

She was more curious than ever now, but she was not to find out more about Matt Harper's life in America because Dorothy's car was turning into the drive at last.

'I'll put the kettle on,' Matt said abruptly, and made a swift exit from the room.

'Julie dear, I'm so sorry to keep you waiting,' Dorothy said breathlessly as she hurried into the room. 'I ran over some broken glass and got a flat tyre. Then I couldn't move the nuts to change it so I had to call out the rescue service. I ought to have phoned you but I'd left my mobile behind. I do hope you've not been worrying about me. Or Ben,' she added.

'No,' Julie lied cheerfully. 'I knew you'd have been in touch if there'd been anything to worry about, and I had Matt to talk to while I waited. He's just gone to switch the kettle on.'

'Good! I'm desperate for some tea, and I expect you are too. Why don't you stay on and eat with us? We'll make it high tea. That's if you've nothing else arranged for tonight.'

As she voiced the invitation Dorothy's smiling glance met Julie's. In that moment Julie guessed that the older woman was hoping she would say she had promised to cook a meal for Dave and his children, or that Dave was coming to share her supper in Jacob's Cottage. Dorothy was going to be bitterly disappointed that she and Dave were no longer an item. It was going to be difficult breaking the news to her, but it would have to be done and the sooner the better.

'No, I don't have anything arranged for tonight, Dorothy, so I'd love to stay and have high tea with you.'

Dorothy hesitated. 'I was wondering if you and Dave were going to eat together...'

'No. We're not.' Julie knew that her answer was harsh, uncompromising, but the pain that seared her every time she thought of Dave Bramley and her shattered hopes and dreams seemed to grow fiercer.

Matt, who was striding into the room, carrying a tray bearing a teapot, mugs and milk jug, came to an abrupt stop. His glance moved from Julie to Dorothy, and back again to Julie before he spoke. 'Am I interrupting anything? Anything private, I mean. I can always make myself scarce if I am,' he offered, with his interrogative stare still riveted to Julie's eyes.

'No, no of course not,' Julie rushed to

answer before Dorothy could get a word in. 'Dorothy was inviting me to stay to high tea, and I was accepting.'

'Good!'

There was open admiration in Matt's face now. Julie found herself irritated by it.

'You probably won't be saying that at the end of the meal when you've been bored out of your mind by hearing us catching up on all the local gossip,' she said tartly.

'I'll risk it,' he said with a smile. 'I've got a lot of catching up to do myself after being away for so long, and it will give me the chance to get to know you a little better, Julie.'

Andrea replaced the small Communion set in the case which rested on her knee. It was at Ben's request that she had come to the hospital today to enable him and Dorothy to share the Bread and Wine in the short and simple service of Holy Communion, which had been such an essential part of their lives during all the years before and after their marriage. It was, and always would be, of the utmost importance to them both. Dorothy had just left them quite suddenly, overcome with emotion she could no longer hide from them.

'Thank you, Andrea my dear, for making this possible for us. It's meant a great deal to us, and given us a chance to offer thanks for

134

my recovery,' Ben said as Andrea prepared to leave him and go on to visit another sick member of her church.

'It won't be long now before you are sharing a service with us at Nyddford,' Andrea reminded him. 'Everyone is looking forward to that.' She held out her hand and Ben enclosed it within his own large palm. 'Especially Dorothy,' she added.

Ben sighed. 'Dorothy has been quite wonderful during these last few weeks. So much more wonderful than I deserve.' He said the words wistfully, and seemed almost embarrassed at having shared them with Andrea.

'Dorothy wouldn't agree with that, Ben. You know she wouldn't.' Andrea spoke firmly. What was in Ben's mind that he should sound so unlike his usual self? He was normally so confident, so self-assured. So proud of the fact that at an age when many men were opting for retirement he was still able to run his own successful business, and more than proud that Dorothy was his wife.

'Maybe Matt would.'

Andrea was puzzled by these words. 'I don't think I follow you, Ben. Maybe Matt would...?'

'Agree that Dorothy has been more wonderful than I deserve,' he said in a low voice.

Andrea waited silently, knowing that there

135

was more to come, and that Ben needed to share it with her.

'I haven't set a very good example, have I, either as a father or a Christian?'

Instantly then she knew what he meant. 'None of us behave as well as we ought to do, Ben. Especially when we are under pressure,' she added quietly.

'The trouble is that once you get at odds with one another and allow it to go on and on it's so hard to mend the gap. Perhaps it's impossible, after so long. What do you think, Andrea?'

She took her time about answering. Then: 'I don't think anything is ever impossible if we want it enough, Ben.'

'I've never wanted anything as much in all my life, except to marry Dorothy,' he confessed. 'I was a fool to let things go on for so long, once I'd got at odds with Matt. Now I'm afraid he might decide to go back to America before we patch things up. Do you think there's any chance of him doing that?'

'I don't know,' Andrea answered truthfully. 'He hasn't discussed it with me. Though he seems to be content enough to go on helping out with your animals.'

'Matt was always good with the livestock.' Ben chuckled as he added, 'With the girls too. If he's taken a fancy to someone while he's been over here, he might not be in such a rush to get back. Dorothy seems to think he has met someone. She says he's been going out dressed up smart as paint some evenings.'

Uneasiness took possession of Andrea when she heard that. Because twice recently she had phoned Julie and asked her if she had thought any more about helping with the Youth Drama Group, and twice Julie had said she couldn't do it that evening because she had a date. Andrea's hopeful enquiry about whether the date was with Dave Bramley had brought a scornful reply.

'Of course not! Dave's old news now as far as I'm concerned. It's someone who's been around much more exciting places than Nyddford.'

Andrea had not made the connection at that time. Now it seemed so obvious that she could not think how she could have missed it. Julie had mentioned meeting Matt Harper when she had been at Ford House to visit Dorothy, and Matt Harper had certainly been around more exciting places than Nyddford. Her thoughts moved on. A partnership between Julie and Matt Harper, even of the most temporary sort, would arouse fierce jealousy in Dave. It would also be certain to cause trouble between the Harpers and the Bramleys.

Eight

Dave scraped his boots wearily on the worn piece of iron which had stood at the back door of his farmhouse for a couple of centuries. He ought to take off the boots before going into the kitchen but as he'd have to go straight back out again to take another look at the ewe that was going to have a bad time giving birth to her twin lambs there was no chance of him doing that. In the lambing shed the ewe was already voicing her distress. He might have to call the vet after all, if he couldn't help her himself, but he didn't want to do that. Vets cost money which he could ill afford.

The kitchen of Abbot's Fold was empty, except for the house cat. The Aga sent out a slow heat, but he had forgotten to refill the kettle that always sat on the hob. Cursing under his breath, Dave made his way to the electric kettle and set it to boil. Then he looked about him at the chaos, and felt the familiar surge of anger rush through him. He'd told Carla that she must clean the place up when she came home from school yesterday. She had seemed to be making a start on it when the phone had rung and she had embarked on a long conversation with Josh Bolton. After that the tidying up had been left behind as she finished off the meal Mrs Grainger had prepared the day before, then she had run out to meet Josh Bolton at the farm gate when he arrived there on his motorbike.

Dave had been furious with her, and given vent to his anger when she came back just before ten. He had told her then that she must clean the kitchen before going to school this morning. It had done no good though, because the clearing up she was supposed to do before she went to school was all around him in the form of dirty pots and pans, a littered table and work surfaces, and nothing ready for the evening meal. He'd have plenty to say to her about that when she came in from school. Something she would not like. There would be no Drama Group for Carla tonight, or any other night until she began to put more help into the house. She was sixteen now, old enough to make herself useful instead of coming up with all the old excuses about having homework to do. The homework never seemed to stop her from going out with the American lad. There wasn't much point to the homework anyway because he couldn't afford to let her go on to university.

Her place would be here when she left school, to keep house and cook for him and Jack. Then he would not need to pay Mrs Grainger to come twice a week. Carla could get a part-time job in one of the Nyddford shops or cafés to provide her own clothes and pocket money.

It was not what Jill would have wanted for their daughter, and it was not what would have happened if Julie had been staying on at Abbot's Fold because Dave knew that Julie would have wanted the same things for Carla as Jill had wanted. Only Julie was not staying on at Abbot's Fold. In fact Julie was hardly ever to be seen at Jacob's Cottage these days, she seemed only to come back to the cottage to change out of her uniform, have a shower, and then go out again dressed as if for a date with this new guy of hers. So Carla would have to put up with the way things were now, at least until things improved on the farm. If things ever did improve...

Julie spotted Carla getting off the school bus at the top of Abbot's Hill, and stopped to ask if she'd like a lift home.

'Yes, please!' Carla gasped. 'The bus was late leaving school, so Dad'll be blazing mad with me again if I'm not back in time to do some cleaning up. He was on at me again last night about not doing it because Josh

140

came to take me to a barbecue at his folks' place. I said I'd do it this morning, but I slept in and didn't have time.'

'Won't Mrs Grainger be coming to help?'

'Not today. She doesn't come till tomorrow. We can only afford her twice a week, and Dad says we really can't afford her then.'

'But I thought—' Julie closed her mouth on the words she was about to utter. Words that would have said she had been under the impression that Mrs Grainger, who had been Ben Harper's housekeeper at Ford House right from the time his first wife became ill until he married Dave's mother, was still having her wages paid by Ben. She ought to have known better. Dave was far too stubborn to have allowed his mother's new husband to pay for the help he needed once his mother had moved out of Abbot's Fold Farm and into Ford House. He was just too pig-headed for words, and quite blind to the fact that he was putting immense stress on this young girl at a time when she couldn't cope with it. If he had asked *her* to stay on at the farm she would have talked him round about it; made him see sense. Only he hadn't asked her, and soon she would be leaving his cottage for good. Two weeks from today...

'I wish you weren't leaving, Julie,' Carla said, as though reading her thoughts.

141

'I have to go, Carla, and the sooner the better.'

'Why?'

'Because there are holiday bookings for the cottage starting soon.'

'You could have come and lived in the house with us. Why didn't you do that?'

How could she answer such a question? Julie wished they had already been at the farm gate so she could have avoided having to do that, but the dairy cows due for milking were blocking the road she needed to turn into.

'It wouldn't have been such a good idea,' she answered slowly.

'I don't see why not. We all get on well together, don't we?'

Julie sighed. 'It really isn't as simple as that, Carla.'

'I mean, if you came to live in our house Dad might get married to you one day. I'd like that. So would our Jack.'

This statement from Carla, who was never afraid to express an opinion whether anyone wanted to hear it or not, brought an unexpected rush of moisture to Julie's eyes. It was going to be hard to know what to say next, she knew as she searched her mind for the right words.

'As I said before, it isn't quite as straightforward as you seem to imagine, Carla,' was all she could come up with. 'You'll understand better when you are just a little older.'

'I understand now how my Dad feels,' the girl told her then. 'I know he fancies you a lot because I've seen the way he kisses you sometimes.'

Julie almost choked when she heard that. Dave was not in the habit of kissing her in the presence of his children. So when had Carla managed to watch those more passionate embraces which until now both of them had thought to be unobserved by anyone?

'I don't know what you're talking about, Carla. Your Dad isn't in the habit of kissing me—' she began hurriedly.

'Not when he thinks we are around,' Carla broke in. 'I've seen him through the cottage window though when I've been slipping out through the old dairy door to meet Josh. That's why I know he fancies you. The only other person I ever saw him kiss like that was Mum.'

The cows were all through the gate that led to the milking parlour at last, Julie saw to her immense relief. So she could drive on into the farm lane and ignore Carla's words. Not forget them though. Because those totally unexpected words seemed to be burning into her brain as she brought her car to a screeching halt in front of Jacob's Cottage and pushed open the passenger door so that Carla would have no excuse to linger and ask more awkward questions. Enough, today, was more than enough. Especially with Dave at that moment striding across the yard to confront his daughter.

'Thanks for the lift, Julie. Thanks a lot!' Carla cried as she gracefully swung her long slim legs free of the car.

Julie remained in her seat as the girl gave her a smile and a wave before turning in the direction of the Abbot's Fold back door. What her father had to say to her would soon banish the smile from her face, Julie guessed. Before their raised voices could reach her through the open window she made a rapid exit from the vehicle and let herself into the cottage. Once in there she shut the door on the row that was fast building up between father and daughter, then leaned into it with her hands covering her ears while she allowed despair to engulf her.

During the first week of this year, when she had moved into this cottage, which Dorothy had offered her at a low rental, she had hoped that before the first of the holiday bookings were due to arrive at the beginning of May David Bramley would have fallen enough in love with her to ask her to stay, if not as his wife, then as his live-in partner. Julie would have settled for such a partnership, if only Dave had said he loved her too much to let her go.

Only Dave had not said any such thing. All

he had said was that she could have a room in his farmhouse instead of buying herself a house in Nyddford. It was the sort of arrangement he might have made with a bed-and-breakfast tourist last summer when his mother was still living in his home. So her gamble had not paid off. Dave had certainly enjoyed being with her, and even appeared to be as much attracted to her as he had been all those years ago before he met and married her friend Jill. Only it had all been just an excuse to share her time, her emotions, and sometimes her bed. Which was why she was now going to take a shower, put on make-up and perfume and the new narrow-strapped emerald-green dress, in time to be ready when Matt Harper called for her at seven o'clock to take her to dinner at a new restaurant in Harrogate.

They had already been out twice since Matt arrived, once to a film, once to the local Chinese. At first she had just felt sorry for Matt, coming all this way to see a parent who would not meet him, then she had begun to enjoy his admiration. It made her feel less used, more appreciated. Now she liked Matt for what he was, a man with his father's best qualities plus that fascinating polish on the personality that came from his experience on the other side of the Atlantic. She would take care not to fall in love with

Matt, but she would certainly make the most of his company and his admiration while he was here. The telephone brought an abrupt end to her musing.

'Hi! Julie! Andrea here. How did you enjoy helping with the Youth Drama Group?'

'Hi! Andrea. It was more fun than I expected. They're all so keen, aren't they?'

'Oh yes. Especially Carla. She's really quite good. I was wondering if you were free to help again this week? I meant to ring you yesterday but I got so bogged down with work that I never got round to it. I hope I'm not too late now.' Andrea waited hopefully until the exclamation on the other end of the line warned her that she was about to be disappointed.

'Sorry, Andrea. I can't make it tonight. I've got a date.'

'With Dave?' Andrea asked hopefully. 'If you have, I don't mind being disappointed...'

'No! Not with Dave.' Julie answered too quickly.

Andrea waited to hear who the date was, but Julie moved on quickly to tell her how her house buying was going, then to ask if she had heard yet when Bill was coming home to Nyddbeck.

'He's not sure, yet.'

'I thought it was going to be the end of this week?'

146

'So did I, but when he rang me yesterday he said his agent had slotted in more lectures and demonstrations than he had anticipated.' Andrea sighed as she recalled how tired, how remote, Bill had sounded during their short conversation. The aching loneliness that she had been aware of before the transatlantic phone call interrupted her preparation for the baptism service to be held in Nyddbeck Church next Sunday was still there for long after Bill's voice had disappeared.

'Don't you wish now that you'd gone with him?' Julie asked. 'All that travelling from one exciting place to another, and being there to hear Bill talk about his art so brilliantly, would have been good for you.'

'Maybe it would.' Andrea paused, then went on. 'It wouldn't have been good for my churches though to have me on the other side of the Atlantic at a time when things are so busy here and neither Ben nor Dorothy are able to help out.'

'Things should improve for you soon because Ben's due home tomorrow,' Julie told her then.

'Is he? I didn't know that. I expect Dorothy will be letting me know not to go and visit him in the hospital. Has Matt been able to go in and see him yet?'

'No, but I'll—' Julie broke off, then added hurriedly, 'I must go, someone's coming for me. I think he's here already. Bye!'

'Bye!' Andrea echoed. It was too late, Julie had already gone.

Matt Harper had brought the low-slung sports car to a halt outside the farm gate and glanced from the farmhouse to the attractive silver-grey stone cottage which was closer to the gate. Should he wait here for Julie? Or was she expecting him to drive up to the door of Jacob's Cottage to collect her? He slid out of the driving seat and felt the clean moorland air sting his freshly shaved cheeks. It was certainly marvellous up here on a late spring day when the clouds were racing one another across the sky as day moved gently towards night. The wild geese were calling to one another as they flew low overhead. It was as unlike the place where he lived in America as anything could ever be. There was a peace here, a stillness, a cleanness that was not to be found in a city. He would miss it when he went back to the States. If he *did* go back to the States...

Of course he was going back to the States. That was where his future was. There was no future for him here, with a father who did not want to know him and who would certainly not appreciate all the time and effort he had put into the family farm and transport business over the last few weeks. Once his father was restored to health it would be time for him to leave. That would not be long now, because Ben Harper was coming home from the hospital to Ford House tomorrow. What would happen then?

'I won't be able to stay on in the house once Dad's home,' he had told Julie a couple of nights ago. 'I ought to move into a hotel before then.'

He did not want to move into a hotel. To do that would hurt Dorothy's feelings and, to his surprise, Matt had discovered that he liked the woman who had taken his mother's place. Decision time was fast approaching, and it was getting harder and harder for him to make his mind up and book a flight. The letters from Susanna ought to have helped, but it was all too easy to put them out of his mind. Especially since he had got to know Julie Craven...

Nine

Julie glanced at the open back door of the farmhouse as she crossed the yard on her way to the gate. She wondered briefly why Matt had parked outside the gate instead of coming right to the cottage for her. Was it because he did not want Dave to see him calling for her? A moment later the thought had been banished from her mind by the admiration she saw so plainly written on Matt's face.

'Wow! You look absolutely stunning, Julie.' He opened the passenger door for her and held it while she slipped into the seat. Then took his place beside her. There was a long moment of silence before he started the engine, a moment during which he bent towards her as though about to kiss her. Julie felt her heart racing as she waited. Then one of the collies began to dash up to the gate, filling the air with high-pitched barking. It was the young dog, Jack's dog, but it was Dave who uttered the curt command to the animal to 'lie down'.

'Dave seems to be permanently on a short

fuse these days,' Matt remarked with a frown as they began to move along the lane.

Julie shrugged her shoulders beneath the soft white wrap. 'It's lambing time. I expect he's short of sleep.'

'He'll be used to that. It's all happened before, surely?'

'It's always a worry though, especially if there's a threat of late snow, as there is this year.'

'Or is it that he's got too used to having all your company in the evenings?'

This question took Julie by surprise. 'I'm not sure what you are trying to say,' she managed to answer at last.

'I was just wondering whether I was treading on Dave's toes in taking you out to dinner. Or would you rather not answer that?'

'The answer should be obvious to you, as I'm here with you and he's back there with his sheep. Dave is my landlord, that's all, and he won't be that for much longer.'

'He'll miss having you in his cottage.'

Julie deliberately misconstrued Matt's words. 'There are holidaymakers due to move into the cottage as soon as I move out. They'll be paying Dave far more in rent for the place than I've been paying.'

'He'll miss the help you've been giving him though, won't he? His mother says you've been very good to him, and to his children.'

'I haven't done very much. Only some cooking at times.' Julie wanted to close the subject.

'His children will miss you. Dorothy says they are very fond of you.'

'I'm fond of them. They are nice kids.'

'They were hoping you'd stay, according to their grandmother.'

Julie forced a laugh. 'You should know better than to believe everything doting grandmothers tell you, Matt.'

'All the same, I can't help being curious...'

Julie had had enough of his probing now. 'There's nothing for you to be curious about. Their mother was my best friend. I've watched Carla and Jack grow up, that's why I'm fond of them, and them of me. Now can we talk about something else, please?'

'Such as?' Matt smiled, but his eyes were serious as he halted his vehicle on the corner of the road which would lead them in about ten miles to Harrogate.

'Your father, and what's going to happen tomorrow.'

Matt frowned. 'Do we have to?'

'I think we should, before it's too late.'

'What do you mean? I thought he was doing well enough now to be able to come home? Or do you know something I don't know yet?'

Plainly, her words had alarmed Ben Harper's son. So her guess had been correct;

152

Matt had a great affection for his father still, in spite of the chasm which had grown between them in recent years. She must help him to build a bridge over that chasm before he went back to the States.

'I know your father is just longing to make things up with you before you go back.'

'How do you know that? Have you been in to see him again?' Matt asked sharply.

'Will you pull into the next parking bay, then I'll answer your questions? This is not the sort of road where you can allow your concentration to relax.'

Matt did as she suggested, then switched off the car engine and turned to look at her intently.

'I had to go into Harrogate yesterday, so I decided to go and see Ben while I was there. Andrea was with him. He had asked her to give Holy Communion to him and Dorothy. When I got there Dorothy had already left, but the curtains were still pulled around the bed so Andrea and Ben didn't know I was there. I heard him say something that I can't pass on to you, but it did indicate that Ben knew he had been unjust in not agreeing to see you.'

'Why can't you tell me what he said?' There was impatience in Matt's voice.

Julie hesitated. 'It was something he would not have said if he had known I was there. The sort of thing he would only have said to

Andrea in private.'

Matt's frown deepened. 'I don't follow you. I don't know what you mean, Julie.'

It was going to be hard to put into words, but she must try. 'It was to do with why Andrea was there, the taking of the Bread and Wine, the words of confession, and absolution.'

'I still don't see...'

'It was something private, something I was not meant to hear.'

'They must have known you had heard it, my father and the minister?'

Julie shook her head. 'No, because I left again while they were still talking. They would not even know I'd been there, with the curtains being drawn around the bed.'

Matt let his breath go on a long sigh. 'So that was what the phone call from the woman was all about.'

'The phone call? Do you mean from Andrea?'

'The minister, yes. She rang just before I left Ford House and suggested that I make a short visit to my father tonight.'

'What did you say?'

'I told her I was not going into the hospital to be humiliated. That I would not visit Dad unless he asked me to.'

'What did Andrea have to say to that?' Julie could guess, but she was still going to ask.

154

'She said it was what Dad wanted, even though he found it so difficult to put into words.'

'So?'

'So I said I thought she shouldn't interfere in what was, after all, a family affair.'

'Oh Matt! How could you? Andrea was only trying to help you; trying to do her job properly, as she sees it.'

'I don't see it the same way. I see this as something quite private between me and my father,' Matt said curtly. 'It's not even as if I go to her church.'

'Your father does. He's an Elder there, and so is Dorothy. They are also friends of Andrea's, which is another reason why she wants to help them before it's too late.'

'Too late?'

'Before you go back to America. I don't suppose you'll be in any great hurry to come back over here, unless you have to?'

'I haven't exactly been made very welcome here, have I?'

'I wouldn't say that. Dorothy has gone to a lot of trouble to make you welcome.'

'In my own home,' Matt reminded her.

'It is *her* home too.'

Suddenly Matt gave in. 'I suppose you're right. Dorothy *has* been very good to me. Perhaps better than I deserve.'

'It won't have been easy for her. She and your father had a long wait to get married, because of what happened to Jill Bramley, and they were so happy. If you had seen them together...'

'I didn't get the chance to see them. I wasn't even invited to their wedding!'

'Would you have come, if you *had* been invited?' Julie's gaze was intent on Matt's face as she put the question. She watched as a dark flush crept over his cheeks.

'Probably not, but I would like to have been asked,' he admitted after a long silence.

'It isn't too late for you to wish them happiness now.'

'Now?' There was bewilderment in the eyes which were so like Ben's.

'Right now! While we are in Harrogate, I mean. It wouldn't take long, and it would mean so much to them.'

Matt shook his head slowly. 'You never give up, do you, Julie? What happens if Dad refuses to see me still?'

Julie smiled, scenting victory. 'You'll have me there to comfort you,' she said quietly.

Matt laughed. 'That's all the incentive I need. So let's be on our way.'

The subject was not mentioned again as they travelled on towards Harrogate through a landscape enhanced by the golden light of a sunlit spring evening. A pale-green haze hung over the trees and hedgerows on either side of the winding road. Beneath them, the grass verges were thickly carpeted with daffodils and crocuses. North Yorkshire was at its tranquil best.

'I'd forgotten just how beautiful Yorkshire could be,' Matt said as they drove through yet another village where houses built of silvery stone clustered around a square towered church.

'It isn't always like this, you know,' Julie reminded him. 'Not many weeks ago some of the villages were under water when the river burst its banks and the floods came. Now there's snow forecast for the end of this week.'

Matt laughed. 'Are you trying to put me off, Julie?'

Julie was puzzled. 'Put you off? I'm not with you, Matt...'

'Put me off staying.'

His reply astonished her. 'Do you mean permanently? I didn't know you were considering doing that.'

'I wasn't, until today.'

'I thought you had a very good job in America?'

'So I have.'

'Won't you be taking a huge risk then in staying over here too long?'

'Yes. They'll only hold my present position open for a month or so, and most of that has already passed.'

'What would you do over here?'

'That depends on my father.'

'You mean you'd go back into the family business if he asked you to?'

'Yes.'

'It didn't work last time, did it?'

'No.'

'What makes you think it would work this time?'

'Dad's older, and frailer. He'd have to listen to some of my ideas.'

'What if he wouldn't?'

Matt considered this for a long moment. 'It would be in my own interest to go along with him, for the time being,' he said.

They were nearing the hospital now, driving alongside the famous Stray where millions of purple and white crocuses flowered on the green acres which encompassed the town. Julie asked no more questions of the man at her side. The answer he had made to her last one lingered uneasily in her mind. She was wishing now that she had not asked that particular question.

Andrea knew she ought to be getting ready for the meeting of the Youth Drama Group at Nyddford Church. The phone call she had shared with Matt Harper had delayed her. It had also made her angry. All she had done was what Ben Harper had asked her to do, make it known to his son that he would be glad to make a start on healing the breach between them. She had thought Matt would be pleased to hear that. Instead he had accused her of interfering in private family matters.

Life was one huge problem these days, and she was lonely. So lonely, in spite of all the demands of her work. So lonely without Bill. It would not have been so bad if there had been a definite date which she could have circled on the calendar above her desk when Bill would be back, but there was not. He had gone to America for three weeks. Then it had become four. Now it could be five. Yes, there had been text messages from him, and a couple of long phone calls. A basket of flowers too, which still stood on her desk even though they had faded. Only there was no tall, bronze-haired, athletic man to be glimpsed from the front windows of her manse as he stood at his easel beside the beck, or strode across the bridge with his dog. Life was empty without Bill.

If the man was not here his dog certainly was, pushing open the study door and gazing at her with longing in his golden eyes while he lashed her with his waving tail.

'You win, Lucky,' she told him. 'We'll have another walk before I go, seeing it's such a gorgeous day.'

She did not have to decide which way to go, Lucky made that decision for her, pulling hard on the lead to drag her down the drive and through the gate of the manse, over the bridge and, with only his usual brief stop to water the grass on the village green, make a left turn into Church Lane. His destination was the same as always, the big square stone house called Beckside where Bill lived and had his studio. All Andrea could do was hang on to the dog and allow him to discover yet again that his beloved master was not at home.

There were primroses growing in the grassy bank close to Beckside, Andrea noticed as they neared the gate. The gate was open, which surprised her and brought a vague uneasiness to her. It could have been left open by the postman, but this was unlikely since Andy, the postie, was a stickler for closing gates. Even as she wondered whether she ought to take a look round in case there had been an intruder on the premises in Bill's absence, Lucky was making that decision for her and leaping towards the house, barking madly.

What happened next was so unexpected that Andrea let go of the dog's lead and watched in astonishment as he launched himself at the man who came round the side of the building from the back garden. The breath caught in her throat as she stared at the man, and stared again, unable to believe what she was seeing.

'Bill!' The word was only a whisper which

died in her throat as the man halted and Lucky leapt up to place long front paws on the shoulders of the black leather jacket.

'I'm sorry to disappoint you,' the man said as she realized her mistake and the joy in her face died. 'I'm not Bill Wyndham, if that's who you were expecting to find here.'

Andrea managed a shaky laugh. 'I know you're not, now I've got over the shock and had time to take a closer look at you.'

'I'm sorry if I gave you a fright, appearing like that. When I heard the dog I was expecting to see Bill.'

'Were you? Didn't you know he was away?' Her voice was calmer now that she had got used to the idea that this man surely must be a member of Bill's family. The likeness in colouring, height and features was uncanny. Though the voice was different.

'I knew he was going away to the States. He told me that when I phoned him the night before he left, but I'm certain he expected to be back before now. It was to be a three-week working trip, Bill said. That's why I was surprised not to find him back here by now.'

'Three weeks became four, because of the extra lectures arranged by his American agent, and now four weeks are turning into five.'

Had she done right to tell the man that? To

161

let him become aware that this house full of valuable paintings was empty when she had no idea of who he was. Her uneasiness was reflected in her expressive blue eyes, so that the man who was unable to drag his gaze away from the beauty of her face knew it was more than time that he introduced himself. He took a step closer to her, pushing Lucky away at the same time, and held out his hand.

'I'm Alexander Ross, a cousin of Bill's,' he explained.

Andrea put her own hand out to meet his and found it firmly grasped. 'Andrea Cameron,' she told him. 'I'm a friend of Bill's.'

Lucky gave voice to a couple of warning barks. His master had told him to look after Andrea and that he intended to do.

'It's all right, Lucky.' Andrea bent to stroke him reassuringly, and moved a pace or two away from Alexander Ross.

Bill's cousin laughed. 'You've got yourself a powerful friend there. He looks ready to tear me apart, yet just now he was friendly.'

'He's not my dog. He belongs to Bill. I'm just looking after him while Bill's away,' she said.

'When will he be back? Have you any idea? Does Bill keep in touch with you?'

Andrea frowned. This man could certainly be Bill's cousin; the likeness was obvious in their looks, but the voices were altogether different. Alexander Ross was as much of a Scot as she was herself. 'Where have you come from?' she wanted to know.

'Mull,' was his answer. 'Do you know it?'

She nodded. 'I went there once when I needed to take a break from my studies. I thought it was a gorgeous place.'

He laughed softly. 'Obviously you were there when the weather was good.'

'I suppose so. I don't remember much about the weather. Only the peace I found there.' The peace she had needed so badly; the peace which had helped her to make the right decision. She pushed that thought away from her and went back to his question.

'Bill should have been coming home this weekend, but now I don't know. Did you come specially to see him? Or were you just passing and decided to drop in?' She looked about her for a vehicle he might have arrived in, but there was none to be seen.

'I'm taking an early holiday, to do some painting and walking, so I decided to base myself at Nyddford and spend some time with Bill while I'm here.'

'Oh, I see. I don't see your car though.'

'My car is at Nyddford. I told you I came to do some walking. I walked over here from Nyddford. A great walk, with some wonderful views.'

'You should try the walk over Nyddmoor while you are here. If you like bracing air and big views that's the place to find them.'

'Is that where you're heading now with Bill's dog?' he wanted to know.

She shook her head. 'No, I wish it were. I've got a meeting to go to in Nyddford at seven so I must be on my way right now.' She was about to leave him when a thought occurred to her.

'As Bill isn't here, can I give you a lift back to where you are staying? Because there's nowhere in this village that you'll be able to get a meal.'

He seemed to hesitate, as though unsure whether or not to accept her offer. Then he smiled, and his smile was so like Bill's that a lump came to her throat.

'I'd like that, thanks, Andrea.'

'Then I'll meet you opposite the church in fifteen minutes.'

She called Lucky to her side, slipped his lead on and walked at speed away from Bill's cousin, but she found herself looking forward to that short journey to Nyddford with him. Alexander Ross was a stranger to her, yet she seemed to have met him before somewhere.

Ten

Julie turned to Matt with her question as they joined the queue of vehicles waiting to enter the car park at the District Hospital. She did not want him to feel that he had been pressured into making this visit because of anything either she or Andrea had said to him. A glance into his face gave her a clue to his state of mind. His mouth was set in a taut line, his strong chin was thrust out in the way she had seen Ben's look when he was being obstinate, and his heavy brows were drawn together fiercely. She began to wonder whether this visit was such a good idea after all, or whether they ought to have gone straight to the new restaurant.

'Are you quite sure about this, Matt?' she asked very quietly.

His head spun round in her direction and his dark eyebrows lifted as he answered. 'Don't tell me you've got cold feet now that you've talked me into it, Julie?'

'Of course not,' she came back at him, too quickly.

'Don't forget, if it doesn't work out, and

Dad sends me away with a flea in my ear, you've promised to be on hand to comfort me,' he reminded her as they began to move forward in their search for a parking place.

'It *will* work out,' she assured him with a confidence she was far from feeling.

'If it doesn't, I'll hold you to your promise,' he warned. 'How good are you at comforting people like me, Julie?'

She had been very good, during recent months, at comforting David Bramley through the trauma of his farming disasters, and the problems of bringing up Carla and Jack on his own, but she had not been good enough to make Dave realize how empty his life would be without her. The thought was so painful to her that she was glad to push it into the back of her mind when Matt found a parking place and she did not need to reply to his question. Hurriedly she opened the passenger door of his car and swung her legs to the ground, walking towards the entrance to the hospital a few steps ahead of him.

'You didn't answer my question, Julie,' he said as he caught up with her.

'Which question?'

'Don't try to fob me off! You know perfectly well which question.' He put a firm hand under her elbow. She found herself disturbed by the strength of his touch.

'Would you prefer to see your father on

your own? Or do you want me with you?'
she asked in a low voice as they shared a lift
with another couple.

Matt did not answer until they were out of
the lift and walking along a corridor. 'I'd like
you with me. It was *your* idea, Julie, so I
want you near enough to pick up the pieces
if Dad has me thrown out.'

She glanced into his face as he spoke, and
became aware then that he was nervous
about the coming visit. Instinctively she put
a hand on his, as she would have done to a
patient who was afraid of an ordeal to come.

'I'll be there to do that, but it won't be
necessary, Matt. Believe me, Ben will be
very glad to see you.'

In spite of her confident words she felt her
heart beating fast by the time they reached
Ben's bedside. It was with a feeling of relief
that they both saw Dorothy sitting there
holding Ben's hand. The older woman's face
reflected the joy their arrival brought to her.
She was on her feet in seconds, a hand on
the flowered curtains to draw them across
and provide a degree of privacy. Then she
took Matt's hand and drew him forward,
close enough to be able to touch the man
who was propped up against a bank of
pillows.

'I think we'll leave you to have a few words
in private,' she said as she lifted a tall vase of
red carnations from the bedside table.

'You'll help me to rearrange these flowers, won't you, Julie?'

It was a command, even though uttered in a gentle voice. Julie hesitated only for a moment, then followed Dorothy and left father and son alone together.

As Andrea closed and locked the door of her manse and went to her car parked on the drive she focused her gaze for a long moment on the figure of the man who was waiting for her on the other side of the beck. In the fading light it would have been easy to mistake him for Bill. There was the same height, the same slender but muscular build. The same thick bronze hair too. All that was missing was the short, neatly trimmed, auburn beard worn by Bill. If only it had been Bill waiting there for her close to her church ... Waiting to share an evening with her. Waiting to make plans for their future with her ... Waiting to tell her how much he loved her...

'This is very good of you,' Alexander Ross said when she brought the car to a halt opposite Nyddbeck Church. 'I hadn't realized that it would begin to get dark quite so soon, and that I might get lost on an unfamiliar walk in the dusk going back to Nyddford.'

'Of course it won't become dark quite as early where you live,' Andrea recalled.

He slipped into the front passenger seat, then spoke again as she put the vehicle in motion. 'I'm not surprised that Bill finally decided to settle here. It must be a great place to live.'

'Yes, it's very peaceful and beautiful for most of the time. It can be rough in winter though,' she conceded.

'Have you lived here long?'

'Since last summer.' She was watching the traffic at the end of Beck Lane where a left turn would take her up Abbot's Hill and from there to Nyddford. It was a notoriously dangerous road junction, where extra care was needed.

'You're a Scot too, I believe?'

'Yes, I'm from Inverness-shire.'

'What brought you down here?'

'My work.'

'Do you mean that you work here in this village?' He sounded surprised.

'Here and at Nyddford, and sometimes up on Nyddmoor.'

'What do you do? Are you in medicine, a nurse or a doctor perhaps?'

'No. I'm a Free Church minister.'

Alexander Ross's long moment of silence warned her of his astonishment.

'I was ordained at Emmanuel Church in Nyddford last year,' she went on.

'So it's all new to you? Your first parish?'

'A new area, yes, but during my training I

169

spent four years on placements in other churches. Not places like this though. They were city churches with inner-city problems.'

'So you'll maybe find it very quiet here? Perhaps even boring?'

Andrea laughed. 'These are quiet places but they are never boring. There are problems here, but they are different ones. The challenge is here too.'

'I don't suppose you see much of Bill, with both of you being so busy?'

Andrea did not answer that. Obviously Bill had not spoken of their friendship to his cousin.

'How did you come to take on his dog?' Alexander asked then.

That question was unexpected. She took her time about answering. 'Lucky was found in my church at Nyddbeck. Someone had shut him in there and walked away without him. I would have taken him myself, only I was going to my parents in Scotland for Hogmanay. So Bill took him instead. Now I'm looking after him while Bill's in America.'

That statement brought a laugh from Bill's cousin. 'I'd say it's the other way round and he's looking after you, judging by the way he warned me off when I tried to shake hands with you.'

Andrea smiled. 'Yes, Lucky's very protective.'

They were on the outskirts of Nyddford now, quite close to Emmanuel Church, and it was almost seven o'clock. 'Where are you staying?' she asked.

'The Golden Fleece, in the market square. If you drop me off at your church I can walk the rest of the way.'

'Here we are then, and there are the would-be TV stars of the future waiting for me,' she said as she turned into the church car park and switched off the engine.

'I thought you said you had a meeting—'

'Yes, a meeting of the Youth Drama Group.'

Alexander laughed. 'It won't be boring then.'

'There's no fear of that. They are all raring to go, and so keen that they need a firm hand.' As she spoke she was already out of the car and locking it as he also alighted. 'I just hope one or two parents will arrive in time to give me some help.'

'Is that likely?' Alexander asked as an outburst of loud laughter came from the group, who were larking about in the porch of the church hall.

Andrea shook her head. 'Not very! They all think it's a good idea to have things like this for the younger church members, but they say they are too busy to spare a couple of hours to help with whatever we are doing.

Yet some of them must have been involved at some time with things like this. I was hoping my friend Julie would be here again. She was such a help last week, but she's got a date tonight so I won't be seeing her.'

'Does Bill help you?'

This was another unexpected question. Bill's cousin was waiting for her answer, even though she felt it was time he made his way to his hotel for dinner. 'I was hoping he'd be here to help, but this trip to America came up just as we had the first meeting. I really must get this lot into the hall before things get out of hand and they become too noisy. You'll be wanting your dinner, too.'

She was turning away from him and moving towards the group of young people, who were now beginning to quieten. His next words stopped her in her tracks.

'I'm in no hurry for my dinner, if I can be of any help to you with your drama group.'

'Are you serious?'

'Yes. You know, one good turn and all that...' The smile she saw on his face, beneath the light shed by the porch lantern, was so much like Bill's smile that her heart gave a sudden lurch.

'I hope you won't regret this,' she said as she opened the door.

He followed her into the hall, with the girls aged from twelve to about seventeen years and the lads who were almost as tall as him, surging boisterously in after them. After that it was all action, noise and buzz as the third rehearsal of a specially written drama based on a modern version of the parable of the Good Samaritan got under way. Andrea made a brief introduction of Alexander first.

'This is Alexander Ross, who has offered to help us tonight as Julie Craven is unable to be here. Mr Ross has come to Nyddford to visit his cousin, Bill Wyndham.'

Then the questions came from one of the older girls, who was a sixth-former at Nyddford High School. 'Are you an artist as well? Are you famous, too? Like Bill Wyndham, I mean?'

Andrea wondered whether the questions would embarrass him, but Alexander Ross took them all in his stride and provided brief, smiling answers.

'I am a sort of artist, but I'm not famous like my cousin. I'm still working on that,' he added with a grin.

'Mum says Bill Wyndham's going to do some programmes on the telly about how to paint pictures, and that some of them are going to be filmed around here,' one of the young people informed him.

'Is he? That means he's even more famous than I realized,' Alexander said with a laugh.

Yes, there were the television programmes due to start filming next month when this part of the Yorkshire Dales was vibrant with the colour of late spring and early summer. So Bill would have to come back to England soon, no matter what his American agent had arranged for him to do over there. The thought brought immense comfort to Andrea.

'Carla's late tonight. I wonder if she's coming?' Andrea asked. 'I don't want to start without her if she's just going to be a few minutes late.' As she spoke, Andrea looked around her at the girls and boys who were already there. 'Do any of you know if she intended to be here?'

'She sure did!' Josh Bolton replied emphatically. 'I wanted to go and pick her up on the bike, but she said she'd make her own way down on the six o'clock bus.'

That would probably be because Dave didn't like his daughter riding on the back of Josh Bolton's motorbike, Andrea guessed.

'We'll give her another five minutes, then we'll need to make a start whether she's here or not,' she told Josh and the others.

Carla did not put in an appearance but the rehearsal went much better than Andrea had expected it could without her. Josh Bolton was in gloomy mood though. Andrea had an idea that if it had not been for Carla talking him into joining the Youth Drama Group Josh would have considered himself too old for such activities. If Carla missed again next week he would probably not bother to come again. With Dave in his present sour mood, it was unlikely that Carla and Jack would be allowed to come to the group or any other at this church, or at Nyddbeck. It was so unfair on them to punish them because things had gone wrong for him with Julie, as they so obviously had if Julie was out this evening with someone else. Andrea wondered again if that someone else was Matt Harper. Then she pushed the thought away from her and gave all her concentration to what she had come here to do. The sixth-form girl who had put the questions to Alexander took Carla's place in the play with enthusiasm, even though she had refused to even consider the part at the first meeting. Andrea guessed that she had Alexander's involvement to thank for this.

'Thanks so much for helping out, Alexander,' she said as the youngsters drifted away to their homes and she was turning out the lights in the hall. 'It made a great difference, having you there. I just hope you won't have missed your evening meal by staying with us all the time.' It was after nine now. How late did the Golden Fleece serve meals?

'Dinners will be over now, but they serve bar suppers until nine thirty. A bar supper will do fine for me,' he told her, adding, 'especially if you'll join me.'

His invitation took Andrea by surprise, so

she was slow in replying. Until that moment, her mind had been so full of satisfaction at the way the rehearsal had gone, and so full of gratitude to Bill's cousin for his help, which had encouraged the young people to give of their best, that her own hunger had been ignored. Now, the prospect of having placed in front of her one of the delicious bar suppers for which the Golden Fleece was renowned was very tempting. Especially as she had not had any food since her sandwich lunch eaten between phone calls.

'Please say you will,' he pleaded.

'I will,' she responded as she locked the hall door behind them and moved to where her car was parked.

Soon they were facing one another across one of the copper-topped tables in the lounge-bar of the centuries-old inn which fronted on to Nyddford Market Place. Andrea felt amazingly at ease in the company of Alexander Ross. Yet until a few hours ago she had never met him, or even heard of him. Bill had never spoken to her of this cousin, who was so like him in age and appearance. Maybe that was because she and Bill always had so many other things to talk about: his work and her own work; their plans for a future together, which this man from Mull quite obviously knew nothing about. He would not learn about that from her, she decided. It was for Bill to tell him, when at last he returned from America. In the meantime she would enjoy this quite unexpected treat of being taken out to supper by a handsome and charming man...

'I'm just praying that all's well behind those curtains,' Dorothy Harper confessed as she and Julie rearranged the carnations, which had no need of such attention. 'I've got a feeling that if it isn't, Matt will book the first flight back that he can get.'

Julie found this statement puzzling. 'I didn't get that impression when he was driving me over here tonight. From the way Matt was talking then, he could be seriously considering whether he might stay over here.'

There was a long moment of silence, then Dorothy spoke again. 'I don't really know that it would be a good thing for everyone if Matt did stay here. It might lead to more problems than we've already got.'

Julie frowned. 'What do you mean, Dorothy? I thought you would be pleased if Matt stayed on to help Ben with the business?'

Another pause followed, until Dorothy spoke again in a troubled voice. 'I was thinking of it more from David's point of view.'

Julie's frown deepened. 'I don't see how it would affect Dave.'

Dorothy was impatient with her now. 'Oh, come my dear, you must know what I'm getting at! You and David were getting on so well until Matt arrived that I was beginning to hope—'

'What you were beginning to hope for just isn't going to happen,' Julie broke in. 'I'm going to buy a little house in Nyddford.'

'Why on earth are you doing that?' Dorothy responded sharply.

'Because I'll need somewhere else to live when the first holiday bookings are due to arrive at the cottage.'

'Surely by now David must have...' David's mother broke off there, uncertain how to go on without being too intrusive.

'He said I could have a room in the farmhouse, when the visitors are due to move into Jacob's Cottage.' Julie could not hide the bitterness in her voice.

'I don't understand...'

'Dave made me that offer just as if I was of no more importance to him than one of the tourists seeking bed and breakfast. The only difference being that I knew I would have to cook my own breakfast, and probably his and his children's as well.' Julie's lips quivered as she suffered the hurt again.

'So you turned his offer down?'

'Of course I did! I'm not so desperate to stay close to Dave that I'm prepared to hang around for ever, waiting for him to make up

178

his mind whether he can commit himself to putting someone else in Jill's place. Time's moving on for me, Dorothy. If I'm not going to marry and have a family of my own, at least I can start finding a permanent home for myself. Buying a place I can call my own, where I can have a big friendly dog and...' Suddenly the anger had gone from Julie's spirit and all that was left was the despair and the heartache.

'Oh, my dear Julie! I'm so sorry.' Dorothy abandoned the vase of flowers and put her arms about the girl she had become fond enough of to love as a daughter.

'I'm fine, or I will be in a minute,' Julie insisted as a tear escaped to slide down her cheek.

'That son of mine needs his head examining if he lets you go. I just don't know what's got into him,' his mother confessed. 'There was me, hoping during all the months you've been living in the cottage, that it was only a matter of time before you and David became partners and there was another wedding on the horizon. You're so right for him, and for his children.'

'Obviously, he doesn't think so.'

'Are you sure you haven't misunderstood him?' Dorothy was desperately anxious to put things right between them.

'Absolutely certain.' Julie sniffed, wiped the tear from her face and blew her nose.

'Hadn't we better go back to Ben now and find out whether he's thrown Matt out yet?'

'Yes.' Dorothy sighed. 'Sometimes I wonder whether all men are pig-headed, or if it's just the ones in my own life.' She picked up the vase of flowers, then turned to Julie with a rueful smile. 'If my husband and my stepson are still at odds with one another when we get back to them I think I'll tip this lot over the pair of them.'

Julie managed to summon up a smile. 'If they are, I'll help you do that,' she said.

Both women were holding their breath when they found themselves facing Ben and Matt. It was not possible in that first moment to guess at what had happened during their absence. Ben was still sitting propped up by pillows; Matt was still occupying the chair vacated by Dorothy. Yet it was evident that there was no need for the vase of flowers to be poured over the father and son. Common sense, and a deeply buried love for one another, had won. There was no air of emotion or excitement about them; they were just sharing a quiet discussion about the prospects for the lambing at Ford House Farm.

Matt rose to his feet and indicated that Dorothy should take his seat. 'It's time we were going,' he said. 'I've booked our table for eight, and it's almost that time now.'

'There's no need to rush away...' Dorothy began.

'We'll see each other tomorrow, when I've finished on the farm,' Matt promised.

'I'll be waiting for you, son,' Ben answered.

Eleven

'Is that really the time?' Andrea looked at her watch in dismay. 'I must be going home; right now.' She rose to her feet and picked up her bag.

'Eleven isn't so late, surely?' Alexander Ross objected.

'It is when there's a dog to be walked, and an answerphone to be checked.'

'Can't you leave the phone checking till tomorrow morning?'

Andrea shook her head. 'No, I can't. There could be someone needing to talk to me urgently, or a request for me to go out to someone who's very ill; perhaps dying.'

That made him frown. 'What can you do, when you get there?'

Andrea took her time about answering. Plainly, he did not understand her commitment to her work. 'I can be there for the sick person, and for their family. There to give help, in any way. Or just to provide comfort when they need it most.'

'I suppose if they are members of your church...' he began doubtfully.

182

'It wouldn't matter to me if they were not members of my church. If they need me, I'll go.'

'What on earth made you choose such a life? A woman like you...'

This time it was easier for her to reply. 'It was chosen for me.'

'Do you mean by your parents?'

That brought a laugh from her. 'Oh no! It was nothing to do with them. I was a married woman when I knew this was what I had to do.'

'Didn't that cause problems for you? With your husband, I mean?'

That was not so easy to answer. 'I suppose it did, in the end,' was the only truthful answer she could give. She hoped he would not want to explore the subject any further.

A new thought came to Alexander Ross then. He was swift to voice it. 'Is your coming out to supper with me likely to cause any problems for you, Andrea? Would your husband be expecting you home earlier?'

'No. The only one expecting me home is Lucky. I must go now—'

'Have I offended you by asking these questions? If so, I must apologize,' he broke in.

Andrea smiled. 'There's no need for you to do that. I'm certainly not offended. I'm just very grateful to you for the help you've given me tonight.'

'I'll be glad to help again next week, if you'll let me?'

Now she laughed. 'If I'll let you! Now you've offered, I'll keep you to your word. That's if you're still here then.'

'I'll certainly still be here. I'm hoping Bill will be too, by then.'

'So am I!'

Andrea's words were so heartfelt that Bill's cousin was puzzled. 'Is looking after his dog getting too much for you, Andrea? Is it one job too many in your busy life? If it is, I can take some of it off your shoulders by coming over to Nyddbeck in my car and giving Lucky some long walks to run off his energy.'

'Do you really mean that?'

'Yes, I really do.' His mouth was smiling but the expression in his hazel eyes was serious.

'Then you're an answer to prayers, because I've got a too-full schedule for the rest of this week. When I made some of the appointments I thought Bill would be back by now, and Lucky would be back home at Beckside. These extra lectures his agent has fixed up for Bill have rather upset my own plans for the next few days.' She sighed as she admitted that.

'If Miriam organized the lectures, she'd make sure Bill agreed to them. She's that sort of girl, is Miriam,' Alexander ended with a laugh. 'A real go-getter.'

Andrea was intrigued. 'You know her then?'

'I've met her, when she's been over here. I wish she'd take as much interest in my work as she does in Bill's. But then, I'm not Bill. I don't have his talent, his fame or his—'

Suddenly Andrea was uneasy. She wanted an end to this conversation. 'I really must go,' she broke in. 'Thanks a lot for the help, and the meal, Alexander.'

He was on his feet in an instant. 'I'll see you to your car.'

She shook her head. 'There's no need, finish your drink in peace. You've earned it! Goodnight, Alexander, and thanks again.'

'What time would you like me to report for dog-walking duty tomorrow?' he asked as she was turning away from him to head for the door.

Andrea made her mind up quickly. She could get up extra early to walk Lucky in the morning; but late afternoon would be difficult if her appointment as guest speaker at a Ladies' Fellowship in a market town several miles away from Nyddbeck overran. 'Could you make it late afternoon please? About five?'

'Yes. I'll be there. I'm looking forward to it.'

'That's because you don't know how energetic Lucky is when he's been shut up in the house all day,' she warned him with a laugh. 'I'm still looking forward to it, and to meeting you again.'

It was definitely time for her to leave him, she knew when she caught the gleam of admiration in his eyes. She was glad of the cool spring breeze which refreshed her warm cheeks when she reached the car park. Bill's cousin was a real charmer, both in looks and personality, and he was sufficiently like Bill to stir a longing inside her which must be pushed right to the back of her mind. Alexander was like Bill, but he was *not* Bill.

When she got back, her phone was ringing and Andrea was surprised to hear Carla's voice. It had a deeply distressed tone which pushed the tiredness out of Andrea's mind and brought a rush of anxiety to her.

'Sorry I didn't turn up, Andrea,' the girl said in a rush. 'I intended to; I really wanted to, but Dad just wouldn't let me leave the house.'

Andrea listened to the long shuddering breaths the girl was trying to control, and waited. Carla would spill it all out if she gave her enough time.

'I'm really sorry I let you down! I *do* want to be in the drama group but Dad says I can't. Not ever again. I said it would be letting you and Julie and the others down, but he said he couldn't care less about that.'

Now the shudders were sobs, deep and heart-rending as Carla went on. 'He says I can't see Josh again either.'

'I don't suppose he means that, Carla. I expect he's just overtired, and maybe worrying about the lambing.' Andrea spoke quietly but before she could utter any more comforting words Carla was putting her right about Dave Bramley's state of mind.

'All he's worrying about is getting his housework done without having to pay for it. I told him Mrs Grainger would be coming tomorrow but he still made me stay at home and clean the cooker and the sink and the kitchen floor. I hate him! I really hate him! I'm not surprised that Julie won't come and live in our house. As soon as I can get away from it I'll be going! Nobody will stop me next time. They won't even know I'm going till it's too late.'

Andrea felt her heart thudding as she listened and cast about in her mind for something to say that would calm the girl. At the same time there was anger building inside her that Dave Bramley should be so blind to what was happening in his home. Carla had inherited her father's volatile temperament and needed now to be given a measure of freedom to enjoy being young. It had seemed, once Julie moved into Jacob's Cottage, that Dave was allowing her some of that freedom. Julie's recent decision to move to Nyddford seemed to have reversed the process.

'Please don't do anything rash, Carla,' Andrea begged. 'Think how it would upset your gran, after all she's been through since Easter. You're old enough now, and mature enough, to know just how awful things have been for her lately while Ben has been in hospital.'

'It *would* upset Gran if she saw what Dad's like these days,' Carla broke in. 'He's so absolutely awful, moaning and shouting, and finding fault with me every time he comes into the house.'

'He's probably tired out after helping to care for Ben Harper's animals as well as looking after his own stock. He might not even realize he's doing it.'

'He does!' Carla insisted. 'As soon as he sets eyes on me he loses his rag. It's not fair! He doesn't go on at our Jack. Why should it always be me?'

No answer needed to be found for that question, since the slamming of the outer door and the sound of Dave's collie barking led to Carla ending her phone call abruptly. This did not banish the disquiet from Andrea's mind. In fact she found herself lying awake for a long time after she had swallowed her late-night drink and said her final prayers of the day, wondering what she could do to help father and daughter

188

come to terms with the way their lives were now.

What had happened to all their lives since Bill went away to America? Things had seemed to be set fair for the Bramleys, for Julie, for herself and Bill, only a few weeks ago. She had been very disappointed not to have Bill here with her at Easter to meet her parents when they came down for a few days, but by then she and Bill had managed to heal the rift her refusal to go to America with Bill had caused. When Ben had suffered his severe heart attack she had been very glad to be here in Nyddbeck to give her support to Dorothy. Until then she had not been aware of how serious was the breach between Ben and his son.

All had appeared to be going well for Dave and Julie too, until Bill left to go to America. Because of their close friendship Carla and Jack were enjoying happier times. Now that was no longer the case and Andrea was certain this change had been brought about because Julie was leaving the farm. Was it because Julie had become attracted to Matt Harper that she was in such a hurry to move out of Jacob's Cottage?

What could she herself do to help all these people who had become her friends? There must be something. She could not think of anything right now, but there was always prayer.

'Tell me what to do, please, Lord,' Andrea prayed fervently.

Julie did not speak to Matt as they walked out of the hospital to the car park. She knew Matt needed this time to be empty of conversation so he could recover from the emotional trauma he had just experienced. He did not need to tell her that he was profoundly disturbed; it had been written in the tension of his shoulders and in the tightness of his mouth which she had been aware of when she and Dorothy had rejoined father and son behind the drawn floral curtains. It was going to be all right now though; the yawning chasm of family discord was already beginning to heal. If Matt stayed on for a while it would heal completely.

'Thanks for being with me, Julie,' he said when they were driving away from the hospital across the green acres of the Stray.

'It was the least I could do, seeing it was my idea,' she said with a smiling sidelong glance at his now relaxed profile.

'It was the right idea, at the right time, though I don't think I could have faced it without you.'

'I think you would have done, especially if you needed to go back to America while Ben's health was still causing concern.'

'I don't think I'll be going back there, at

least not permanently.'

'Are you sure about that? You weren't, earlier in the evening,' she reminded him.

There was a long silence before he spoke again. 'That was before I found out how much Dad wanted me to stay here. How much he needed me,' he added in a low voice.

By this time they were at their destination, one of the hotels on the other side of the town. The hotel was old, having been there since the days when Harrogate was a leading spa resort frequented by the rich and famous, but the restaurant was new and elegant. Julie had not been there before and was looking forward to finding out whether it was as good as it looked. She was by now ravenously hungry.

'Have you been here before, Matt?' she asked after they had been shown to a window table.

'No. I've been eating at home with Dorothy, except for the times I've been out into Nyddford with you.'

'How did you know about this place then?'

'The local paper gave it a good write-up. We'll soon see if it was justified.'

By the end of the meal, during which they avoided any mention of their hospital visit and spoke only of things of general interest, they were agreed that the good write-up was more than justified. The food was of high quality and superbly presented, the wine excellent, if expensive, and the service friendly and efficient.

'We must do this again,' Matt said as he slipped Julie's jacket around her shoulders. 'Soon.'

'You mean it, about staying here then?'

'Of course. I'll be starting to look for a property tomorrow.'

Julie was startled to hear that. 'Here, in Harrogate?'

'No, in Nyddford. Or thereabouts.'

'You don't intend to stay on at Ford House then?'

Matt laughed. 'Not for very long. I don't want to cramp the style of the newly-weds. I'm still finding it quite hard to believe how much they care about each other.'

'They had to wait a long time for their happiness,' Julie reminded him. 'They were in love when they were very young, then both married someone else. They only got together again after Dorothy was widowed and your mother had died. Even then, the wedding they planned for a year earlier had to be postponed because of Jill Bramley's death. When they finally got married, last New Year's Eve, it seemed like a happy ending to us all.' She sighed, then went on, 'We were shocked when Ben had his heart attack so soon afterwards. We had walked behind him earlier that day as he carried the

Easter cross up Abbot's Hill and he walked like a young man, so straight and proud.'

'The silly old fool shouldn't have been doing a thing like that! No wonder he took ill!' Matt burst out. 'Why the hell didn't Dorothy stop him?'

Julie laughed. 'What on earth makes you think anything Dorothy said would stop your dad from doing something he thought of as his right, and his privilege?' she asked.

'Then Andrea Cameron should have stopped him. What sort of minister is she to encourage a man of his age to get up to such stupidity?'

'She's a very good one; the right one for Nyddbeck and Nyddford. Don't let your father hear you say otherwise or you'll soon fall out again,' Julie warned. 'Andrea did suggest that it might be better for one of the younger men to carry the cross, but Ben wouldn't have that. In fact he was offended by the very idea of it.'

'And look where his stubbornness got him! Look where he finished up – in intensive care!' Matt burst out.

As Julie listened to him in silence, she recalled Dorothy's words uttered only a couple of hours earlier about wanting to knock sense into the heads of the men in her life. Dorothy was right, they were all pigheaded, and she would tell this one so right now.

'If you weren't so pig-headed you'd know by now that Ben won't care how much he's gone through recently, as long as he's got you back. He'll think it a small price to pay.'

They had left Harrogate now and were well on their way back to Nyddmoor when Matt slowed down and pulled the car into a parking space which in daylight would have given them a wonderful view of the moorland landscape, with the ruined abbey rising starkly in the distance. At this time of night they were surrounded by darkness, with only scattered pin-points of light to mark out the isolated farmhouses and cottages. Julie waited for what she was half-expecting to happen; for Matt to pull her into his arms and begin to kiss her. Maybe try to make love to her. It hadn't happened on their few previous outings, but they knew each other better now and she was already aware that he was strongly attracted to her. How was she going to handle it if that was what he intended? Could she even contemplate making love with anyone else when she was still so overwhelmingly in love with Dave Bramley?

The thought, and the ache it brought to her mind and body, was banished by what Matt Harper said next as he switched off the engine and turned his head in her direction.

'Do you really mean that, Julie? Do you believe Dad thinks it worth suffering all that pain, and almost dying, just to have me back here again?' His voice was so low, so hesitant, that she could hardly hear him.

'Yes, I do, and if you were not so thick-skinned you wouldn't even have to ask that question.' Her own voice was sharp with censure. Because she had shared so much of Dorothy's fear and anguish at the thought of losing Ben, she was not going to spare his son from facing up to the truth.

'Oh God, if only I'd known! If only I'd had any idea, I wouldn't have wasted so much time. What if he dies now, Julie? What if I've left it too late to try and make up to him?'

Suddenly then the tears were pouring down Matt's face and he was dropping his head on to the hands that still rested on the steering wheel so that Julie should not witness his distress. She let him weep for a while, knowing that he needed the release that tears would bring. Then she put a hand on his shoulder, offering tentative comfort.

'It's not too late, Matt,' she murmured. 'Ben *is* on the mend, and you being here will speed things up, believe me.'

He gave a long sigh and lifted his head. 'I have to believe you, since you have more knowledge of these things than I have. I'm sorry if I've embarrassed you. I'll get you home now.'

'There's no hurry. Take your time, calm down first. There'll be no one waiting for me with a shotgun because I'm late home,' she told him with an attempt to lighten the atmosphere.

It seemed to work. Matt blew his nose, then managed to smile as he said, 'Not even Dave Bramley?'

Instantly her face closed up, her sympathy for him was banished. 'What makes you think anything I do could concern Dave Bramley? I'm not his sister, or his daughter...'

'Or his wife,' Matt finished for her.

'What on earth made you say that?' she demanded fiercely.

'Something Dorothy hinted at. Something she hoped would happen.'

'You shouldn't take too much notice of what people say when they are under the sort of stress that Dorothy has been living with recently,' she hit back, then added, 'I'm just renting David Bramley's cottage until I can move into my own property.'

'I'm glad to hear that.' Matt put an arm about her shoulders and drew her close as he said the words: 'Very glad.' His kiss was long and warm, and not unpleasant. Her response to it led him to kiss her again, and again.

Suddenly then she began to feel trapped; heading for a situation she was not yet ready for and needed to avoid. 'We ought to be moving, I have to be on duty early tomorrow morning,' she reminded him as she strugged free of his embrace.

'Right, I'll take you home then.' He started the car, then turned to say softly, 'There'll be other times when you don't have to be at work early, won't there?'

Julie did not answer.

Dave saw the vehicle moving along the lane that led to the farm as he went to make his late-night check of the hen houses. There had been a fox about recently. The worry about the fox and the damage it could do was banished from his mind when the car stopped at the farm gate. It could only be Julie coming home, even though it was not Julie's car. His footsteps halted and he stood quite still for a long moment as Matt opened the driver's door and went round to meet Julie as she stepped out into the moonlight. He heard her laugh softly at something Matt said to her and he watched as Matt bent his head over her face. Then he turned his back and strode away as Tyke and Brack started to fill the air with the sound of their barking.

So it was true; Julie was seeing Matt Harper. She was probably going to invite him into the cottage for coffee. Perhaps for more than coffee ... The idea of what could follow the coffee, once in possession of his mind, would not leave him. Temptation was strong inside him to walk back to where he would have a good view of the cottage so that he could see whether the lights were on in the front rooms. Or if they were already switched on at the back where the bedrooms were. He fought against the temptation, and almost lost. Even as he turned his body to walk back so that he could find out whether there were indeed lights showing in the back of Jacob's Cottage, a swift surge of revulsion engulfed him and stopped him in his tracks. He would not allow himself to lose his self-respect by spying on Julie. If she wanted to give Matt Harper the privileges she had once shared with him, he must accept that.

After all, what did he have to offer Julie that could compare with what Ben Harper's son had? All he possessed was a family farm which was losing money; an overdraft, and two difficult teenage children! Matt Harper had it all on offer: a choice of whether to go back to his highly paid position in America or stay in Yorkshire and take over the prosperous farm and transport business in a few years when Ben retired. There was no just comparison to be made.

Yet he had been so certain, such a short time ago, that Julie was not ambitious for the things money could buy. He had been sure that what she wanted was what was here all around them: the peace and beauty, the carrying on of a tradition of farming which had been satisfying for his father and his grandfather and his great grandfather, and which would in time be continued by young Jack. Julie had seemed so interested in the life of the farm, and the work which changed with the seasons. How could he have read her so wrongly?

Because he had been a bloody fool, he knew in a spurt of revelation that shocked him into facing the truth. Because he had lacked the courage to put Julie's love to the test by asking her to marry him and make her life with him and his children. He had thought there was plenty of time for him to get round to it; that they could just go on as they were, snatching brief hours of love and companionship in Jacob's Cottage when his children were not around. After Ben Harper had collapsed and been taken into the District Hospital, those periods of time had become shorter and much less frequent as Dave had taken on some of the work at Ben's farm to make life easier for his mother. So he had not become aware that Julie had someone else in her life until it was too late. God, what a bloody fool he had been! So lost was he in berating himself that he did not hear Matt's car drive away, or see Julie walk alone into the cottage.

Dorothy Harper had been in bed for a long

time before she heard Matt's car come to a halt in the drive below the spacious en-suite bedroom she normally shared with Ben. Her prayer book was open in her hand, but the peace of mind and relaxation which so often enveloped her after she had spent a few minutes in prayer was far away from her tonight. She knew she would not sleep for the anxieties that were jostling one another in her tired mind. She had thought that once Ben was out of danger the sleepless nights would be a thing of the past; that she would drift happily off to sleep planning the special meals she would make for Ben when he came home, the friends who would come to spend pleasant hours with them over tea, and the drives to the little church at Nyddbeck for the services which meant so much to both of them. Most of all Dorothy was looking forward to that time they would spend together here in this beautiful four-poster bed which Ben had bought for their marriage; a time to share love.

It had never occurred to her that the arrival of Ben's son at Ford House would have brought another set of problems for her to worry about. Problems which might have far-reaching consequences for her own son and her beloved grandchildren. How was she to know that Matt Harper would take such a fancy to Julie Craven that he was already seriously considering abandoning his excellent job in America in order to stay in Yorkshire and become involved with Ben's business?

How was she to know that her David, already on the point of asking Julie Craven to marry him, would lose his nerve and leave the way wide open for Julie to decide that she had waited long enough for Dave to commit himself to her and was moving out of Jacob's Cottage, and at the same time into a close friendship with Matt? What an idiot her David had been to let things come to this pass! Why had he not asked for her advice, as he so often did about family or farming matters? Did he really imagine she didn't know how close he and Julie had become since Julie had been living in the cottage?

A wry smile lifted Dorothy's mood as she recalled going unexpectedly to the farm one afternoon a few weeks ago to drop off a birthday present for Julie, and finding her car parked at the gate but no answer to her ring on the bell. Without giving a thought to what she was doing, Dorothy had gone round to the back door in time to see David's bare shoulders wrapped around Julie as she struggled to pull on a silk robe. It had been good to hear them laughing; good to know they were happy together. Very good to glimpse the joy there could be for them and the children in the days to come. She had not known then that her son would be pig-headed enough to let it all go wrong.

'Please, God, show me how to help David put things right again,' Dorothy prayed as she heard Ben's son enter the house. 'Please don't let me regret asking Matt to come home.'

Twelve

As Andrea had anticipated, her return from the market town where she had been the guest speaker for a ladies' group was delayed by a spring thunderstorm. This resulted in so much surface water lying on the winding riverside road that she was forced to keep her speed right down. So she was not surprised to see the unfamiliar estate car already parked outside her manse. It was still raining hard. The man who was behind the steering wheel would be regretting ever having made his offer to walk Bill's dog for her, she guessed.

Inside the manse, Lucky was already giving her a noisy welcome home. The moment she got the front door open he threw himself at her, sniffing happily at her damp jacket and licking her wet hands lovingly. Andrea stroked his floppy red-gold ears as she spoke to him. 'Sorry, Lucky, you're not going to get a very long walk tonight.'

By the time she had slipped off her jacket Alexander Ross was ringing the doorbell. She hurried to admit him. 'Hi! Alexander.

Thanks for coming in such grotty weather. I wondered whether you'd have second thoughts when the storm broke?'

'A promise is a promise,' he reminded her with a wry grin. Lucky had now transferred his attentions to Bill's cousin and was lashing him enthusiastically with a wildly waving feathery tail. 'But we won't be going as far as I had hoped, Lucky, my lad,' he told the dog.

'I feel bad about you going at all,' Andrea confessed.

Alexander laughed. 'It won't be the first time I've got wet walking someone else's dog.'

'You don't have a dog of your own then?'

'No, not now.'

'I thought, with you living on Mull, it's such a perfect place for walking...'

'I agree, only I don't live there all the time. I travel a lot. My work takes me away far too often for me to have a dog of my own.'

'Your painting? You did say you were an artist too?' Andrea was curious about this man who had told her so much about himself, yet kept other things back.

'I'm not a professional artist, like Bill. I'm just an amateur. Now, let's have this lead on you, Lucky, and get rid of some of your energy.'

'There's an umbrella, if you'd like one?' she offered.

'Could be a good idea!'

Andrea reached for the large multi-coloured brolly which stood in a container in the space under the staircase and handed it to him.

'So you're a golfer,' he remarked. 'Perhaps we could...'

'No,' she replied quickly. 'It was my husband who played golf.'

'Won't he mind my borrowing it?'

'Hardly. He's been dead since last July.' Andrea said the words quietly, and without emotion. She caught the startled glance thrown her way by Alexander before she moved to check her answerphone.

'Oh God, I'm sorry! I had no idea. Some of the things I said to you last night...'

'Please don't worry about that. I should have told you last night when I had the opportunity. I hope you don't get too wet. There'll be some tea when you come back.' She hoped he wouldn't linger to apologize again, and was relieved when the front door closed behind him. It was time now to check the answerphone messages to find out if there was anything from Bill.

There was, right at the end of the requests for visits or appointments, a short message but one which sent her heart thumping madly. Bill said he was in North Carolina for yet another lecture and demonstration. 'Only two more to go, and then I'll be on my way home. I've told Miriam that I've had enough; more than enough. So I'll be on that plane whether she likes it or not. I can hardly wait to see you, my love.'

The message was cut off abruptly there, but it was enough. Enough to send her spirits soaring, and fill her heart with thankfulness. 'Thanks a lot, Lord,' she murmured as she headed for the kitchen to fill the kettle and set it to boil. Next time Bill went to the States, she would make sure she went with him, instead of letting him go alone to have his tour extended time and time again by this woman called Miriam. She was feeling slightly uneasy about the woman called Miriam; the woman who could decide what Bill must do. The woman Bill's cousin said was a real go-getter...

When Bill's cousin came back, preceded by the bounding, shaking, dripping-wet red setter, Andrea was waiting with a large towel for Lucky and a big mug of tea for Alexander. 'Help yourself to sugar and cake,' she told him as he settled his tall figure on one of the kitchen stools.

'As for you, Lucky, your master will be home by the weekend. So just you mind and behave yourself until then. Right?' she said sternly as she began to towel the dog vigorously.

Alexander almost choked on a laugh. 'You sounded just like my mother then!' he told her. 'She thinks I'm still her wee boy.'

Andrea's face clouded when she heard the last few words. They brought back sharply, painfully, the memory that was buried deep in her heart. The memory of her own wee boy, Andrew. She pushed her sadness aside and said, 'I suppose we never really grow up to our mothers. Mine still thinks I don't get enough to eat when I'm busy, so she brings me shortbread and Dundee cake whenever she visits, or sends it with anyone who's coming within twenty miles of here.'

'It's great stuff,' he commented after taking a large bite out of a generous slice of the richly fruited cake.

Andrea glanced at her watch. There was a meeting of the church Elders at Nyddford that evening to discuss the urgent repairs needing to be done to the church roof, and she had paperwork to catch up on before then, so she hoped Alexander would not linger to talk to her when the tea and cake was finished. As though able to read her thoughts, he stood up and reached for his Barbour.

'You said you had a heavy work load today, so I'll be on my way. Thanks a lot for the tea and cake.'

'Thanks a lot for walking the dog,' Andrea responded. 'It was good of you to help.'

They were in the hall now, accompanied by Lucky, who hoped he might be in line for another walk. Alexander held out his hand, a beautiful hand with long tapering fingers. 'It's been my pleasure to help you, Andrea,' he said softly. 'If I had known there was someone like you here I think I'd have found time to visit Bill long before now.'

Andrea felt warm colour flood her cheeks in response to the admiration she recognized in his eyes. She withdrew her fingers from his, wondering whether she had made a mistake in accepting his offer to walk Bill's dog. He was flirting with her, of course. Perhaps he flirted with every woman who was around his own age and reasonably attractive? She was unsure of what his status was; they hadn't discussed whether he was married, or had a permanent partner, during the hour or so when they shared the bar supper the previous evening. Certainly he was not yet aware of her own relationship with Bill, though it was likely that Bill would soon reveal their plans to him when he returned. In the meantime, she must play it cool. Lucky turned out to be useful in that respect. As the front door opened he shot out of it at speed.

'Damn!' Andrea said under her breath. She knew it would take ages to get him back if he went over the wall into Dave Bramley's beckside pasture, and she was already pushed for time.

'I'll catch him,' Alexander called as he set

off in pursuit of the excited animal, who stopped to give them both a laughing glance before leaping over the wall.

There were ewes with their lambs in the field. There was a man in the field too, jumping down from a tractor to find out what all the fuss was about. It would be Dave, Andrea guessed with a sinking heart, and Dave in his present sour mood would be more than likely to blow his top. She soon found she was right about that.

'Get that bloody animal under control,' Dave was bellowing as Alexander followed Lucky over the drystone wall.

Andrea moved swiftly in the direction of Dave, guessing that Lucky would by now have caught sight of the collie, Tyke, and be racing over the grass to join him in what he took to be a game, but was in fact Tyke's work of gathering the sheep. The air was full of noise now, there was Lucky's excited bark, Tyke's snapping warning to the younger dog to keep his distance and not interfere with his sheep, and intermingled with it all the panic-stricken cries of the lambs and their mothers. Then came another roar from the farmer.

'Are you bloody deaf? Didn't you hear what I said? If you don't move that dog I'll bloody move it for you.'

There was no need for Dave to do that. Tyke had done it for him, turning quick as a flash on the red setter as Lucky bounded up to him. A couple of growls, a yelp from Lucky as the collie gave him a nip, and it was all over. Lucky turned tail and made for the manse with drooping tail and lowered ears. Andrea caught hold of his collar as he came back over the wall, subdued and whining for sympathy.

'You're a bad, bad dog!' she scolded.

'Will that cause problems for you with the farmer?' Alexander asked as he joined her. 'I don't think any harm came to the sheep, but if it had done he could have complained to the police. Or even shot the dog. As it was, I think Lucky got the worst of it.'

'I'm sorry it happened though, because Dave Bramley isn't in the best of tempers just now,' she told him with a sigh.

'I suppose you can't blame him for losing his rag. Farming's going through bad times. My parents are in farming, so I know a bit about that.'

'Are you in it too?' He couldn't be, not with those beautiful hands.

'No, not now. I'd better be on my way, and leave you to get ready for your meeting. Can I walk Lucky for you again tomorrow? I'd like to.'

Andrea laughed. 'Are you serious, now you know what a disaster area he can be?'

'Yes, I'll risk it. Providing you'll have supper with me afterwards,' he added.

She was relieved to find that she did not need to make an excuse; that there was a genuine reason why she could not accept his invitation. 'Oh, I'm sorry I can't; there's a church meeting here tomorrow.'

'Another meeting? Don't you ever get an evening off?'

She smiled. 'I get a day off every week, in theory. It doesn't always work out in practice.'

Bill's cousin was perplexed. 'Why do you do it? There must be other careers...'

'Not for me,' she said with conviction.

'I'll see you tomorrow. Same time?'

'Same time; unless you've changed your mind.'

'I won't do that,' he declared, before striding through the rain to his car.

Was Bill's cousin going to become a problem with his obvious admiration for her? Andrea pushed the unwelcome thought away from her and went to her study to collect the notes she needed for the Elders meeting.

'I knew I should have gone to the drama group!' Carla told Josh as they made their way out of Nyddford High School. 'I told Dad I'd be letting Andrea down, and that she'd have to get someone else to take my place. Was Sara Hall really brilliant, or are you just winding me up?'

Josh hesitated. He knew he'd got it wrong by praising Sara instead of keeping his big mouth shut. Now Carla would be more upset than ever about her dad keeping her grounded on the farm. He didn't understand what it was all about, the way Carla's dad could be so friendly to him one day and so damned cussed another. He couldn't work it out at all. Most of the guys he'd met up with since his own dad had come from the States on this exchange with a teacher from Nyddford High were great guys. Sometimes Carla's dad was a great guy, but right now he was just a pain in the ass.

'Sure, Sara was pretty good, but I liked it better the way you played the part,' he said now. 'I mean, you kinda got it right. Like it was supposed to be. Sara was overworking it a bit. Maybe because we had this new guy come to help Andrea instead of Julie.' Josh hoped he'd got it right. He really liked Carla; she was so cool, yet so smart. All that long shiny hair and those legs that seemed to go on for ever...

'Which new guy? Do you mean someone from church?' Carla asked sharply.

Josh shook his head. 'No, not from the church. I've never seen him there. This guy's just here on a visit to see the artist, Bill Wyndham.'

Carla frowned. 'Bill Wyndham's away in America. He's doing some lectures and

212

things over there to do with his pictures.'

Carla still thought Bill Wyndham was pretty special, but not in the way he had been special to her a few months ago. She felt a hot wave of embarrassment wash over her as she recalled the way she had pestered Bill, even asking him to let her go and live with him at Beckside! Bill must have thought her the ultimate slag, but he had been patient with her until she had gone over the top one day. He had lost his rag with her then. She had been planning to run away from home after that, only then Josh Bolton had turned up at Beckside to bring Bill's dog home. Once she had got a good look at Josh's thick blond hair, his amazing blue eyes, and his real neat bum, she had changed her mind about leaving home.

'Bill's due back any day to do some things for television, so Alexander's going to stay on and help with the drama next week. Sara really went crazy over him. That's why she said she'd take your place in the play,' Josh's voice broke into Carla's racing thoughts.

'Huh! Just like Sara Hall! She wouldn't take the part when Andrea first asked her.'

'I guess she wouldn't have taken it on last night if Alexander hadn't been there. She was telling everyone afterwards that he was going to stay on in Nyddford because he fancied her.'

'Did you believe her?'

Josh laughed. 'I guess not. He seemed to fancy Andrea more than her. I saw them go off together afterwards in her car.'

'Oh!' Carla was taken aback. 'I always thought Andrea was interested in Bill Wyndham. I'm sure...' She stopped, then went on. 'Only Bill isn't here, is he?'

'This guy, Alexander, says he's Bill Wyndham's cousin.'

'Why did he come here when Bill was away?'

Josh shook his head. 'Don't ask me.'

Carla made her mind up. 'I'll make sure I get to drama group next week,' she said, 'even if I have to sneak out when Dad thinks I'm doing my homework.'

Josh Bolton grinned. 'I'll come and pick you up,' he said.

'Don't bring your motorbike anywhere near the farm house, Josh, or you'll give the game away,' she warned.

'I'll leave it at the end of Abbot's Lane, where the bus shelter is. Will you meet me there?'

'You're on!' Carla was jubilant. 'I'm not going to be a prisoner in my own home just because my dad has fallen out with Julie.'

Josh turned round, his face full of laughter. 'What do you mean, Carly? What gives with your pop and Julie?'

'Nothing! Now!' Carla's tone was derisive. 'It was going like a bomb between them,

214

only they didn't think I knew. Then suddenly it's all off, Julie's buying a house in Nyddford close to the health centre, and Dad's like a bear with a sore head. He's always nagging me or shouting at me to do more housework or cooking. He'll be worse than ever now he's seen Matt Harper bringing Julie home. I bet that's why Julie wasn't helping with the drama last night; because she was out with Matt Harper.'

The arrival of the school bus, an ancient vehicle well festooned with mud from the lanes of a dozen Yorkshire Dales villages, brought their conversation to an end as they joined the scrum of senior students all trying to force themselves and their school bags, sports gear and musical instruments on to the entry platform at the same time. It was chaotic. There was no chance of them being able to sit together as the Nyddford Crawler chugged into noisy, reluctant life and began to weave its precarious way out of the market town.

Life wouldn't be as much fun when there was no Josh Bolton at Nyddford High, or living in Nyddbeck village, Carla decided. There would be no more barbecues shared with the friendly American family, no more hair-raisingly exciting rides on the back of Josh's motorbike, no more secret meetings in the summer-house at Beckside, which Bill Wyndham had forgotten to lock before he went away. Life would be dull, dull, dull. Life would be dead boring when Josh went home in early July, and now there was no prospect of her dad and Julie Craven getting together to make life better for all of them. Carla sighed as the Nyddford Crawler began a smoky, groaning ascent of Abbot's Hill.

If the worst came to the worst, after Josh went back to America, and Dad wouldn't let her go on to college, she would go back to her plan to sneak out late one night and hitch a lift to somewhere like Manchester or Birmingham. Somewhere she could get a job as a waitress or a barmaid, and find a flat or a bedsit. She wouldn't tell Josh what she was planning though, because he would be sure to try and talk her out of it. So it would be best not to tell him...

The thunderstorm of yesterday had cleared the air and left behind a pale-blue sky with floating white puffs of cloud. The air was perfumed with the scent of lilac from the heavy mauve and white blossoms which hung over the stone wall that enclosed the manse. Today Andrea was home earlier than she expected to be from her round of home visits to some of the more elderly and unwell members of her churches. After the hours spent in small, over-warm rooms she was longing for fresh air and exercise. If

Alexander Ross had not promised to come and walk Lucky for her again she could have taken Bill's dog for a long walk on Abbot's Moor. Perhaps Alexander wouldn't come? It could be that this bright beautiful day would have tempted him to drive farther afield to one of the places where the riverside walks would not be still clogged with mud after the cloudburst. Yet even as the thought entered her mind she knew that Alexander would come to the manse again today.

He arrived at a few minutes to five. The windows of his low sporty car were wound right down to allow the breeze to ruffle the thick auburn hair that grew down over the collar of his purple shirt. As the car came to a stop he reached over to the back seat to bring out a sheaf of flowers, starburst lilies and huge carnations expensively dressed with satin ribbons. Andrea, who was in the front garden pulling out weeds, felt a frisson of delight at the sight of them. This was swiftly followed by a pang of dismay.

'Hi there! Are you about ready to go?'

Andrea frowned. 'Go where?' She was mystified. A glance down at her jeans and T-shirt was all it needed to remind her that she was dressed for gardening, or dog walking. Or both.

'Ready to go to your latest meeting, or whatever.'

She shook her head, smiling. 'Not today. I've caught up on the paperwork this morning, and done the sick visiting this afternoon. So that's me off the hook for a few hours.'

Alexander beamed at her. 'So you could come with me and Lucky; show us one of those great walks Bill was telling me about,' he suggested.

Andrea hesitated, then made up her mind. Going dog walking with Alexander was a much better option than staying at home to do the weeding.

'Yes, I'll come with you,' she said.

Thirteen

As she and Alexander made their way over the bridge and along Church Lane in the sunshine, Andrea felt her spirits rising. Bill would be back in a couple of days! He had promised that he would. They would be able to walk Lucky together then, and talk about all the things that had happened while he'd been in America. Bill might be surprised to find Alexander still here.

'I believe you're daydreaming, Andrea,' Bill's cousin said as they reached Beckside and Lucky almost pulled her off her feet in his effort to drag her through the open gates of Bill's home.

Andrea covered her embarrassment with a laugh. 'I was wondering who had left the gates open,' she said. 'Bill keeps them closed because of Lucky.'

'Perhaps the postie?' Alexander suggested.

'No, it won't be him because he keeps a few sheep on a smallholding and he knows how vital it is that dogs don't run loose at this time of the year.'

'Yes, I felt bad about Lucky dashing into

your neighbour's field. I hope it didn't cause any problems for you afterwards with the farmer.' Alexander turned a concerned face to her as he pulled Bill's gates closed.

'No. I usually get on quite well with Dave Bramley now, his mother is a friend of mine, but things have all gone wrong for Dave recently and he's on a short fuse.' She frowned as Dave's problems rushed into her mind, then went back to wondering about those open gates. 'Maybe we ought to take a look round to make sure Bill hasn't had unwelcome visitors while he's been away?'

'Yes, I think we should,' he agreed.

'Did Bill send you a key for Beckside when he knew you were coming down?' she asked.

Alexander shook his head. 'No. My visit was arranged at short notice, and as I planned to stay in hotels down here there was no need for him to send me a key.'

'Perhaps we should just look through the windows then?' Bill had left a key with her, but for some reason she did not want to share that information with his cousin.

So they peered through all the ground-floor windows of the spacious studio home. They could see no cause for concern. By now Lucky was sniffing happily about the back garden and making his way to the summer-house. Andrea followed him. She saw then that someone had certainly been in the summer-house because the door was not quite closed and there was an empty bottle on the round teak table. Next to it was a chocolate wrapper. No damage had been done but someone had certainly made use of the place. They had used it very recently because there was a lingering hint of perfume about; a perfume which was vaguely familiar to Andrea. A fragrance which was popular with the teenage girls who came to drama group...

Instantly then, as she recognized the musky scent, a girl came to mind. A girl who had used this place once before when she was chasing after Bill. Carla must have been here recently; probably with Josh Bolton since her father would not let them meet either at the farm or at church events. The empty bottle on the table had held a cheap wine, possibly bought by Josh, who was almost eighteen and looked older than that. Dave Bramley would really lose his rag if he found out that Carla had been drinking here with Josh in Bill's absence.

'Looks like someone's had a party, doesn't it?' Alexander said as he joined her.

'Yes, I'd better get rid of the evidence before Bill comes back.'

'Won't he want to know about it?'

'It's best if he doesn't know,' she decided.

'Why?'

'He might guess who it was.'

'So?'

'If it's who I think it was, the family have enough problems to deal with right now without any more.'

'You really care about these folk, don't you, Andrea?' There was surprise evident in his voice.

Andrea sighed. 'Yes, I really do. They were very good to me when I first came here, when I had no one else to help me.'

'Did Bill come into that category?'

The question was unexpected. Andrea was not sure how to answer it, so she gathered up the bottle and the sweet wrapper and hurried to dispose of them in the waste bin. 'Shall we get on with our walk now?' she suggested.

Julie Craven was busy packing books into a cardboard carton in the big, pleasant living room of Jacob's Cottage. There was really no need to start preparing for her move as early as this, but she was filled with such restlessness now that she had committed herself to buying the house in Nyddford that she was unable to let any of her daylight hours pass in inactivity. Not having anything to do with her hands meant going to stare out of the window which overlooked the farmyard in the hope of seeing Dave going about his work. Since Dave's work was based here he could be glimpsed far too often moving from one farm building to another, or coming out of the back door of the farmhouse after a meal or a tea-break. Every sighting of Dave brought a fresh stab of anguish to Julie. So she had begun the emptying of bookcases and cupboards, not because she had any real heart for the task but simply because she was too tense to be able to relax in this place where for a few months she had been so happy and so full of hope for the future. Now it was a place where she knew nothing but despair.

She knew she was spending too many hours alone in this cottage now. Even Carla and Jack did not seem to drop in on her as they had been in the habit of doing a few weeks ago. Surely Dave had not forbidden them to come and see her? He would not be that vindictive, would he? She pushed the thought aside as Tyke's furious barking warned of a vehicle stopping at the farm gate. It could be Andrea, who had said she would drop in this morning on her way back from visiting Ben Harper.

Her spirits lifted when she saw her friend crossing the yard, heading for Jacob's Cottage. 'Hi! Andrea. Come in. I'll put the kettle on for coffee,' she said.

'There's good news; Ben's going home later today.' Andrea followed Julie into the kitchen as she spoke.

'Oh, I'm so glad! Dorothy will be over the moon to have him back at Ford House.'

'So will Matt, I imagine. You'll know more about that, won't you?' Andrea smiled as she made the teasing remark.

'What do you mean?' Julie spun round in the act of pouring hot water on the instant coffee.

'Well, you are quite friendly with Matt, aren't you? Dorothy was saying how grateful she was for your help in getting Matt to go in and see his father.'

Julie's frown deepened. 'I thought the reason Matt left his job in America and came home was because he wanted to see his father.'

'Matt came because he was sent for, even though he was not willing to go to the hospital until he was certain his father would be glad to see him. You were the one who made him change his mind,' Andrea reminded her.

Julie gave a wry smile. 'It wasn't easy to do. Matt only agreed to go providing I would be standing by to comfort him if his dad threw him out.'

Andrea laughed. 'Matt certainly seems to have gone overboard for you, Julie.'

Julie sighed. 'I wish I could say the same for me. I like Matt; he's good company, but that's as far as it goes.'

'Perhaps you haven't given yourself long enough yet for anything else to develop?'

Julie shook her head. 'The trouble is, he's

not Dave. There's never really been anyone for me except Dave. I tried so hard to fall for someone else after he married Jill, but it just didn't work.'

'I thought, after Ian died, that there would never be anyone else for me.' Andrea stirred her coffee thoughtfully. There was no need for her to say any more than that. It was Julie who had noticed, and then made her aware of the fact, that Bill Wyndham was in love with her.

'When's Bill due back?' Julie wanted to know.

'Any time now. There was a message from him a couple of days ago, when he was in North Carolina. He said there were only two more lectures or demos lined up for him to do then he was coming back, whether his agent liked it or not.'

'I hear this cousin of his made quite an impression on the drama group kids?' Julie gave Andrea a speculative look as she made this remark.

Andrea laughed. 'He certainly made an impression on Sara Hall! When I asked her to take the leading part she didn't want to know. Yet when Alexander suggested it she not only played it, she overplayed it! Alexander was very good with the youngsters; he seemed to know what he was talking about, and they certainly listened to him. I was really glad of his help. None of the parents turned up to give a hand.'

'So glad that you had supper with him afterwards at the Golden Fleece, I believe,' Julie teased. 'I'm almost tempted to offer to help with the drama group again myself this week, if only to see this guy who's made such an impression on Sara Hall.'

'Your offer's accepted, whether you're serious or not,' Andrea said before Julie could change her mind. 'Who told you about the supper at the Golden Fleece?'

'I can't remember. It's difficult to keep anything secret in a town as small as Nyddford,' was all Julie would say.

Later, as she was leaving the farm, Andrea saw Dave crossing the yard with a sickly new-born lamb in his arms. She stopped to speak to him, knowing an apology was due. When he guessed that was her intention it seemed at first that Dave would turn about to avoid meeting her. Then she spoke his name and he came to stand close enough so that she could see the face of the little creature tucked inside his jacket, and hear the faint distressed cries. Dave was so patient with the creatures in his care, yet with his children, particularly Carla, he was so different. Andrea thought of the wine bottle and the chocolate wrapper left behind in Bill's summer-house and guessed that if Dave even suspected that Carla had been partying there with the American boy, there

226

would be a fresh storm waiting to erupt about the girl.

'I won't keep you, Dave,' she said quietly. 'I know it's your busiest time. I just wanted to say how sorry I am about Lucky getting into your field. I'll make sure it doesn't happen again,' she added, crossing her fingers.

'I've enough problems on my hands right now without having my animals put at risk by out-of-control dogs,' he said curtly.

Andrea took a deep breath then let it go ready to speak again. 'There'll be one less problem for you to worry about now because Ben's coming home from hospital today.'

Dave's features relaxed only slightly. 'That was one of my mother's problems, not one of mine.'

Andrea tried again. 'I'm sure you'll be pleased, for her sake.'

He shrugged that off in silence, with a slight movement of his muscular shoulders. Andrea was beginning to lose patience with him. Then, as she was leaving him and turning to give Julie a goodbye wave, he spoke to her again.

'I don't suppose you'll bother to come up here again when she's gone from the cottage?' His voice was harsh, his face set in stern lines. Yet there was an expression in his eyes that made her feet come to a halt. Those dark-grey eyes mirrored a depth of desolation that appalled her.

She knew she must play for time, and go very carefully. 'What makes you think that, Dave?' she said quietly. 'I had begun to believe that all of you at Abbot's Fold were my friends.'

'I'd been thinking that Julie was my friend, that she would be here for me and my children, and all the time she was planning to move away without saying anything to me.'

'Only because she knew there were holiday lets booked since last year for the cottage, and that you needed the money they would bring in.'

'I told her she could come and stay in the farmhouse, that there was plenty of room there. She didn't have to go looking for a place to buy.'

As Andrea saw the resentment in Dave's expression she could guess at the hurt that was behind it. Dave was a highly intelligent man, but an inarticulate one. Having heard Julie's side of the story earlier she could now sympathize with both of them. Both had too much pride to be able to give the other the benefit of the doubt. Both were afraid of being hurt. What could she do to help? Only offer up a quick prayer for guidance...

'Why don't you talk to Julie about it? Ask her why she made up her mind in such a hurry. Give her the chance to explain. There will be a reason.'

'The reason is that she's met someone else; someone who has a lot more to offer her than I have. Someone who's only staying on here to make sure he takes over his father's business as soon as possible. Julie's going out with Matt Harper now, that's why she's leaving here.' Dave's voice was burning with bitterness.

'I'm quite sure you're wrong about that, Dave. Please give her the chance to explain. Please go and talk to her,' Andrea pleaded.

'And find myself snubbed again? Not likely!' he hit back.

'You won't be,' she began.

'Why don't you save your advice for those who ask for it? Why don't you mind your own business and leave me to get on with my own life?' he responded angrily.

Andrea sighed. 'If that's the way you want it, Dave, there's nothing more I can say. I'm sorry; very sorry, for you and Julie.'

With that, she strode quickly to her car before he could see how upset she was.

Bill Wyndham felt a great surge of thanksgiving wash over him as he reached the familiar landscape of the Yorkshire Dales. It was homecoming in the very best sense of the word. Here was a place he had come to over a year ago because a large international company which had a base in Yorkshire had commissioned a series of watercolour paintings from him for their prestigious new offices. He had expected to be in North Yorkshire for only a few weeks, but the region had captivated him so much that he had extended his stay in Jacob's Cottage until he was so reluctant to leave that he had even begun to consider buying the place when it came on the market. Two things were against him doing that. The first was that the cottage was not large enough to allow for him to have a decent studio there without building on a substantial extension, which would have meant him having to apply for planning permission and perhaps endure a long wait before being allowed to build his studio. The second was that Carla Bramley had begun to make a nuisance of herself by following him around and trying to persuade him to let her go and live with him. That had been an alarming experience.

Yet if it had not been for that experience he would never have got to know Andrea when he asked her to help him discourage the girl. So deeply had he fallen for Andrea that, in spite of his early misgivings, he was soon eager to change his own way of life so he might share her life. He was aware that this would mean him staying put in the village of Nyddbeck for most of the year rather than travelling extensively to paint his pictures wherever fancy, or commissions, took him. It would also mean him sharing some of Andrea's work at the little church in Nyddbeck and the larger church in Nyddford. Already it had led to him playing the organ sometimes for services in those churches, even though he had drifted away from going to church regularly in his teens.

Sharing Andrea's life and her faith would demand immense commitment from him. Yet he had no qualms about that. All he longed for was to stay close to Andrea always; to work in the studio home he had bought in Church Lane in order to be near her, then, when she was ready, to marry her and share a family with her. He had missed her terribly while he had been in America. When he discovered how many extra lectures and demonstrations his agent had booked for him to do, he had been tempted to cancel them and get on the next available plane home. He hadn't done that because he was essentially a straight-dealing man and was honest enough to admit to himself that even with his talent he would not have done anything like as well without Miriam to guide and manage and publicize his work.

Miriam had not been pleased with him for taking this flight home today at such short notice. She had wanted him to stay on and meet a couple of people she said were interested enough in his pictures to offer him commissions, but there had been an urgency in him all of a sudden to get back to where he could talk at length to Andrea and convince her that they should marry very soon. He was tired of keeping their love a secret from all the people who had become their friends in the village and in the market town of Nyddford. What he wanted to do was to tell the world that he loved Andrea, and she loved him. It would not matter then if they were seen touching hands or embracing.

Bill had had more than enough of secrecy about his relationship with Andrea. He knew it was nine months now since her husband had been killed in a car crash. It was time they set a date for their wedding, and the sooner the better. He had been angry with her for refusing to go to America with him and there had been a coolness between them for a time, which he knew must have hurt her. Yet he had also known that it must have been a difficult decision for her to make because Andrea was a warm-blooded woman who was eager to put the memory of her past unhappiness behind her and share his love and his home.

Now that he was back home he intended to convince her that they should not wait any longer before announcing their engagement and that they should marry in late summer. Inside his jacket, close to his heart, was the ring he had bought in America. He could not wait to show it to her, and to place it on her finger. It would not be long now before he would be able to do that. There below him, nestling in a hollow at the foot of the fell, was the village of Nyddbeck. He slowed down the speed of the car he had hired at the airport and halted for a moment to stare down at the tower of the church emerging from the foliage of horse chestnut, oak and beech trees. They would marry there in the little building where he had come to realize that he would not have to pretend to share Andrea's faith. Faith had been waiting there for him to reach out and take it into his life.

Seconds later he was on his way again down the long winding hill, turning carefully at the foot of it to drive alongside the beck and then over the bridge to come to a halt outside the manse. Elation filled him. She would be so surprised to see him, a day earlier than he had told her in his last phone call. Disappointment hit him when he saw there was another car already on her drive. That meant he would have to wait till her visitor had gone before he could give her the ring.

Andrea had seen him getting out of the unfamiliar car. She was already opening the door to him, with Lucky pushing past her to reach his beloved master. Bill could not wait

to pull her into his arms. He was taken
aback when she pulled away from him, even
though her face was alight with her joy at
seeing him.

'It's so good to see you, Bill,' she said
breathlessly.

Over her shoulder, emerging from the
kitchen, Bill caught his first glance of the
man he did not think would still be here. He
had thought that Alexander would have
moved on now; gone back to his hectic life.
Why was his cousin still here? Why was he in
Andrea's home?

Fourteen

'Hi there, Bill! It's great to see you, man!'

Alexander seized Bill's hand and shook it heartily. He was so obviously pleased to see him that Bill felt ashamed to be wishing his cousin anywhere but here. So he forced a smile to his face as he returned the handshake. 'It's good to see you're still here, Alex,' he said. 'I guessed you'd have got fed up of waiting for me to come home and moved on.'

'I did intend to do that, at first, then I began to get to know the place, and some of the people, and I found I didn't want to leave in a hurry. I suppose that's what happened to you?'

'Yes, something like that.' Bill was eager now to move on from the greetings and find a way of getting Andrea to himself, if only for a few minutes. First though there was Lucky, clamouring to be made a fuss of. Obviously his dog had missed him greatly. Had Andrea also missed him a lot? He was moving towards her now, with his dog still leaping madly up and down with excitement and Alex blocking the way into the big living room of the manse.

'I'll put the kettle on for coffee,' Andrea said.

She still had not recovered from the shock, and the joy, of Bill's sudden appearance a day ahead of his scheduled return. There was also a quite unexpected feeling of reticence inside her about greeting Bill in the presence of his cousin, who knew nothing of their feelings for each other. Her hands were shaking slightly as she lifted the kettle to the tap and set it to boil; her heart was racing and there was hot colour in her cheeks. Why hadn't Bill let her know he was coming home a day earlier than planned? If he had done that, she could have prepared a special meal for him, and cancelled the visit she had arranged for tonight with the Rainbows and Brownies.

'Andrea, darling! Are you glad to see me?' Bill whispered as he came to put an arm about her.

'Oh, Bill, so glad! It's seemed such a long time.' Emotion was almost choking her in the moment before he kissed her.

'Too long, my love. Far too long, and then Miriam wanted me to fit in another meeting with potential clients at the last minute. That's when I decided I'd had enough.'

'Why didn't you let me know you were coming back early?' she wanted to know.

'I thought I'd like to surprise you.'

'You certainly did that!' she laughed.

Bill was frowning now. 'What's he doing here?'

'Alexander? He's here because you invited him, and then had to be away when he came.'

The frown deepened. 'I meant what's he doing here in your manse? I wouldn't have thought...'

'He's here because he offered to walk Lucky for me.'

'How did that come about?'

'I met him when I was walking Lucky one day. I saw him at Beckside when we were walking past on our way up to the moor. In fact he gave me quite a shock at first because I thought he was you.' Andrea chuckled at the recollection.

Bill was not amused. 'Me? How could you think he was me when I was in America?'

'Because he looks so much like you, the same height, the same build, the same colouring, and about the same age. Lucky took to him at once.'

'We may look alike, but we certainly don't have that much in common.' There was something in Bill's voice that Andrea found perplexing.

'I thought Alex was an artist too...'

'He doesn't paint, at least not professionally. He's a photographer.'

'He didn't tell me that.' Andrea was even more puzzled.

'They wouldn't be your sort of photographs,' Bill said bluntly.

Before Andrea could ask him why not, Lucky came bounding into the kitchen, taking the sound of spoons making contact with mugs to mean that biscuits would be on offer. So the awkward moment, and the time for asking questions, passed. They joined Alexander in the living room to drink the coffee and make the sort of general conversation that for the time being helped Andrea to forget the uneasiness which had invaded her when she became aware that Bill was not too pleased to find that his cousin had stayed on to wait for his return, and was on friendly terms with her and Lucky.

More awkwardness arose when Lucky made it plain that it was time for his walk. After a glance at her watch, Andrea said, 'I don't think I've time to go on the walk after all, Alexander. Would you mind very much going on your own? You know the way now, don't you?'

There was a moment of silence during which Andrea could feel Bill's intent stare moving from his cousin's face to her own. Then Alex began, 'Why don't you come with me and Lucky, Bill? I guess you'll be ready for a breath of fresh air after your flight.'

Bill hesitated, and seemed for a moment about to refuse, until Lucky leapt up to give him yet another welcome home. He laughed then and picked up the dog's lead as he made for the door. 'I expect you're right, Alex, a breath of moorland air will do me good. We mustn't hold you up if you've a meeting to go to, Andrea. What is it tonight?'

'Rainbows and Brownies at Nyddford Church, so it's an early one.'

Alexander laughed. 'It won't be quite as chaotic as your drama group, will it?'

Andrea smiled. 'No, and it will finish earlier.'

'You can put me down to help with that again next week,' Bill's cousin said over his shoulder as he followed Bill and Lucky to the door.

'Will you still be here then?' There was an edge to Bill's voice.

'Sure! I've no more assignments booked until June. I've heard that some of the local stately homes and National Trust properties are worth visiting then for the gardens. So if I stay on for a while I could get some good shots then for the calendar companies.'

'You didn't tell me you were a photographer,' Andrea said, without thinking.

'Didn't I? I suppose that's because we had so many other things to talk about.'

239

'If you've an early meeting, Andrea, we ought to be going,' Bill broke in as Alexander seemed inclined to linger in the back porch.

'Yes, I really must get moving.' Andrea was uneasy about something that was building up in the atmosphere; a coolness towards his cousin that was becoming more evident every time Bill spoke to Alexander. This was perhaps because Bill was suffering jet lag after his journey home. It was certainly unlike his usual demeanour. Bill was such a relaxed person, so pleasant and easy-going.

'Why don't you join me at the Golden Fleece again for supper when your meeting is over?' Alexander's voice broke into her thoughts as she was turning back into her kitchen. 'And how about you, Bill? If you're back earlier than expected I don't suppose you'll have any arrangements made for tonight.'

Bill did not answer. Instead he strode away from the manse, holding firmly on to Lucky.

'Sorry, I can't. I have my sermon for Sunday to prepare when I get back tonight,' Andrea said into the silence that followed Alexander's invitation.

Frowning, she watched the two men walk towards the bridge that spanned the beck. Bill had plainly been put out to find Alexander with her at the manse, and was still in a strange mood. Was he jealous of his cousin?

240

Surely not? Surely he could trust her, as she had trusted him when he was on the other side of the Atlantic? He had been very abrupt when he told her about his cousin's work as a photographer, almost as though he meant to belittle it. It was all very puzzling, but she would have to put it out of her mind now and give all of her attention to her own work. This was not going to be easy now that Bill was back and her whole being ached to be alone with him. They would have so much to say to one another, so many experiences to share. Would Bill come to see her tonight when she was home from her meeting and he was back from his supper with Alex? She longed for Bill to do that.

Matt and his father were deep in discussion about the immediate future of the farm and the more long-term prospects for the transport business, so Dorothy left them to it and went to the kitchen to start making scones and cake to offer the many friends and neighbours who would drop in at Ford House to welcome Ben home. It was so good to have Ben back home again, an answer to all those prayers she had said so constantly from the time he had collapsed after carrying the Easter cross up to the traditional place on Abbot's Hill.

She had been so afraid then that she and

241

Ben had left it too late to marry, and that she would become a widow only a few months after being a bride. There had been nightmare days and sleepless nights when she had paced the floor at Ford House, pleading that Ben should be restored to health, if only for a few more years of happiness. Dorothy was a realist; she knew that when you married for the second time in your late fifties you could not expect to share as many years as she had shared with Jacob Bramley, her first husband. There had also been another reason why she had prayed that Ben would be granted a few more years of life. She had desperately wanted him to become reconciled with his only son.

Ben had never spoken about the rift with Matt which had resulted in Matt taking a job with his girlfriend's father and staying over in the States ever since. When she had gently tried to lead him into sharing his hurt with her, Ben had shut her up instantly by saying it was all part of the past and a part that he did not wish to be reminded of. He would not even agree that his son should be sent an invitation to their wedding. Dorothy had been deeply troubled by this refusal, which had marred her happiness.

At the back of her mind, and surfacing from time to time right up until Ben's heart attack, had been the remark she had overheard during their wedding reception. The remark had been made by a distant relative of Ben's, a man who had not been as successful as Ben had become after combining a transport business with his farming activities.

'There'll be nowt to come to Matt now our Ben's wed again. It'll all go to her, the house, the business, the farm and the brass,' the man had said bluntly.

Dorothy had not been surprised to hear this relative of her new husband expressing this view. It was fairly common in farming circles for discussion of money matters to take place at family weddings and funerals. There was no element of nosiness or spite intended by the speaker. It was simply well-meant concern on his part for Ben's absent son who could not be here to look after his own interests.

'Aye, and then it'll all finish up at Abbot's Fold Farm with Dorothy's lad,' a second opinion had added.

Dorothy had moved quickly out of hearing and soon been caught up in talking to other wedding guests, but she had not been completely able to banish those words from her mind. Thinking about them made her feel uncomfortable. She had not married Ben because he was a wealthy man; she had married him because she loved him. During the first few weeks after their marriage she had tried to persuade him to change the will he had made leaving everything he possessed, apart from bequests to the church and a couple of charities, to her. Ben had refused to listen.

'You've been my reason for living these last few years, my love,' he had told her. 'I was full of bitterness when Matt refused to stay in the business with me. I had nothing to live for then until your Jacob was released from his long illness and you were free to marry me. Since then you've become my whole world. You, and my church, are enough for me.'

There had been a huge lump in Dorothy's throat as she listened, and moisture in her eyes, but mention of the church which meant so much to both of them stirred her conscience and urged her to remind Ben of family loyalties.

'You could have grandchildren that you know nothing about, Ben. Young people who are of your blood and could mean a great deal to you if you gave them the chance. Grandchildren are such a blessing. They bring so much fun, and interest, and joy.'

'I've got your grandchildren to do that for me now. Young Jack's shaping up well, and Carla's showing signs of turning out to be a grand young lass. So don't let's hear any more about the lad who turned his back on me.'

Now the lad who had turned his back on his father was here in Ford House, and Ben was back in his home. It was time for him to put things right. If he did so, Matt would probably stay on to continue helping with the farm and transport business. That was what she wanted to happen, but there could be a heavy price to pay for it. Because if Matt stayed on in Yorkshire he would almost certainly go on taking Julie Craven out. Then Julie would lose contact with David, and all her own cherished hopes of Julie taking Jill's place in her son's life would be dashed. Surely her David was not going to just stand by and watch Matt Harper take over more and more of Julie's life? What was wrong with the lad? Couldn't he see that if only he had said the right words Julie would never even have begun to look for a house to buy in Nyddford?

Why hadn't Julie spoken out to David, taken things into her own hands as so many young women seemed to do these days? Dorothy could understand why Julie had got tired of waiting. After all, she was about the same age as Jill had been, so she must be thirty-five or -six, and eager perhaps to have a child of her own. Soon though it would be too late for Julie to start a family with David because Matt was making no secret of his fancy for her. Once Matt became aware of

Dorothy's own long friendship with Julie he had encouraged her to tell him more about her. At first she had not suspected that he was intending to start dating Julie. When she did discover they were going out together she was bitterly disappointed. It was not that she did not like Matt by that time. Rather it was that her heart ached for David; for the reticence and what she guessed was his stiff-necked pride about asking the girl she was sure he loved to share the uncertainties of his farming lifestyle.

It was not too late though to try and knock sense into her son's head. There were a few days left before Julie would move into her new home. So Dorothy doubled the cake mix and made up her mind to drop in unexpectedly at Abbot's Fold Farm and take scones and a cake for her grandchildren.

As she drove back to Nyddbeck, Andrea's ears were ringing still with the more lively of the Brownie and Rainbow songs which had brought her time with them in Nyddford Church Hall to an end. The little girls had been proudly showing her the simple gifts they had been making to help raise money for the repairs needed to the church roof. It would take thousands of such items to pay the huge bill when the work was done, but they were not to know that, and every little helped. Worrying about the state of the church roof had brought on a nagging persistent headache, and she was unable to shake off the memory of Bill's unexpectedly cool attitude when he found his cousin at the manse. Perhaps it would be better if Bill did not come to see her at the manse after having supper with Alexander, she decided as the lights of the village came into sight. Then she could have a leisurely bath, a milky drink and some aspirin before finishing off her sermon. At least there was no late evening dog walk with Lucky to be done tonight.

She had checked the answerphone, dealt with the most urgent calls, and was about to run her bath when her front door bell rang. It was probably Bill, but in case it turned out to be a stranger she left on the safety chain which Bill had fixed for her before leaving for his American trip.

'Can I come in, or is it too late?' she heard Bill ask as she fiddled with the chain.

'Of course you can come in. I was wondering if you'd come—'

'I know it's late,' he broke in, 'but I had to see you. I couldn't wait to find out what's been going on while I've been away.'

'Going on?' Andrea stepped back from the front door to allow him to come into the hall. She wondered why he had not gone round to the back door, the kitchen door, as most of her friends did. 'I'm not sure I understand what you mean.'

'Between you and Alex, I mean.'

His voice was curt, rough almost. Bill had never spoken to her in such a tone before. What was it all about? 'I'm still not with you, Bill.' Her own voice was crisp. 'Would you like to explain?'

'I'm talking about Alex being here when I arrived, and about the meal he said you had with him last week at the Golden Fleece.'

'I told you, he came here to walk your dog.'

'And you as well, by what he said. Then he wanted you to have another meal with him at the Golden Fleece. Would you have gone, if I hadn't come home a day early?'

Andrea frowned. 'No, of course not. I'd promised to spend time with the Brownies.'

'You could have gone later, like you did after your drama group finished.' Bill's voice was accusing.

Andrea had heard enough. She was tired and the headache was worse now. Disappointment was simmering below the surface of her mind. This was far from being the sort of reunion with Bill that she had been dreaming of, and longing for.

'What is this? What's eating you, Bill? Surely you don't resent your cousin helping me with your dog? Or with my drama group?'

'You didn't need to go to supper with him.'

'I'd had hardly anything to eat since breakfast, so I was tired and hungry, and Alexander had missed out on the hotel dinner because of helping me with the drama group. Not many people would have been prepared to do that when they were on holiday.'

'Alex wouldn't have been prepared to do it if you'd been middle-aged and ugly.' Bill's face was tight with disapproval.

Andrea was fast losing patience with him. 'That's rubbish, Bill, and you know it.'

'It's true. Alex wouldn't have got involved with you and your church drama if you hadn't been a beautiful young single woman.'

'I'm not a single woman, I'm a widow.' She knew as she uttered it that her remark was unwise, but it was too late now.

'You're also a church minister who has to watch out for her reputation, as you pointed out to me when I wanted you to come to America with me,' Bill reminded her.

'One meal out with a man who's a visitor to the area doesn't make a scandal,' she hit back.

'It could do when the visitor is Alex Ross.'

'Alex Ross?' Andrea was perplexed.

'Alex Ross, photographer to the tabloid press.'

'I still don't know what you're getting at...'

'Don't be so naive, Andrea. Alex specializes in photographing the pop stars, the ones who make the headlines with their outrageous behaviour. Because of that he's not everybody's favourite person, so he sometimes makes enemies.'

'Why did you invite him to stay if you don't like him?' she wanted to know.

'I do like him, I always have. It's just that I don't always like what he does with his cameras. We don't see much of each other these days but he phoned me just before I left for the US and said he was taking some time out from his work and would like to see me. I thought I'd be back before he arrived, but of course I was delayed.'

'So he waited to see you,' she reminded him.

'Or was it to keep on seeing you, Andrea?' he suggested.

Anger was seeping away from her now and being replaced by bewilderment and hurt. 'Surely you can trust me, Bill, when you know I love you?'

There was a long moment of silence during which she waited for him to close the distance between them and take her into his arms. Then awareness that it was not going to happen took over and her throat began to ache with grief for what they were losing.

'If you had loved me enough you would have spared a few days from your work to

250

come out and join me, as I asked you to. Will your work always come between us, Andrea?' he said quietly.

He did not wait for her answer but turned away from her and walked slowly out of the manse. She heard the door close after him, followed by the sound of his footsteps walking away.

Fifteen

At least there was a good crop of lambs this year, mostly healthy and with no ewes lost and no call to send for the vet. Dave sighed as he looked down at the little creature he had slipped inside his jacket as the mid-April breeze sharpened and took on an icy edge. If only all his problems could be dealt with as easily as would be the care of this new-born lamb! He had thought, when his mother told him just before her marriage to Ben Harper that she was giving him the deeds of Jacob's Cottage to help him over the hard times the farm had been through during the previous years, that his luck was on the turn at last. His heart had been full of gratitude for her love and generosity. There were holiday lettings already booked which would have to be honoured, but he had decided he would not take on any more. Instead he would sell the cottage and use the money to reduce his overdraft and buy essential equipment needed for the farm.

Dave had not been so pleased when he heard that his mother had offered the cottage to Julie Craven for the months until the holiday lettings began while Julie looked for somewhere to live close to her new job at Nyddford Health Centre. He had never felt comfortable with Julie since he had spoken out of turn to her at Jill's funeral and seen the stricken look in her eyes as his words put the blame on her for Jill's death. Back at the farmhouse after the funeral, he had looked around for Julie so he could apologize but she had not gone there with his family and friends for refreshments. After that Dave was unable to meet Julie without remembering with shame his bad behaviour. So he had taken the coward's way out and ignored her.

Yet when Julie had taken up his mother's offer and was preparing to move into the cottage he had soon found himself looking forward to seeing her about the place; actually offering to help her and allowing her to help him sometimes with his children. There had been the day he had given way to a sudden impulse and bought a plant for her when he was in Nyddford on market day. Her response, when she reached up and kissed him warmly on his lips, had been totally unexpected. His own reaction to that kiss had been even more surprising.

So it had all begun, the days of companionship, laughter, joy, and hope for the future. The snatched hours of shared love while Carla and Jack were at school; the meals shared with his children in the farmhouse or her cottage. What the hell had gone wrong then? How had it come about that Julie began looking at properties in Nyddford without saying anything to him first? There had to be a reason for that. Was the reason Julie had got tired of him tied up with the fact that Matt Harper had come back to Nyddford and begun to take her out for the sort of expensive meals he could not afford to offer her?

It had to be the reason. While she had been living in Jacob's Cottage Julie would have had plenty of opportunity to observe at close hand what a struggle he was having to keep his farm profitable. At the same time, as a friend of Dorothy and Ben Harper, she would be aware of the different life-style she would be able to enjoy if she became Matt Harper's partner. Soon, now that his father was home from hospital and recovering from his heart attack, Matt would either return to his prestigious job in America or stay on here in Yorkshire and take over the family business from his father. Matt had a lot to offer someone like Julie. Far more than he had. All he could offer her would be a life of hard work and tight budgets. It was no contest, as far as he was concerned. Which was probably why she had laughed at his offer of a room in the farmhouse. He was not sure, now, exactly how he had made that offer. All he could recall was the way she had looked when she refused his offer. Her mouth had been quivering and hot colour had stained her cheeks bright with anger. He had longed then to reach out for her, to crush her in his arms and tell her he loved her and could not bear the thought of her leaving. Only the damned words would not come up from his heart to his mouth. While he had stood there struggling to speak, Julie had closed the door on him.

Andrea had guessed at his feelings and urged him to tell Julie how he felt about her, but she could have no idea of how afraid he was of being turned down by Julie if he didn't get the words right. Words came easily to Andrea; they were the tools of her profession. For him, words were a stumbling block He could never manage to get them right when he needed them most. Soon it would be too late – Julie would have left Jacob's Cottage and, unless he bumped into her by accident, he would never see her again.

Why couldn't he get it right with young women? He'd upset Jill by making a fuss about her going back to nursing, even though they needed the money. He'd upset Andrea soon after her arrival in Nyddbeck by turning away her offer of help when his mother was ill. He was constantly upsetting

Carla, often when she didn't deserve it. What the hell was wrong with him? Was he turning into a moron?

Only with his animals was he able to be himself; a man who felt a duty and a responsibility towards all the living creatures in his care, for as long as they were in his care. Why could he not show the same gentleness to his daughter, and to Julie? Why? Why? Why? The question was still hammering away in his brain as he carried the weakling lamb into the farmhouse kitchen and placed it in a blanket-lined box close to the Aga.

As Andrea walked from her manse to the church to prepare for the Sunday morning family service her heart felt heavy in spite of the sunshine that gilded the stonework of the bridge and the cottages which lined Beck Lane. There were late daffodils still flowering beneath the trees on the village green and a froth of purple and white blossom cascading over the cottage garden walls. Birdsong mingled with the cries of the lambs that came drifting down from Abbot's Moor. It was the sort of morning when all should have been well with her world. All was not well with her world though, which was why she was making her way to the church earlier than she need have done to spend some time in private prayer.

'You're early this morning, minister,'

Norman Carter greeted her when she reached the post box set into the wall of his cottage. 'Couldn't you sleep?'

'It was too nice a morning for me to stay in bed,' she said as she bent to stroke his old dog.

'You'll be missing your dog-walking now that Bill Wyndham's back home, won't you?' the elderly man said. 'Why don't you get a dog of your own? Grand company they are.'

'I might do that,' she told him as she turned into Church Lane. 'I'll see you later, Norman, I hope.'

'Oh yes, I'll be there. I like the family service. I enjoy seeing the children acting out their plays and taking part in the stories instead of sitting there all bored and silent like we used to do when I was a lad.'

Andrea walked on towards her church, but her eyes were not looking that way. They were staring into the distance, to where Bill's home could be glimpsed. When she reached the gate that led into the church-yard her footsteps slowed, then came to a halt. Was that Bill she could see at the top of the Monks' Steps? Did the bark she could hear in the distance belong to Lucky?

When the figure was near enough for her to confirm that it was Bill Wyndham she wondered whether he would have caught sight of her waiting by the church gate. Slowly he descended the steps to come nearer to her, but when he reached the foot of those steps he did not walk on to join her. He seemed not even to be aware of her as he turned into the entrance to Beckside and was no longer visible from where she was standing.

Lucky had been left behind, but not for long. The young red setter spotted Andrea, then made for her, barking joyously and waving his feathery tail happily.

'You'd better go back to your master, Lucky, or you'll be in trouble,' Andrea told him after making a fuss of him. 'I don't think he likes me this morning. Go home, boy!' she ordered. 'Go home!'

There was a lump swelling in her throat as she watched him go, looking over his shoulder a couple of times as though perplexed because the two people he loved most in all the world quite suddenly did not love each other. So it was more than just over-tiredness and jet lag which had got into Bill last night and made him stalk away from her after uttering that final hurtful, unjust remark. Surely it could not just be because she had shared a meal with Alexander, and accepted his help with the drama group? This was a side of Bill's character he had not shown her before. How was she to deal with it, because deal with it she must. Otherwise the relationship which had been growing steadily stronger between them during the last six months would be ruined.

There was only one way, as far as Andrea was concerned, to find out how to save the friendship which had turned to love between herself and Bill. It was the way she found an answer to most of her dilemmas. She made her way into the porch and unlocked the heavy oak door of the little church. It was cool inside the building. Almost at once the familiar feeling of peace and serenity enveloped her. As she walked slowly to the front pew and sat down the scent of hyacinths and carnations from the pedestal arrangement close to the lectern drifted over her. She bent her head over her hands and began to pray.

Dear Lord, where did I go wrong this time? Is this wonderful relationship I had with Bill going to fall apart as my marriage to Ian did? Is there something lacking inside me that I'm not yet aware of? Something I ought to know about...

The heart searching and the prayers brought no ready answer as she remained there, with the only sound to be heard that of a blackbird singing in the cherry tree close to the main door of the building.

Lord, I wanted so much to love and be loved again. To be loved by a man like Bill. A man so caring and talented that he's become a great blessing in my life; someone I can't bear to lose. Is Bill a blessing I didn't deserve, Lord?

She raised her eyes at last to the east window, as though hoping to find the answer there. Light poured in a colourful stream through the stained glass. Memory came to her then of the day she had come here to seek the solution to the hardest decision she had ever had to make in her life. Her heart had been filled with pain then because of her discovery that her dead husband had given another woman a child. Then, after she read the words inscribed at the base of the east window, she had known what she must do. Doing it had been immensely difficult. Perhaps something equally difficult was required of her today?

I need to know, Lord. Please tell me. Am I not meant to share my life with Bill? Must I go on with my work here alone?

This time no answer to her prayer came flooding into her mind, as there had been to the prayers about whether or not she ought to reveal to Ian's mother that there was a baby boy fathered by Ian waiting to be loved by her. The revelation had brought such joy and comfort to Ian's mother that Andrea knew she had made the right decision. Nancy had found faith again soon after she found her new grandson.

'You're here early this morning, Andrea.' Dorothy Harper's gentle voice broke into the silence.

Andrea turned her head to smile at her friend. 'It was too nice a morning to stay in bed, so I thought I'd come over early and say a few extra prayers.'

'I had the same thought myself. I feel I have so much to give thanks for, Andrea. It's so good to have Ben back home with me. He wanted to come to church with me this morning, but I persuaded him to give himself a few more days before he starts going out and about again.'

Andrea laughed softly. 'I bet that wasn't easy to do!'

'No, but I had Matt there to back me up, and to keep Ben company while I'm out. Matt's being very helpful, which is another thing I'm very thankful for.'

The arrival of the organist sent Andrea hurrying to greet him, and to allow Dorothy a few minutes of privacy. As she welcomed Brendon May, a regular organist at both Nyddbeck and Nyddford Church, Andrea could not help wishing this had been one of the Sundays when Brendon was unable to be with them because if Brendon had not been here Bill would probably have been asked to play the organ, so he would have been forced to speak to her. As it was, she found herself hearing from Brendon about his forthcoming visit to play the organ in a West Country cathedral. Brendon was a lovely man, but he was not Bill. Andrea sighed as she left him and went to thank the door stewards for coming early too.

'There'll be a lot of people here today, I think, with it being a nice morning and a family service as well. We could get a few parents in with the children. If they're not all at the supermarket in Nyddford,' Norma Barker said with a wry grin.

'I sometimes wonder if we ought to try taking a short service to the supermarket; the sort of thing the supermarkets have taken to doing on Remembrance Day. What do you think, Norma?'

'It could be worth a try. If we can't beat 'em, let's join 'em,' the older woman said with a laugh as she picked up a stack of hymn books ready to hand out with her words of welcome.

Andrea could hear children's voices outside in the porch. 'Everyone seems to be here early this morning,' she said. Everyone except Bill. Would Bill come to church this morning, as he had got into the habit of doing since he came to live in the village?

Later, as she lifted her eyes from the prayer book to send her voice to the back of the church with the opening prayers, she was able to catch a glimpse of the familiar auburn hair in one of the rear pews. Her voice faltered momentarily, then steadied. She frowned as her mind began to question why Bill should choose to sit so far back in the building when he usually liked to sit mid-way down on the days he was not occupying the organ seat. Then another glance showed her that the auburn hair did not belong to Bill but to Alexander. Disappointment destroyed her concentration for a moment.

After the words of blessing shared with the congregation at the end of the service, she made her way to the place inside the porch where she shook hands with some people, shared a hug with those she knew well, or spoke individually to each of the children. Although having occupied a seat at the rear of the church Alexander could have been first out of it, but he did not seem to be in any hurry to leave. In fact he seemed to be delaying his departure while he talked to a few of the teenagers he had met at the drama group. Carla Bramley was not with them; neither was Jack, Andrea noticed. Almost everyone had either gone home or to the church hall for coffee before she found herself shaking hands with Alexander.

'Hello, Alexander. I'm glad you came,' she told him.

'So am I! Perhaps I should do it more often? What do you think?' His hold on her hand strengthened as he said that.

Andrea laughed. 'It won't do you any harm; it might even be good for you,' she said.

'I'd find it easier to do if you were always there.'

This time his words made her feel uncomfortable. She took a step backwards, hoping to release her hand from his grasp. 'I thought Bill might have been here,' she heard herself say, even though she had not intended to mention Bill's absence.

'I think he's taken Lucky for a long walk,' Bill's cousin told her. 'At least, that's what he said he was going to do. If you've nothing planned already, Andrea, perhaps I could take you out to lunch somewhere?'

She forced a smile to soften her refusal. 'Sorry, I've got my mum-in-law coming down from Durham for lunch today.'

Alexander shrugged his muscular shoulders. 'I'll have to make do with my own company then, but I'm looking forward to helping you with the drama group again this week.'

'Thanks a lot, but maybe you'll have moved on again by then, now that Bill's back home,' she suggested.

'No, I'll still be here.'

His words refused to be banished from Andrea's mind as she left the church after rushing down a cup of coffee she did not want in case Bill either called at the manse or telephoned her. She was beginning to wish she had not accepted Alexander's offer of help with the drama group, or with the

264

dog-walking. His presence here in the village was beginning to make her uneasy.

Since Bill did not contact her, she was glad of Nancy's company that Sunday to take her mind off her heartache for a few hours. Nancy was looking so much better nowadays as time began to soften the shock of her son's sudden death. At first she tried to avoid talking about Jamie, the grandson she had not known about until Andrea had told her of his existence. Then, after the first few sentences exchanged about her drive down from Durham, Nancy began to talk about the plans for Jamie's christening in the village church close to his home, the Raven Falls Hotel. Andrea listened patiently, glad of the happiness she was able to see reflected in Nancy's face. 'How very thoughtless of me!' Nancy Cameron stopped in mid-sentence and put out a hand to touch her daughter-in-law's clenched fingers. 'More than thoughtless; totally insensitive! Please forgive me, my dear?'

Andrea nodded, aware now of the tears that sparkled in Nancy's eyes, the eyes that were so like Ian's had been. 'There's nothing to forgive, Nancy, so please don't upset yourself. It's the most natural thing in the world that you should enjoy talking about your grandson.'

Nancy's hold on her hands tightened. 'Not to you, my dear girl. Not to you!'

Andrea managed a smile as she replied. 'I'm so pleased to see you happy again, Nancy. So glad that things have worked out well for you, and for Jamie.'

'You'll never know how grateful I am, Andrea. Telling me about Jamie gave me something to go on living for again. We all need that, don't we?'

Andrea nodded, unable to speak for the lump that was filling her throat. Then she changed the subject by saying that she ought to be checking the oven to see how the chicken in wine was doing. 'Pour yourself a sherry, Nancy. You know where to find it,' she said before making a hasty escape to the kitchen.

Once in the kitchen she did not go to the cooker but went instead to stare out of the window which gave a view over her back garden wall of the rising ground which belonged to Abbot's Fold Farm. Sometimes from here she would catch sight of Bill taking the right-of-way footpath that ran down the edge of the field and ended at the ancient stile set into the drystone wall under the great oak tree. As though her very longing for him had magically conjured up the man, Bill came into view, walking slowly, rather than in his usual brisk manner.

Her heart began to race at the sight of him. Bill, with his tall, athletic build, his thick, wavy bronze hair and his short well-trimmed beard glowing in the sunlight. Bill whose artistry could bring to vivid life on canvas the beauty of moors, dales, rivers and mountains. Bill, whose talent could stir her spirit when he brought to life on the church organ great musical compositions, or the hymns of Wesley, Watts and Graham Kendrick. Bill, whom she had grown to love against her will. Was he on his way to see her, to put things right with her?

The meal in the oven was forgotten as she kept her eyes glued to the figure clad in a bright-blue shirt and dark cords, the figure that seemed to be stopping and starting, maybe as the dog with him stopped to pick up all the exciting scents that dogs were able to find in such places. There was a longing inside her to dash out of the manse and run up the hill to meet Bill; to tell him that she loved him and would always love him; that Alexander Ross meant nothing to her, except that he was Bill's cousin. To tell him she would marry him now just as soon as he said the word. No more worrying about what the gossips would think...

Her hand was already opening the back door, her feet were stepping over the threshold, her mind leaping ahead to what she would say before Bill could say anything. Then Lucky came bounding down the hill, ignoring Bill's commands in his eagerness to get to Andrea. He cleared her garden wall in one graceful spring and flung himself at her, barking a welcome. Andrea tried to free herself of the long red-gold forelegs the dog had placed on her shoulders while he lashed her with his wildly waving tail. Bill again gave voice to a sharp command. Lucky again ignored him. Bill seemed reluctant to come any closer, even though Andrea now had a firm hold on Lucky's collar.

So they stood, only a few yards apart, with the atmosphere between them becoming so tense that even the young animal became aware of it and began to whine as he lay down and placed his head on his paws.

'Bill—' Andrea began.

'So you even persuaded Alex to go to church!' Bill broke in.

'I didn't! I was expecting to see you there, not him.'

'I couldn't trust myself to watch him mischief-making again without causing a scene, and your church was not the right place to do that.' Bill rubbed a hand over his right eye as he spoke, a gesture Andrea had come to know indicated that he was keeping a tight hold on his temper even though his voice was low.

She took a deep breath to calm herself. 'I had come to think that it was *our* church, Bill; the place where we would be married,' she said quietly.

'That was before Alex turned up and started to muscle in.'

'You're quite wrong about that,' she began.

'Not according to him. He's talking about staying on here to do some work; something different from what he usually does.'

'Why should you be upset about that? How can it affect you – us?'

'I've been through it all before, Andrea. Only this time I'm not going to let him get away with it.'

With that Bill clicked his fingers to summon Lucky to his side and went over the stile and from there to the bridge that would take him home to Beckside. He did not even look back at her.

Sixteen

'We won't be able to meet at Beckside any more,' Carla told Josh as they waited together for the school bus to take them to Nyddford High School. 'Bill Wyndham's back from America. I saw him walking his dog on the moor this morning.' She shivered as the chilly spring breeze cut through the fashionable jacket which was not part of her school uniform, and not warm enough for this late April day.

Josh put his arm about her waist and squeezed. 'We'll find somewhere else to go, honey. I guess we can always go back to my place. Mom won't mind.'

'It won't be like being on our own though, will it? Really on our own, I mean.' Going back to Josh's home meant someone could walk in on them at any time; Josh's young brother or sister, for instance. Though she did like Josh's mum and dad, and the young kids. She'd miss them all so much when they went back to the States in July. Only a few weeks from now they'd be gone. Oh, what would she do without Josh. She bit hard on her lips as the thought brought a burning sensation behind her eyes.

'We'll find a place. Maybe in Monks' Wood. There'll be places there to be on our own.' His arm dropped from Carla's waist as the Nyddford Crawler came into sight and chugged to a noisy halt in the layby at the top of Abbot's Hill. He stood aside politely to allow Carla to enter the bus ahead of him.

Carla liked his good manners, even though she would probably have scoffed at such behaviour from any of the local lads. Josh was different. He was from America, and he was amazingly cool with his blond hair, vivid blue eyes and neat bum. Josh was bright too, clever in a cool sort of way that meant he didn't ever have to brag about what he could do. He was planning on being an architect after his years of university in America were over. They were not able to sit together on the school bus because after picking up from villages over a wide area it was already almost full. She would see him tonight though because, somehow or other, she was going to get to the drama group. It would mean defying her dad, but that was *his* fault. If he hadn't gone all mean on her again and said she was not to go to anything at Andrea's church she would not have had to lie to him.

Could she get Jack to say she was over at

Jacob's Cottage with Julie if Dad asked where she was? It might be worth a try. Soon Julie would not be living in the cottage so there would be no chance of using her as an excuse, but she'd try it tonight, and then meet Josh in the old sheepfold and ride to Nyddford on the back of his motorbike.

Jack knew there would be trouble as soon as his dad came storming into the kitchen while he was catching up on his favourite Australian soap, eating a thick cheese sandwich he'd made for himself, and trying to finish off the homework he was supposed to do last night. He hadn't done it last night because he'd fallen asleep after helping Dad mend a wall that a passing lorry had broken down while taking one of the Abbot's Hill bends too fast. It was dark when they had finished doing that but his dad had said they couldn't leave it till morning in case any of the lambs found the gap and got out on to the road. Then there had been a sleet shower and the wool cap he wore well down on his forehead had been frozen to his eyebrows. When they got back home Dad had made him a big mug of cocoa and given him a slice of the cake his gran had brought for them. Jack had fallen asleep with the cake in his hand, so when he overslept this morning and missed the school bus Dad said it didn't matter because he could do with a rest.

'Where's your sister?' his father was asking now.

Jack looked about him, startled out of his daydream about going to live in Australia when he was old enough. It was always hot and sunny there, with no sleet showers when it was almost summer, and there were millions of sheep he could work with. He'd have to take Brack with him, of course, because Brack had the makings of a champion working dog. Wandering Joe had told him that, and Wandering Joe knew all about dogs.

'I asked where Carla is. When are you going to answer me, lad?'

Jack didn't like the sound of this. Dad often got snappy with Carla, but not with him. That was because they worked together every day before Jack went to school and when he came home again. He knew his father was waiting for an answer, so he'd have to come up with something soon. To delay his reply he looked about the kitchen as though he might be able to see his sister sitting on the old sofa, or at the sink washing the dishes. He even looked at the box where the weakling lamb was recovering, but there was only Brack to be seen there, close enough to be on guard but not too near to panic the little creature.

'Well?'

He'd have to say something, but he didn't

really like telling lies to his dad. Not proper lies, that is. It was different saying you were out of bed and getting dressed when you were still under the duvet and wishing you could stay there and not go to school. There was no way he could look Dad in the eyes and say Carla was with Julie in the cottage, it was best just to look down at his shoes while he said it.

'She's with Julie.'

'Where?' his father demanded.

'In the cottage.' Jack kept his eyes downcast and began to scuff up the hearthrug with his heels.

'If she's in the cottage she's not with Julie, because Julie's gone out again. So why would Carla be over there on her own?'

'I don't know, Dad.' Jack knew his face was bright red, and not with the heat from the Aga. It was what happened when he was embarrassed.

'So let's have the truth; where is your sister?'

'She's gone out, Dad.'

'Where has she gone? Speak up, lad!'

'I'm not sure. She's gone with Josh.' It was a relief to be able to tell the truth about that at least. Though it hadn't made a lot of difference, Jack knew, because his dad's face was now black as thunder.

'Has she gone on the motorbike?'

'I don't know, Dad.' That was true anyway.

'Why don't you know? Did he come for her on it?'

'I didn't see him. She just went to meet him.' All of a sudden Jack couldn't take any more of this. It wasn't his fault that Carla had gone out when she'd been told to stay in. He guessed she'd probably gone to the drama group again, but he wasn't going to say so. It would only cause another row and there were too many rows these days between Carla and Dad. When Mum had been here it was different. So different, and so good. There had been hot food and drinks to come home to because Mum arranged her hours at Nyddford Health Centre to fit in with school times. There had been lots of talk, and lots of laughs. His mum had loved to laugh. He could see her now in his mind laughing at the antics of the latest kitten. Only he couldn't really see her at all because his eyes were full of tears. When they began to run down his cheeks he bent his head right down so his dad wouldn't see them.

It was his young collie, Brack, who saw the tears; sensed the misery that her young master was trying so hard to hide. Whining her sympathy, she left her place beside the lamb and came to place her head on Jack's knee. Automatically, he put a hand on her head, so she reached up and began to lick his face.

Dave, about to rebuke her and send her

back to her place, paused, looked again at his son, then realized what was happening. 'Don't upset yourself, lad,' he said gently. 'It's not your fault.'

'I couldn't help it, Dad. Honest! I didn't want her to go because I knew you'd be mad with her and there'd be trouble, like there always seems to be these days between you and our Carla. Only I couldn't stop her from going.' The words came out of Jack with some difficulty and were interlaced with sobs and hiccups.

Dave felt a lump forming in his own throat as he looked more closely at his son, who was growing to be more and more like his mother as he grew older. What would Jill have thought if she had heard him going on at the lad for something which certainly wasn't his fault? Shame rose in a bitter tide inside Dave as the thought entered his mind.

'It wouldn't have mattered if Julie hadn't gone out, would it, Dad?' Jack said as he scrubbed the moisture from his face with the sleeve of his sweater. 'You wouldn't have known that Carla wasn't over in the cottage with her, would you? You wouldn't have minded if she'd been with Julie. You never do mind us being there.'

Dave swallowed the angry denial that rose so swiftly to his mouth. How could he deny the truth of what young Jack was saying?

Instead he sighed, walked across the kitchen to lay a swift, affectionate touch on the boy's shoulder, then moved away to switch on the kettle. 'We'll have some coffee, lad, then you can come out and see the last of this year's lambs. I came in to tell you that the last ones were triplets. Good news, eh?'

'Yeah! Good news, Dad! Can I have a chocolate biscuit before we go?'

So the bad moment was over, but not erased from Dave's mind. He was used to having problems with Carla. It was the age she was at now, but he was not accustomed to the sort of thing which had happened tonight with Jack. The episode had shaken him. It had filled him with doubts about how he would cope in future, especially when Julie was no longer there in Jacob's Cottage to listen to the problems he knew Carla and Jack had got into the habit of sharing with her.

Andrea was not looking forward to the drama group meeting. Usually it was fun, and something of a challenge to put Bible teachings into the right context for present-day life. Starting this group had been dicey because during her work experience at the placement churches where she had done some of her training she had found it almost impossible to get any parents involved. The enthusiasm of the teenage girls and boys had more than made up for her doubts.

Of course it would have been easier if some parents had become involved. She had been hopeful of Josh Bolton's mum, who had been quite keen to take part, but there were younger siblings to be looked after in her home and the only night the church hall was free for the drama group to meet turned out to be the one when Josh's dad had agreed to teach American Football at Nyddford High School.

At least there was help from Julie sometimes, if she was not going out with Matt Harper, and Bill's cousin Alexander had certainly proved useful. So it was a pity Andrea had to hope that Alexander would not put in an appearance at Emmanuel Church Hall tonight. How could she prevent him doing that without offending him? This thought had been wandering in and out of Andrea's mind ever since her meeting with Bill last Sunday, and she was no nearer to finding a solution to it.

Alexander ought to have been gone from Nyddford by now. Why wasn't he? Was he truly staying on in Nyddford to take photographs of the scenery for a new project he was working on? Or was it that Alex was, as Bill had put it, trying to muscle in on Bill's friendship with her? 'I've been through it all before, but he's not going to get away with it this time,' Bill had said with that aggressive tone in his voice which seemed out of character to her. Just what had Bill been through with Alex before which had made his voice so thick with bitterness when he told her that?

With these thoughts lying heavy in her mind, Andrea found herself hoping and praying that when she reached the church hall Julie Craven would come to help her, but that Alexander Ross would not. It hurt so much that Bill was keeping his distance from her still, and it mystified her. If Bill *was* so jealous of Alexander why didn't he just tell his cousin that he was wasting his time because he and Andrea were partners? Or had Bill changed his mind about wanting to marry her because of her refusal to join him in America? This thought was so unbearable that Andrea pushed it away from her as the spire of Emmanuel Church came into view.

As usual on drama nights, there were several teenagers hanging around the gate that led into the church car park. They scattered as Andrea gave them a warning salute. She was pleased to notice that Carla Bramley and Josh Bolton were among them. So Dave had relented and allowed Carla to come after all. She was not so pleased when, as they all surged into the hall, Alexander Ross strolled in after them.

'I thought perhaps you'd have moved on now,' she told him after they had exchanged greetings.

'Didn't I tell you I was staying on here to take some pictures for a project I've had in mind for some time? I was certain I had done.' His smiling glance held a hint of mockery. 'Or perhaps I expected Bill to pass it on after I told him.'

'I haven't seen much of Bill since he came back. I've been very busy with my work, and I expect Bill's been spending time with you, showing you round and all that,' she said.

Bill's cousin was frowning. 'He doesn't seem to want to spend much time with me; says he's got a lot of work to catch up on.'

'I suppose he will have, after being away twice as long as he expected to be.'

'Thanks to the lovely Miriam, who likes to get her own way,' Alexander said with a grin.

'I suppose if she's his agent he'll have to go along with her plans.'

'She was more than that to him a couple of years ago.'

Andrea frowned. 'What do you mean?'

'She was almost part of his family. He was engaged to her sister, Gina. They shared a home and were going to make it permanent. Then Gina went to stay with Miriam and decided working in America was a better bet as far as she was concerned. Bill took it very badly, but I don't suppose he's told you about that?'

'As a matter of fact, he has.' Abruptly Andrea brought the conversation to a halt and went to call the young people to order. The conversation came to an end and the rehearsal got under way, with Carla back in the main role because the girl who had substituted for her failed to arrive.

'That girl's got real talent,' Alexander said as the rehearsal came to an end. 'She must be an asset to you.'

'She is, when her father allows her to come,' Andrea agreed.

'Surely she's old enough to please herself where she goes?'

'She's only just sixteen, a volatile age. I just hope her father knows she's here tonight.'

'What do you mean?'

'Her father's been through a bad time, and because of that he wouldn't allow Carla to come to any of the church activities. If she's here tonight without her dad's permission there'll probably be trouble brewing in her home, and it could involve me.'

'Why? Why should it involve you, Andrea?' There was concern in Alexander's eyes as he walked with her to the door of the church hall.

Andrea sighed. 'It's a long story, and I don't think it will really interest you.'

'But everything about you is of interest to me.'

Andrea was dismayed to hear that, but she made no comment as she locked the door behind them and turned to where her car was parked.

'That's why I'm staying on here longer than I first intended to,' Alexander said.

She swung round to face him, frowning. 'I understood that you were staying on to take some photographs for a new project?'

'There's that as well. I want you to be in some of the shots.'

That startled her. 'Me? Why on earth would you want to have me in your pictures?' As she said the words she thought they would have been better left unspoken.

'Because you're a very beautiful woman, and a beautiful woman photographed against the sort of scenery to be found in the Yorkshire Dales could be a winning combination.'

Her frown deepened until it was almost a scowl. 'I don't have time to pose for photographs. You must know that.'

'Not even if those pictures could make a lot of money for your church?'

'What do you mean?' In spite of her tiredness and her wish to be on her way home, Andrea found herself wanting to hear more.

'You've got a problem with this church roof, haven't you? I believe it needs a major repair which will cost a lot of money. Am

I right?'

She nodded. 'I don't see how your photographs could help with that.'

He laughed. 'The right sort of pictures, taken by someone like me and produced as a super calendar in time for the Christmas market, might well raise a great deal of money. In fact it would be certain to do that with the right sort of marketing and publicity.'

Andrea was silent for a long moment. Then: 'Are you joking, Alexander? I think you've got to be. You can't possibly be serious.'

'Why not? I do know what I'm talking about; the sort of speciality calendars that promote a good cause. Your church needs the money to pay for the repair; you've got the looks; I've got the camera and the knowhow. It can't fail.'

'How can you be so sure of that? You'd need to sell an awful lot of calendars to pay the bill that's coming for the roof. It would be a limited market for them, just the immediate area of Nyddford and Nyddbeck. We might not even cover the cost of producing it.'

He laughed. 'With my name on it we would, I can promise you.'

'But by the autumn there'll be so many other Yorkshire calendars on sale...'

'Not with your face and figure, and my

professional name on them. Plus the fact that they'll go on sale while there are still plenty of tourists about. But we can't go on discussing it out here when we are both ravenously hungry. I haven't eaten since a sandwich lunch in a pub, and I don't suppose you've done much better. Let's go to the Golden Fleece again and have a bar supper.'

Andrea opened her mouth to say that she could not spare the time. Then heavy drops of rain began to fall and reminded her of the wet patches which would soon begin to seep through the roof of this church if the rain became heavy and prolonged. She did not want to have supper at the Golden Fleece with Alexander in case Bill came to hear of it and the rift between them grew wider than it already was. Yet the possibility of being able to raise money to help her church with this major repair could not be ignored.

'I'll have to ask you if you'll give me a lift to the hotel, Andrea, because I left my vehicle in the hotel car park and walked here.'

Put like that, reminding her of his help and her own obligation, how could Andrea refuse to drive to the prestigious local inn with Alexander Ross occupying the front passenger seat of her car? Once there, how could she resist the enticing aroma of good food being excellently cooked which drifted in through the open window? By the time Alexander had led her to a small table set within an alcove and brought her a glass of wine she was beginning to forget her doubts and to listen to his plans for the calendar.

'I was already toying with the idea of doing scenic shots rather than my usual stuff,' he told her as they waited for their seafood platters with fondant potatoes to arrive.

Unease stirred inside Andrea. What had Bill said about his cousin's work? Something about his pictures not being her sort of thing? A sudden vision of the more lurid pictures used in some tabloid newspapers caused her to gulp down her drink too quickly. Surely Alexander was not involved with that sort of thing? Yet why shouldn't he be? It was not illegal to take that sort of shot, or to publish it. Though it was certainly not to her taste...

'I'd need to be very careful about my appearances in these photos, and the sort of publicity they might generate,' she began hesitantly. 'I'm still fairly new here, so I can't afford to stir up any gossip. It can make life difficult at times, but it's the way things are. So I have to accept it as part of my job. Do you understand what I'm trying to say, Alexander?'

He smiled, then reached across the small table to touch her hand reassuringly. 'Of course I understand, Andrea. I wouldn't want to do anything which might cause problems for you, but I would like to help with the one you've already got with your church roof.' He laughed, then went on: 'I can't offer to get up there and do any of the hands-on stuff myself; I don't have the skills for that, but I do have skills with my camera that have given me a very good standard of living.'

'And very long holidays,' she responded lightly, thinking of how he had extended his stay in the Dales by two extra weeks already.

'This is not entirely a holiday though. I came here to do some work, as well as take a break. I was hoping to get some publicity shots for Bill's coming exhibition of pictures in York, but he seems to have rather gone off that idea since he came back.'

'Has he? Why should he do that?'

'Search me! It wouldn't have taken long, but he says he can't spare the time.'

'There's his television series starting quite soon, the filming for it, that is,' she said. 'He seems to be over-tired, or jet-lagged, still. Maybe that's why he's not too keen to take on anything else just now?'

Alexander's rusty eyebrows were drawn together in a frown as he replied to that. 'He knew it was on the cards before I came here. We'd talked about it on the phone. Maybe it's just that he doesn't want me to stay on here...'

Andrea had no doubt that this was the truth, but she could hardly say so. Plainly the friction which had arisen between the cousins had worsened. It was with relief that she saw the waiter on his way to their table with two beautifully presented platters of salmon and shellfish. The need for her to answer, to reassure Bill's cousin, could be avoided this time.

Thinking about it later as she drove back to Nyddbeck, she decided that the sooner Bill's engagement to her was made public the better. If Alexander stayed on then to take his photographs it would prove that he was not trying to 'muscle in' on Bill's relationship with her. When she got back to the manse she would ring Bill and tell him she was ready to set a date for their wedding, and that he could make it public by putting an announcement in the *Yorkshire Post* as soon as he liked.

Seventeen

Carla knew she was in trouble the moment she walked into the farmhouse kitchen. There was something in the air, an atmosphere of heavy silence like you got before a storm. The silence was there because both the television and the radio were switched off, which was unusual at this time of day, and her dad was sitting on the old sofa with the *Yorkshire Post* still neatly folded beside him. He was probably already gathering words together to pour out his anger because even though she had cleared the dishes from the table and washed them she had gone out soon afterwards without saying where she was going. She slipped off her fleece jacket and tossed it on to the rocking chair then moved to fill the kettle to make coffee.

'I wonder what your mother would have thought of you encouraging your young brother to tell lies so that you could go out with a lad when I said you were to stay in and get some food prepared for tomorrow?'

Her dad's voice was quiet, but it wouldn't

stay quiet for long once she started to answer back. For the time being she was not going to do that. She was just going to make coffee and pass a mug to him as if he had asked for it. That way he just might simmer down.

'Didn't you hear what I said, Carla?' He spoke a little louder now.

'Yes, Dad. I heard you, and I didn't ask Jack to tell lies for me. He thought I really was over in the cottage with Julie.'

'You knew Julie was going out, yet you still told him to say you were over there.'

'I didn't know she was going out! I thought she was staying in to do some packing, but she must have changed her mind.'

'So Jack tried to cover up for you, and found himself in a situation he couldn't cope with. Then he got upset. Your mother wouldn't have liked that.'

'It wouldn't have happened if she had been here! She wouldn't have stopped me from going to the drama group, she'd have been pleased I was going.'

'She wouldn't have been pleased to know you were going on the back of a motorbike with that young lad.'

'Mum would have liked Josh. I know she would!' Carla hit back. 'Julie likes him, and she was Mum's friend.'

'I'm not interested in Julie's opinion of Josh, I'm only interested in finding out why you went out on his motorbike when I said you were not to. You knew I'd said you were not to go, yet you went out to meet him.'

'It was the only way I could get to Nyddford. If Julie had been going to help Andrea, like she sometimes does, she would have given me a lift. Only she was going somewhere else.' There was a hint of hysteria in Carla's voice now which should have warned Dave to ease off, but it didn't.

'Her leaving here will be all for the best. She won't be able to encourage you to go against my wishes in future,' he said sharply.

'She didn't! She never does! She always takes your side. And her leaving won't be for the best because I'll have no one to talk to then. No one who really cares about me like Mum used to do!'

To his horror Dave saw the sparkle of tears rush into Carla's lovely eyes, to be brushed angrily away as she dashed past him and made for the hall, then the stairs. The slamming of her bedroom door told him that he had got it all wrong again; that his daughter had been in need of someone to listen, not to criticize. Tonight he had failed both of his children, though he had managed to put things right with Jack. He knew he had left it too late with Carla. She would be up there in her bedroom sobbing her heart out, and he guessed that if he went upstairs and knocked on her door she would ignore him. Through no fault of his own, he was failing as a farmer, but his failure as a father could not be blamed on anyone except himself.

Daylight was fading and dusk fast approaching, but in spite of that Dave strode out of the house and made his way up to the place on the moor where he knew he could weep, or rage against fate, without anyone else knowing. He went alone, leaving Tyke to stand guard over his children.

As the lights of the village came into sight Andrea felt excitement rising inside her. In a few minutes she would be home. It would be time then to phone Bill, to tell him that the waiting was over for them and she would marry him this summer. She could not wait to do that. So eager was she to contact him that she left her car on the drive, unlocked, and dashed into the manse to pick up the phone in the hall. As she did so she noticed that the answerphone was showing a blinking red light. In the act of dialling Bill's number, she hesitated. It could be an emergency call from someone needing her help. Her mind raced over the names of people in her flock who were ill at home or recovering in hospital. There was Wilf Postlethwaite, almost ninety and still living alone on his isolated farmhouse. There was Jane Lindsay, fighting a nervous breakdown after the collapse of her marriage. There was Samantha Brown, pregnant at sixteen and being pressured by her parents to have an abortion. There was also Ben Harper. Surely though, if it had been Dorothy needing her help, she would have used the mobile number Andrea had given her for emergency use?

As that reassuring thought came into her mind she caught sight of her mobile phone lying on the chair next to the telephone table. She sighed. How stupid of her to leave it behind when she rushed out to drive to Nyddford. It was not something she did very often. What if there had been a call from Dorothy needing her help? She must run through the answerphone messages before she contacted Bill, and hope there was nothing too serious requiring her immediate attention. There was only one message for her. It was from Bill. What Bill had to say brought disbelief to her then a slow tide of resentment. The disbelief was so strong that she ran the message through again in order to be quite certain of just what Bill had said.

'Where the hell have you been, Andrea? I've been trying to contact you on your mobile and got no response. I need to talk to you very urgently. Please ring me as soon as you get back and I'll come over to see you.'

Just like that. Businesslike words delivered in a tone that was brusque to the point of rudeness, and with no hint of warmth or affection. What was it all about? There was only one way to find out. Andrea tapped out the familiar numbers with fingers which were unsteady and waited with a thudding heart for Bill to respond. She did not have long to wait.

'Bill Wyndham speaking.' The voice was harsh. It held something Andrea did not like. Had Bill been drinking? He liked a beer, or a glass of wine, but he did not usually overindulge in alcohol.

'It's Andrea, Bill,' she said with less than her normal confidence, then waited for words of explanation to follow.

'So you're home at last! I've been waiting for hours to talk to you.'

'It was drama group night at Nyddford. Didn't you remember, Bill?'

'Since when did a teenage drama group go on until this time?'

'What do you mean?'

'It's after eleven o'clock. Where the hell have you been?'

Andrea took a deep breath, then let it go on a long sigh. This was going to be tricky. She could tell the truth and say that she had been to the Golden Fleece for supper with Bill's cousin, but Bill would not like to hear that. He would want to know why she had gone there with Alexander. Her explanation that it was to discuss Alexander's idea for fund raising for the repairs to her church roof would not go down well with Bill in his present truculent mood. So it would be best to skirt round the truth without telling an untruth, if she could manage to do that.

'I've been deep in discussion about raising money to help pay for the repair of Emmanuel Church roof,' she said, after some hesitation.

'While I was waiting here to discuss something much more serious with you,' he snapped.

'What can be more serious at the end of a very wet winter than the fact that my church roof is leaking and we don't have the money to pay for it to be put right?' she asked quietly.

She heard him utter a heavy sigh, a sound of exasperation which told her that he was not in the mood to listen to reason.

'I would have thought your own good name, and your reputation, were more important than the fabric of one of your church buildings.'

Her heart was hammering now. 'What on earth are you talking about, Bill?'

'I'm talking about you going around with Alex Ross while I've been away in America.'

'My going around with Alexander? I don't know what you're trying to say, Bill.'

'I'm wondering why you've been spending so much time with him when you've only just got to know him.'

'Because he's your cousin, and when he found I was looking after your dog he offered to help out with that when I was pushed for time.' She was beginning to feel resentful of Bill's attitude. There was something in it that she did not want to hear, but which could not be avoided now. 'I don't know why you should be so annoyed about that.'

'Because I know what he's like,' Bill answered curtly. 'He's been telling me how friendly you've become with him.'

'Don't be ridiculous!' Andrea was tempted to slam the phone down. Instead she clung on to it with tense fingers. 'We've only been walking your dog together a few times, and he's helped me with the drama group.'

'And had supper with you afterwards at his hotel in Nyddford.'

'I'd had nothing to eat all day, and was starving when he invited me to eat with him.' Andrea's throat felt dry as she waited for Bill to go on and ask about where she had been tonight until so late. This was a side of Bill that she had not encountered before. She was uncertain how to cope with him while he was in this mood.

'Did he come to help with your drama group again tonight?'

'Yes, but I didn't know he intended to be

there.'

'What happened after the drama club finished? Why couldn't I get in touch with you?'

'Because I was still—'

'With Alex?' he broke in harshly.

Andrea was silent, longing for this futile questioning to finish. She was exhausted after too long a day, and thoroughly disheartened by the way things were going with Bill.

'I suppose you were letting Alex talk you into having your picture spread all over this calendar that's supposed to be going to make a fortune for your church?'

'I don't know why you should be objecting to that. It will be just pictures of some churches, with me in the background of one or two,' she said, and knew it to be a mistake as the words were leaving her mouth.

'So you *are* letting him talk you into this calendar business?'

'Why not? I don't feel I have the right to turn down any offers of help when we need the money so urgently.'

'You'll regret it, if you do go ahead. The pictures could turn out to be an embarrassment for you and your church.'

'Why? He's a professional photographer, isn't he?'

'Not the sort who specializes in taking shots of churches. He does tabloid stuff; pop

296

stars, publicity chasers, so-called models. Didn't he tell you that?'

'He just said he was a professional photographer. As I don't have time to read the tabloids I'm not familiar with his work, or his name. To me he's just your cousin.' There were doubts in Andrea's mind now. Serious doubts. Yet they needed that money so much...

'He's certainly able to earn a lot of money with his pictures. I just wouldn't have expected you to go along with this suggestion.'

'I don't know yet whether I will or not, but I have to think about it. I don't know anything except that you don't seem to trust me any more, Bill.'

There was a silence so long that she began to wonder if Bill had walked away from his phone. Then he spoke again, harshly. 'It's him I don't trust.'

'Yet you invited him here? Why did you do that if you don't trust him?'

'I didn't invite him, he just rang the night before I left and asked if we could meet while he was here. I was hoping he would have moved on before I got back, but of course once he had got to know you he had no intention of moving on.'

They were going round in circles, and getting nowhere. She had to end it before she burst into tears of frustration. 'Don't go on, Bill, please! I've heard enough. In fact

I've heard too much and I can't stand any more.' Her breath caught in her throat; her eyes stung; her hands were trembling as she put down the phone.

What had happened to trust? What had happened to friendship? What had happened to love? Andrea dropped her head on her arms and began to weep for the promise of happiness which had brightened her life for a few months and was now beginning to fade away.

'How about tomorrow night, Julie?' Matt said as he reached across from the driving seat to kiss her mouth with strength and warmth.

'It's moving day tomorrow. By the time I've got all my stuff into my new house all I'll be wanting will be a long hot bath and an early night,' Julie answered.

'I could come and help you settle in,' he offered with a grin that gave her an idea of what sort of help would be on his mind.

'You'll be working, won't you?' Julie did not want him to help her settle in. She was not sure that she wanted to go on with this friendship, especially now she knew Matt intended to stay on in Yorkshire and become a partner in Harper Farm Transport. Matt was becoming too possessive, and quite difficult to discourage. Maybe it had not been such a good idea to start going out with him in the first place, but she had been feeling so indignant with Dave for using her time and affection for all those weeks without making any real commitment to her that she had thought it would do him good to see someone else taking her out. Also, she added honestly to herself, she had been quite attracted by Matt Harper's dark good looks and powerful personality. At one stage, after only a few dates with Matt, she had begun to wonder whether at last she had met someone who would help her to move on from her eighteen years of hopeless love for Dave Bramley. Only it had not worked out like that because the thought of moving out of Jacob's Cottage tomorrow to a place where she would not be able to catch a glimpse of Dave every day was really hurting. How was she going to cope with it?

'Yes, I'll be working until the evening.' Matt's face sobered as he added thoughtfully, 'The transport business needs a lot of work putting into it. Dad wants me to take that on and become a partner. Which would mean me staying on here rather than going back to the States. I need to do a lot of thinking about that.'

'Was your position there a much better one than you'll have here if you go in with Ben, and then take over the business yourself one day when he retires?' She wanted him to focus on his future rather than on trying to make the most of the present by holding her too close. There was always the possibility that Dave would be alerted by the restlessness of his collie and come out to investigate. To be seen coming or going from the cottage with Matt was one thing; to be seen trying to evade Matt's bolder caresses was something else.

'In one respect it was certainly a much better prospect, because the boss's daughter had me lined up for marrying into the family,' Matt told her.

Julie was startled. They had touched on the subject of his life in America at times, and talked of what had sent him out there in the first place. She had known that there was someone he had formed a relationship with while in America, but up until now Matt had not revealed that this woman was his boss's daughter.

'How does she feel about you staying over here for so long?'

He shrugged his powerful shoulders. 'She wanted to come over and join me.'

'Why didn't she do that?'

'Because I didn't want her here,' he said bluntly. 'It would have complicated things. Things like going out with you, Julie.'

She did not ask any questions about that. There needed to be distance between them this evening because she was feeling vulnerable and did not want to be tempted into embarking on anything she might later regret.

'Are you going to ask me in for a coffee?' he asked as a beam of light from a torch shone out from one of the farm buildings.

Dave was doing his late-night inspection of buildings and animals. She would not be here when he did that tomorrow night. Or any of the nights after that. A few weeks ago he would have been tapping on her window before sharing a hot drink with her, side by side on her sofa. Sometimes they had let the drinks go cold while they shared love. Though Dave never stayed the night in the cottage. Always they were both mindful of Carla and Jack needing their father to be with them in the farmhouse.

Tonight, remembering the bitter-sweet snatched moments with Dave, Julie watched the beam of light moving in the distance knowing that Dave would have seen Matt's car outside the cottage. A sudden surge of rage filled her because Dave had thrown away all that had promised to be so good for them and for his children.

'I asked if you were going to invite me in for a coffee, Julie?' Matt repeated.

At that moment the beam of Dave's torch turned full in their direction as Dave stood quite still for a moment as though unable to decide whether or not to come any closer to the car. A mood of recklessness enveloped

Julie then. She would show Dave that if he didn't want her Ben Harper's son certainly did. A moment later she was sliding her legs out of the vehicle and turning to Matt to say loudly, 'Yes, we'll have a drink to celebrate my last night here, and the start of my new life away from here.'

She hurried to open the front door of Jacob's Cottage and usher Matt inside.

Dave turned away from the sight of them, hating Matt Harper's guts and at the same time cursing himself for not telling Julie how much he wanted her in his life for good. He should have done that before Matt Harper came back to Yorkshire. Now it was too late.

Eighteen

Bill Wyndham stared down at the telephone he was still holding in his hand and asked himself how he, a mature man, well educated and well travelled, could have been stupid enough to upset the woman he loved by allowing his jealousy of his cousin to boil over as it had done. He'd really gone over the top, and given Andrea the impression that he didn't trust her, when in fact it was Alex he could not trust. Instead of listening to her side of the story, he'd let his anger take over and spoken words which must have deeply wounded Andrea.

The jealousy had been there right from the moment he had arrived at the manse a day earlier than Andrea expected him, eager to take her in his arms, only to find Alex there. Things had not been right between them since then. Little things, stupid things, kept cropping up to spoil what should have been wonderful days of reunion, and planning for their life together.

Was that because Alex was still here? A couple of years ago Alex had come between him and Gina by putting doubts into her mind about settling for family life in the country with an artist, so that Gina had taken herself off to work near her sister in America instead of marrying him. He should be grateful to Alex for that, because if he had not come to Yorkshire to make a fresh start he would probably never have met Andrea. Never been enthralled by the beauty of her face; never come to admire the dedication she gave to the people she had come to this village to serve; and never come to love so deeply the loveliness of her spirit.

Oh God, what sort of life would he have without Andrea? Where would be the joy, the shared love and companionship, the shared home and family? He had risked losing all that simply because he had wanted to have Andrea to himself as soon as he arrived back in Nyddbeck. Only his plans had gone awry because Alex was there. If he hadn't been so exhausted by all the extra work packed into his lecture tour, as well as by finishing the book illustrations, he would have kept his cool. Because there really wasn't much wrong with his cousin Alex except immaturity and irresponsibility. He ought to tell Andrea that without delay, if she would listen to him. It would be his own bloody fault if she would not listen!

Already he was tapping out Andrea's number, and listening at the same time to the heavy beat of his heart. Why did she not answer her phone? Had she gone to bed? Or had she been called out to someone in need of her help? He waited for her answerphone to tell him he could leave a message, but this didn't seem to be operating. What was he to do now? Certainly he could not go to bed himself and expect to get any sleep with so much on his mind.

It was Lucky, suddenly grumbling in his sleep, who reminded him of what he ought to do. 'Time for a walk, Lucky,' he said.

His dog yawned and stretched, rose from his rug and began to wag his tail enthusiastically. Bill clipped on his lead and walked with him to the end of Church Lane, from where he was able to see lights shining out from the ground floor windows of the manse. He walked on as far as the triangle of green, where Lucky made a brief stop, and from there crossed the bridge over the beck. Now he was able to see Andrea's car parked on the drive of the manse. So she was at home still, and had not gone to bed even though it was midnight. Had she not answered his phone call because she was unwilling to speak to him again?

Even as the thought came into his mind his dog was making for the open gates of the manse, going at a speed which showed his determination to go visiting at this home where he was always made welcome. Bill followed, knowing that even if his dog was made welcome he might well not be. It was a risk he had to take.

As he lifted his hand to press the bell on Andrea's front door Lucky let go of several joyous barks. 'Quiet, Lucky!' Bill ordered, placing a restraining hand on the dog's collar. Lucky became quiet, even though he was trembling with excitement. Bill waited, feeling the tension mount inside him. At first he thought Andrea was not going to come to the door, even though he could hear a radio playing softly from somewhere inside the house. Then there was another sound, that of a bolt being withdrawn. A moment later the heavy oak door opened a few inches and a beam of light poured out to illuminate the porch. In the strong light he was able to see Andrea as he had rarely seen her before, with her hair in disarray, her eyes red and swollen and her slim shoulders sagging beneath the blue silk robe she had dragged hastily around her. Looking downwards he saw that her feet were bare. He lifted his eyes again and was appalled by the misery which was etched on her face. Was his lack of trust the reason for this? Shame engulfed him.

'Andrea, darling, I'm so sorry!' He stepped forward, dropping Lucky's lead as he did so; forgetting everything except his need to put things right with her. 'Please let me come inside and talk to you. I have to explain...'

'You've already done that,' she said in a low toneless voice that was utterly unlike the way he had ever heard her speak before.

'I haven't! You've got it all wrong. So wrong.'

'No, Bill!' Her voice was fierce now. 'You're the one who's got things wrong. Only I'm not prepared to go over it all again with you tonight. I've had enough for one day! More than enough! You've been different ever since you came back from America. I thought at first it was because you were tired and jet-lagged, and that you'd soon be over it, but you're not. You are worse than ever; even jealous of your own cousin because he's trying to help me!'

'I thought you would understand...' he began, then knew he had said the wrong thing again.

'You're the one who won't understand, Bill! All I was doing was trying to make your cousin feel welcome here, as I hoped soon to be part of your family. I was not to know that you didn't like him. You hadn't even told me he was coming to see you.'

'I didn't know until the night before I left, and I didn't tell you then because Alex is a person who's inclined to change his plans at short notice if something better turns up. If *you* hadn't turned up in this village, a young and beautiful woman, Alex probably wouldn't have bothered to wait for me to come home.'

'Since he did wait for you, why didn't you tell him how things were between us? Make it clear to him that he was wasting his time, if indeed *I* was the reason he was staying?'

Bill sighed. 'Because we agreed, didn't we, that we wouldn't tell anyone until we told your parents, together?'

Andrea bit hard on her lips because tears were threatening again. 'We were going to do that at Easter when Mum and Dad came down, only this agent who turns out to be your ex-partner's sister had other ideas.'

Bill hesitated. 'So Alex has been putting you in the picture about that! He didn't need to. I'd already told you about Gina, and why things didn't work out with her.'

'I began to wonder, when your jet-lag should have been over with, if you had seen her while you were over there and were having second thoughts about her,' Andrea said slowly, revealing the thought which ought to have been banished from her mind when Bill finally came home but which, once Alex had told her who Miriam's sister was, refused to be forgotten.

'I didn't see Gina, or wish to see her. All I did was work and travel, work and travel, and all the time long to be back home in Nyddbeck with you, Andrea. Please believe that!'

Andrea took a long time to answer him, a time during which she fought against the longing to just fling herself into Bill's arms and forget all about their differences. Bill was reaching out his hands to her when her phone began to ring. Instantly then she switched off, turning away from him to step back into her hall and pick up the receiver.

Bill waited in the porch, hoping against hope that the call would be a wrong number and that they could go back to that moment when he knew it would have been so easy for them to put things right. He was still standing there, listening intently and praying unconsciously that Andrea would put down the phone and walk into his arms, when the realization came to him that it was not going to happen like that. Instead it seemed that once again her work was going to come before her personal life. Her voice came to him clearly as she begged someone on the other end of the line to calm down, though he had no idea whom she was talking to.

'No Jane! You mustn't! Wait until I get to you. I'll come right away, I promise. You must wait because there'll be no one to take care of Kerry and Elliot until I get to you. So wait! Wait! Please wait for me, Jane,' she insisted.

Already she was replacing the phone, untying her robe and making for the stairs to run up to her bedroom. She seemed to have forgotten that Bill was there, which indicated to him that this was a matter of the utmost urgency. He remained where he was, determined to stay until she came down again, which she did almost at once. She was wearing jeans and a sweater now, with shoes on her feet.

'Sorry, Bill,' she said breathlessly as she reached for her car keys, her mobile phone and her bag. 'We'll talk later.'

Then she was closing the front door and on her way to her car. Bill watched from the porch as she drove off at speed without a backward glance at him. He looked down at the dog, who had begun to wag his tail as soon as he saw that Andrea was wearing outdoor clothes – dog-walking clothes – then he rubbed his knuckles over his rusty eyebrows and sighed deeply.

'Too late again, Lucky,' he said. 'Too bloody late, again!'

Once inside Jacob's Cottage with Matt, Julie wondered whether she had done the right thing in asking him in for a drink. Before the door was closed Matt was putting his arms about her and reaching his lips down to meet hers.

'I'll get the wine,' she said, then remembered that the wine had been packed along with most of her food and drink ready for the removal tomorrow. 'Will coffee do, Matt?'

'Anything will do, so long as I have you to myself for a bit longer.'

His words made her feel more uneasy than ever. She'd make the coffee then tell him how tired she was. That would be true; she was tired. Not physically tired because she was accustomed to long and busy days spent either on her feet or driving in all weathers about the scattered rural practice served by Nyddford Health Centre. Her weariness was emotionally based. It was all to do with the failure of her relationship with Dave. Where had she gone wrong there? Why had her hopes of being able to share the rest of her life with Dave and his children come to grief? Grief was the right word for it, because now that she would be leaving this cottage within twelve hours she had been forced to accept that there was no longer any hope of restoring even friendship with Dave, and she had wanted so much more than friendship. The loss of hope had been tearing her apart during these last few days when she had only left the cottage to go to work just in case Dave came to beg her not to go but to stay and move into the farmhouse with him. It was not going to happen now, and the sense of bereavement within her was the same as she had felt when Jill, Dave's first wife and her own close friend, had been killed.

If she had been as strong in faith as Andrea was, she would have prayed that even at this late stage a miracle would happen, but if Andrea had been praying for her, which Julie was certain she had been, that miracle would have happened before now and she would not be leaving Abbot's Fold Farm for the last time tomorrow. She sniffed back the tears as Matt spoke from the doorway of the kitchen.

'Are you having problems, Julie?'

'No.' She kept her head bent over the mug she was stirring.

'You forgot to put the coffee in, darling,' he pointed out.

She laughed shakily. 'I must be even more tired than I thought I was.'

'Here, let me do it. You go and sit down.'

She did not argue with him but went into the living room and dropped on to the sofa there, needing time to gain control of herself. A couple of minutes later Matt joined her.

'What's it all about, love?' he asked as she gripped the mug with hands that were not quite steady. 'It's not just tiredness, is it?'

Julie shook her head before she tried to sip some of the hot liquid.

'Would you like to talk about it?' he asked quietly.

'It's a long story, and it doesn't have a

happy ending,' she whispered.

'I've heard plenty of stories like that. I'm willing to listen to another.'

'You won't like this one.'

'I haven't liked some of the others I've heard.'

Julie drank deeply of the coffee while she tried to marshal her thoughts and decide whether or not to share them with Matt. It was so hot still that she began to cough, which brought more tears to her eyes. Matt took the mug from her and set it on the coffee table. Then he put an arm about her shoulders and drew her head close to his own.

'Take your time,' he murmured. 'There's no hurry.'

All at once then, as he stroked her hair, Julie forgot that he was Matt Harper, local lad made good in America and come home to take over a successful business from his wealthy father, a supremely self-confident, even arrogant, man who like many other Yorkshire men said what he thought even if it was the wrong thing to say. This Matt Harper was patient and gentle, more the sort of man his father had mellowed into since falling in love with Dave's mother. So she didn't feel pressured by him. Instead she began to feel at ease with him, comfortable with him in a way she had not felt before.

'I hoped I wouldn't be leaving here tomorrow,' she began hesitantly. 'Because I knew if I left I wouldn't ever be coming back.'

Matt's arm tightened about her. 'Wasn't the idea of this place just to give you somewhere to stay while you looked around for a place to buy? That was what Dorothy told me.'

'Yes. I knew I couldn't stay on in the cottage because of the holiday bookings.'

'So?' he prompted.

Julie was silent. This was not going to be easy. Matt would not like what he would have to hear if she shared it with him.

'So,' he prompted again.

'I hoped Dave would ask me to move into the farmhouse with him.' She spoke hurriedly, wanted to get the worst bit over with quickly.

'Did that seem a possibility *before* you moved in?'

'No, it was only a hope then.'

'And after you moved in? Was that when it became a possibility?'

'Yes,' she said on a long sigh. 'It seemed to be quite likely then because Dave was beginning to come out of his grief for Jill. He was spending time with me here, and asking me over into the farmhouse for meals. I've always got on well with the children, so there didn't seem to be any real difficulty there...' Her voice tailed off. How much more could she tell him without saying too much?

'You've always got on well with his mother too, haven't you? She's very fond of you.'

'I'm very fond of her.' They were moving to safer ground now.

'So she was hoping that you and Dave would get together. She must have had grounds for thinking you would?'

'Yes, I think so. You see, I knew Dave before he met Jill. I was going out with him, and Jill was my friend. Then when he met Jill he really fell for her, and married her quite quickly. They were really happy together.'

'And she was still your friend?'

'Yes. After she was killed, Dave blamed me for encouraging her to go back to nursing when the children went to school. Because if Jill hadn't done that she would not have been going out to give pain-killing injections to a patient on that stormy night when a tree came down on her car.'

'It wouldn't have been easy then for him to ask you to go and live in his home, would it?'

'Not at first. It would have been later, after I'd been living in this cottage for weeks and we had become...' She could not go on to tell him the rest. He was a mature man, an experienced man, so she should not have to spell it out for him.

'Partners.' He supplied the word for her.

She nodded. 'I thought, I hoped, when I reminded him that I'd need to move out when the holiday bookings for the cottage were imminent, that he'd suggest I moved in with him.'

'But he didn't?'

She shook her head. 'No. At least not in the way I'd hoped he would.'

Matt raised a thick, black eyebrow when he heard that. 'You meant marriage?'

Julie hesitated. 'I meant commitment, sharing his life and his home and children; having a child of our own.'

'He didn't offer that? Was that why you went and bought a house in Nyddford, Julie?'

'He said I could have had a room in the farmhouse.' She tried to laugh as she said that but it didn't work. 'Just as if I was a tourist seeking a bed-and-breakfast booking!'

'What did you say to that?'

'I said, "No thanks," and I meant it!'

'The man's a bloody idiot.'

'Or I just don't measure up to Jill,' she said quietly. 'Jill *was* a pretty special person.'

Now Matt was angry with her. He shook her shoulders gently. 'You're pretty special yourself, Julie.'

'Obviously Dave doesn't think so...'

'Then he's even more of an idiot than I already take him to be. I wish the chances that were open to him had been open to me.'

Julie was lost for words. She waited for what Matt would say next. The world outside the cottage was silent. No animal sounds to be heard, not even the rattle of the collies' chains. Or the noise made by Dave as he opened and closed the doors of farm buildings to check that all was well. Dave would be in bed now, and maybe wondering about her and Matt. He would be aware that Matt's car was still parked close to the cottage. How would he be feeling about that?

Matt turned her head so that he could look into her face. 'When I asked you if I could come in for a drink I was hoping for much more than that, Julie,' he told her. 'What I wanted was to find out how you felt about me moving into your new house with you. Not as an unpaid lodger but as a partner, paying my way and seeing how things worked out for us. Whether or not we might make each other happy on a long-term basis. Maybe a permanent one. I've been attracted to you right from the start, even though I knew you didn't feel the same way about me. When I heard you were moving away from here and buying a place of your own it helped me to make up my mind about staying here and going in with Dad. That led me on into thinking seriously about it being time for me to settle down to family life. I want my own children to have the sort of good stable childhood I enjoyed. Then I realized that I wanted you there too. Only I'd picked up hints from Dorothy about you and her Dave. So I decided to find out tonight exactly where I stood in your life.'

Julie sighed. 'I think you know that now, don't you?'

Matt smiled. 'I know where I did stand, until tonight, but you're moving out tomorrow, Julie, and moving on with the rest of your life. I know you're not happy right now, but I think once you're away from here that could change. We could make it change! We stimulate one another; I like a woman who has a mind of her own, and I know you don't find me repulsive. We are both ready for a new beginning. Why not make that beginning together?'

He did not wait for her answer but closed his lips on hers in a long and searing kiss. There was comfort for her in being desired by a man like Matt, a handsome, intelligent, successful man who would provide the family she longed to have before it was too late. The kiss led to another, and another, and might have gone on from there to the point of no return if it had not been for the small sound that broke into the silence. Julie stiffened in Matt's embrace, took a firm hold on the hand that was caressing her and listened. There was the sound again.

'What is it?' Matt whispered. 'I thought...'

'There's someone outside the front door.' Her heart began to lurch. Was it Dave, listening outside the cottage door?

'It'll be an animal...'

'It isn't!' She was on her feet and across the room swiftly to pull open the door.

The girl who stood there was sobbing quietly, and shaking as though frozen to the marrow.

'Carla! Come inside, quickly!'

For a moment the girl seemed unable to take in what Julie said. Her arms were resting on the lamp bracket at the side of the door and her head was bowed over them. The lamp had gone out and all around her fog swirled, concealing Matt's car and almost, but not quite, deadening the melancholy noise of her crying.

'Come inside, love.' Julie almost had to drag her away from the lamp and guide her into the house. Once inside she closed the door. By then Matt was on his feet, and frowning.

'Who's this?' he wanted to know.

'Dave's daughter. Put the kettle on and make a hot drink,' Julie told him. 'Quickly, she's in shock. I have to find out what it's all about.'

Matt left them and went to do as he was bid.

Nineteen

When Andrea reached the top of Abbot's Hill and prepared to make a left turn for Nyddford she was dismayed to find a thick wall of fog ahead of her. It meant she would need to slow down when what she had hoped to do was gather speed on the wider, straighter road. Fortunately at this very early hour of the morning there was little traffic about. It was the sheep you had to watch out for as they wandered from one side of the road to the other, or worse still lay down and went to sleep on the tarmac surface.

Her throat was dry with anxiety, her hands gripped the wheel with unnecessary force, and her mind was alive with the jumble of prayers that she would not be too late because of the fog in reaching Jane Lindsay. She must not be too late. She dare not be too late, because if Jane did what she was threatening to do, two young children would be at risk.

'Dear Lord, let me get there in time. Please let me get there in time!' She found she was saying the words aloud as she drove with agonizing slowness, picking up speed whenever she came to a clear patch and dropping down again each time there was a blank white wall obscuring sheep, drystone walls, ditches or other hazards on the few miles of road. Her relief was tremendous when the eerie orange-yellow glimmer of overhead lighting told her she was on the edge of the market town.

Where then would she find Jane Lindsay's home? All she had was a road name and a number. Fourteen Nyddford Gardens. Those were the newish houses on the other side of the town. She had never visited Jane Lindsay before, and had met her only a few times when Jane had brought her two young children to one of the family services at Emmanuel Church. Now Jane was in desperate need of her help.

The house was in darkness upstairs but lights shone out from the hall and the bay window at the front. Andrea parked her car in the road outside and ran up the drive, knocking and opening the front door at the same time. As she stepped inside the hall the silence all about her was ominous. It set her heart racing with fear as she pushed open the door that led into a sitting room. She was not surprised to find the girl she had come to help lying sprawled across the low brightly patterned sofa.

'Jane! Jane! Wake up! Wake up!' To add emphasis to her words Andrea grasped Jane by the shoulders, having first made sure that her head was well back to keep the airway open. She began to shake her vigorously, which brought forth a groan and movements from hands that attempted to push her away.

'Wake up, Jane!' she ordered sharply.

'Leave me alone. I told you I don't want to go on without Tim,' Jane cried.

'You *have* to go on without him. You've got two children asleep upstairs. What will happen to them if you are not here? Think about that,' Andrea urged.

'I can't think about it any more. I've tried coping without Tim and it doesn't work. It never will work!' This last sentence ended with a cry of despair that brought a lump to Andrea's throat but she continued to grasp Jane's shoulders even though by now her own arms ached with the effort.

'Tell me how many of those tablets you've taken, and let me see what they are.'

'Tranquillizers. The doctor gave me them to help me cope, but I can't cope. I never will be able to cope without Tim.'

'Never is a long time,' Andrea told her briskly. 'How many tablets have you taken?'

The girl sighed. 'Not many. Not enough. I lost my courage and rang you instead.'

'Thank God for that! Now I'm going to

ring your doctor.'

'No!' The girl was in a panic. 'I don't want him to know. He might take my children away from me if you tell him.'

'How many did you take, Jane? You must tell me or I *will* send for him.'

'Only two, just a double dose. I wanted you to come. I needed to talk to you and I guessed you would come if I told you what I'd tried to do.'

'You didn't need to take any. I'd have come anyway if you needed me. Now, let me go and make some tea for you. Then we'll talk about what you can do.'

'I *can't* do anything. I can't think straight. I can't cope.'

'You will, when you've had some tea and we've talked about it.' Andrea straightened up and made her way to find the kitchen, and the kettle. As soon as she had set the water to boil she went back into the sitting room, where, as she had expected, Jane was weeping. She stared down at the girl and began to pray, then moved her mind back to the training she had undergone about how to deal with this sort of situation. By the time she had prayed that she'd got it right, the kettle was boiling, so she made a pot of strong tea, put it on a tray with a couple of mugs, sugar and milk, and carried it into the sitting room.

'You'll feel better when you've had this,'

she said.

'I feel sick,' Jane exclaimed.

'Then go and be sick. I'll come with you.' Andrea half lifted her to her feet and supported her as she made her way to the downstairs toilet.

A few minutes later they were back in the sitting room, Jane with a freshly washed face and Andrea pouring out the tea.

'Thanks.' Jane managed a weak smile as Andrea handed her the mug. 'I don't mean for this – you turning out in the middle of the night to help me. You see, I don't have anyone of my own here.'

'You've got your children,' Andrea reminded her.

'I mean no friends or relatives. We haven't been here long enough for me to make any friends.'

'What brought you here? Was it your husband's work?' Andrea asked.

Jane gave a long sigh. 'Yes. We came from London because Tim wanted the children to grow up in a better environment, and there was a teaching job going at Nyddford High. Tim and me came to the Yorkshire Dales for our honeymoon, and we loved it. It seemed the ideal place to bring up a family. Only I didn't know that in less than a year we wouldn't be a family any more.' She began to cry again. Andrea put down her mug and went to hold her hand.

'Try to keep calm and just tell me what's gone wrong, if you feel able to. If you would rather not, I'll understand.'

'It all seems to have gone wrong since we came here,' the other girl began. 'First the house wasn't ready, so I had to stay with my parents and the children in Devon for a couple of months. Then I had to get the moving done on my own. Things kept going missing or not fitting in properly, and Kerry started with asthma. Because we had no one to baby-sit I wasn't able to go with Tim to the school events or to any of the school staff who invited him to supper. There just seemed to be so many times when Tim had to go out on his own, but I never realized then that he wasn't on his own at all; that there was someone with him.'

Andrea waited for her to go on, even though she could guess at what was coming.

'It was one of the other teachers. She had been inviting Tim to her place while I was still down in Devon with my parents. Now he's moved in with her.' As the sad story was told, in such a few words, Jane began to cry again. 'I'm sorry,' she gasped.

'Don't worry. You'll feel better when you've shared it all with someone,' Andrea murmured. That was how it had been with her; after she had shared her sense of shock and failure with Bill.

'Will I?' Jane sniffed and tried to dry her

eyes at the same time.

'Have you told your parents yet?'

Jane shook her head. 'No. I know I'll have to tell them but I put it off because Dad isn't too well. He has a bit of a heart problem. They'll want to come up here when they know what's happened, so I've been putting off telling them. I suppose I've been hoping that Tim would come home again,' she confessed.

'Perhaps he will. It could be something he drifted into because you were not here.'

'That wasn't my fault!'

'I'm sure it wasn't.'

'What am I going to do? How am I going to tell the children? Will Tim try to take them to live with him? I couldn't bear that.'

'You probably won't have to. If he's been a good father he won't want to cause them any more bewilderment than they'll already be feeling. What have you told them, Jane?'

'Just that daddy's work is keeping him away from home just now. What else could I say?'

Andrea could not answer that. All she could do was to go on asking about the children, how old they were and whether they were at school yet. She discovered that they were not.

'I intended to start them both at playgroup as soon as we were settled, then see if I could go back to part-time work. Only

Kerry had asthma very badly so I was not able to do that.'

'What do you do? Your work, I mean?'

'I'm a school secretary. That's where I met Tim. We worked at the same London school. I wish we'd stayed in London now,' Jane ended with a wobble in her voice.

'You did what you both thought was the best for your children,' Andrea tried to comfort her.

'It wasn't though, was it? Down there they had a mum and a dad. Up here they've only got a mum. A mum who can't cope on her own!'

Andrea took a deep breath, and prayed for the right words. 'You *will* cope, Jane, once you get used to the idea of being on your own.'

'How do you know I will? You can't possibly know how I'm feeling.'

Andrea sighed. 'I do. I've been through it, or something similar to it, myself. I had a husband, once, and I had a child, once.'

The words, so calmly and quietly spoken, shocked the other woman into a long silence. Then: 'I'm sorry I said that. I didn't know. I suppose I haven't been here long enough to know that you're on your own too.'

'I'm a widow. It happened soon after I came here, on the day of my ordination. Our little boy had died of meningitis when he was only three.'

'How can you go on believing, after that? Doesn't it get in the way?'

Andrea knew that she had shocked Jane out of her own trauma. 'It does, sometimes,' she confessed. 'Though never for long. The loss of my little boy led me to start training for the ministry, and brought me here to a place I love.'

'What about the death of your husband? How did you cope with that?'

Andrea was silent for a long time. Then: 'It was very sudden; a road accident. The people here and in Nyddbeck were so good to me that I felt able to go on with my work here.'

'Do you think I'll be able to go on one day, Andrea? I do want to be able to do that, for the children's sake.' Jane's lovely eyes were pleading for reassurance.

'I'm certain you will. You've taken the first step on the way already, by not taking any more of those tablets. Now, why don't you go to bed and try to get some sleep? You'll need all your energy to keep up with two small children all day. You're lucky to have them, you know,' Andrea reminded her.

'Yes, I know.' Jane reached up to kiss Andrea's cheek. 'You'll never know how grateful I am, Andrea. You've been such a friend to me tonight.'

Andrea smiled in spite of her weariness, as

she answered. 'I'll be there for you again if you need me.'

'Will you say a prayer for me and my children, please?' Jane asked as they went to the front door together.

'Yes, of course, and I'll see you again soon.'

A few minutes later Andrea was driving very slowly back to Nyddbeck through a fog so thick that the early dawn light was not able to penetrate it. Her thoughts lingered on the troubled girl she had just left. She must keep in touch with Jane and see if there was any practical way she could help her. It might be worth starting a group for younger women at Emmanuel Church, a sort of up-dated Young Wives Group. With the estates of new houses growing fast on the outskirts of the market town there could be other girls like Jane needing to find friendship. So it might go well.

'I think you'd better be going, Matt. There's nothing more you can do to help here. I'll have to get Dave to come over,' Julie said as she took another long look at Dave's daughter. What a state the girl was in. There was mud running in streaks down her tear-wet face, her hair was damp and dishevelled. Earth clogged her shoes and clung to her jeans. Where had she been to get into this state? Why was she still out at long after midnight? She could not be out with Dave's permission. A cold tremor of fear shook Julie as she considered one or two possibilities. She closed her mind to them and gave all her concentration to making decisions about what to do next.

'No! No! I don't want Dad. If you ask him to come I'll run away again.' Already Carla was on her feet and ready to go.

'Sit down, Carla!' Julie said crisply. 'I'm not going to do anything at all until you've told me what all this is about. After Matt's gone,' she added as Matt brought in a mug of milky coffee and put it into Carla's shaking hands.

'I'll go now, if you're sure I can't do anything else to help.' Matt made for the door. 'You will ring me if you need me, won't you, Julie?'

'Yes, I will,' she promised. 'Drive carefully, won't you?'

'I'll ring you tomorrow,' he told her. 'Or rather, later today.'

They were alone then, the young girl who was still recovering from a frightening experience, and the nurse who had been her mother's best friend.

'Finish drinking your coffee, then we'll talk.' Julie moved quietly about the room, giving herself time to think and Carla time to calm down. She could hear the long shuddering sobs which the girl could not yet manage to subdue.

'You won't send for Dad, will you?' she asked in the middle of one of these.

'Perhaps it would be better if I came over with you to talk to him,' Julie suggested thoughtfully. 'I don't suppose he knows that you are here, does he?'

'He thinks I'm asleep in my room.'

'He'd be shocked if he saw you as you are now. We need to get you cleaned up a bit before you talk to him.' A terrifying thought hit Julie as she finished speaking. Had Carla been attacked by someone; by some man? If so she must not be cleaned up until the police were informed.

'How did you get into that state, Carla?' she asked gently. 'Did someone molest you? Or try to molest you?'

Carla did not answer at once but stared down at the hands which were clenched in her lap.

'Did someone hurt you? Or try to hurt you? You must tell me, Carla, or I won't know the best way to help you.'

Still the girl was silent. Julie tried a different approach. 'Why were you out so late?'

'I was running away. I had to!' Carla's voice was vehement.

'Why?' Julie stared down at the girl she had known since her birth, willing her to answer truthfully.

'Because I had another row with Dad. He

accused me of making our Jack lie for me.'

'Did you really do that?' Julie wanted to know.

'I didn't mean to. It wouldn't have happened if Dad had let me go to the drama group like I wanted to. I *had* to be there because I was taking the leading part. When I missed the rehearsal last week someone else did it, and she wasn't any good. Only Dad said I couldn't go tonight; that I was to stay at home.'

'But you didn't?'

'No. I arranged for Josh to pick me up in the old sheepfold at the top of the hill and take me to Nyddford on his bike. I told Jack I was coming over here to you, so when Dad asked where I was Jack said I was with you. Only Dad had seen you going out with Matt Harper, so he knew I was not here. He was in a black mood; a real black mood, when I came back. He went on and on at me till I couldn't stand any more.'

'I expect he was worried about you going on the back of the bike,' Julie said quietly.

'He won't let me go anywhere! He wants me to stay in the house all the time when I'm not at school and do the work and the cooking. I told him I can't do that and my homework as well, but he won't listen. He doesn't listen to anything we say to him now.'

'So you decided to run away?' Julie guessed. 'Where were you going?'

'Somewhere like Liverpool, or Manchester, where I could get a job and a place to live on my own.'

'How were you going to get there? Was Josh involved with this?'

Carla shook her head vigorously. 'No! No! When we talked about it Josh said I'd only make things worse if I ran away, and that I should wait until you and Dad got things sorted between you then everything would be all right again.'

Julie felt her throat begin to tingle. 'What did Josh mean by that?'

'He said when people had been used to being together, like you and Dad had been, they got bad-tempered if someone else came on the scene like Matt did with you.'

'But you didn't believe him, did you? That's why you ran away, I suppose?'

Carla nodded. 'I kept thinking it would be OK when Dad asked you to move in with us, or even to get married to him. Only it didn't happen. I knew you were leaving tomorrow. So I decided to go tonight. Only things went wrong.' As she finished speaking the girl shuddered, then clasped her arms about her ribs and fought another outbreak of hysterical sobs.

Instantly, Julie moved to enclose her shaking body in a hug. 'Take your time, love,' she whispered. 'Just try to calm down and then you'll find it easier to talk.'

A long, deep sigh signalled when this was going to happen. 'This van stopped when I was walking through the fog on the main road. I could just see that it said Manchester on the side, so I thought that would do for me. The man opened the door and told me to get in, but there was something about him that I didn't like. So I said I'd changed my mind about having a lift. He grabbed me and began to say foul things to me. I was really frightened then. I hadn't quite shut the door, and we were only just beginning to move off, so I gave the door a big shove and sort of fell out onto the muddy grass. I thought at first the man was going to come after me, but just then a lorry caught up with us so the van driver put his toe down and disappeared. Oh, Julie, he was so horrible; so obscene; so vile. He was huge and he smelled awful. When he grabbed me and tried to drag me back he tore my sweatshirt.'

'But he didn't touch you? Touch your body, I mean?'

'No. Just my clothes. He was the pits; a monster; a brute. If you'd heard what he said...'

'So you won't be hitching lifts again, will you?'

Carla shivered violently. There was no need for her to answer.

'Now we must tell your dad where you are, because if he looks in your room and finds it empty he'll be in a panic.'

'Do we have to? I'd rather not...' Carla began to sniffle again.

'Yes, we do have to, right now. It's after one o'clock,' Julie told her.

'You won't make me go back tonight, will you? Please let me stay here, Julie.'

Julie considered this. 'I'll see what your dad says. You'll have to sleep on the sofa if you stay because the bedding is all packed away.'

'I don't mind, as long as I can stay with you.'

'I'll bring you the duvet from my bed.'

'I'm so tired...' was the last thing Dave's daughter said before she fell into an exhausted slumber.

It was time then for Julie to ring Dave and put him in the picture. She knew he would be furious, but she had to risk that. He sounded half-asleep when he answered her call, but a moment later he was fully alert when he heard that Carla was with her in Jacob's Cottage.

'What the hell is she doing there? I thought she was asleep in her own room,' he said.

'It's a long story, Dave, but I'm not going to start telling it tonight because I'm just about out on my feet and I need to be up early tomorrow. I just wanted to let you know Carla was safe.'

'Why shouldn't she be safe? I don't know what you're trying to say...'

'I'm saying she tried to run away from home tonight, and she had a bad experience, but she's safe now and fast asleep. That's all I'm saying tonight, Dave. I'll see you early in the morning. Please don't come over tonight because I won't open the door to you.'

She could hear him protesting, but left him to it and put down the phone. Tomorrow morning would be soon enough for what she had to say to him.

Twenty

Bill woke from his sleep in the deep leather armchair reluctantly. His body felt cramped and uncomfortable and his mouth was dry. He ought to have gone to bed after bringing Lucky back from Andrea's manse, but there had been a faint hope in him that when she returned to her home from the emergency call-out Andrea would telephone him. Or even perhaps call at Beckside when she saw that there were still lights showing.

It had not happened like that though. Instead Bill had first prowled restlessly from his living room to his kitchen and back again, then decided, as he felt so unready for sleep, to use the night hours to work in his studio. In the studio he found himself unable to concentrate on any of the tasks which at other times he would have found easy to become absorbed in. He was forced to admit then that he had got himself into one hell of a mess since returning from America, and now he could neither work nor relax enough to sleep.

Having admitted that, he flung himself

into his favourite armchair, poured himself a large malt whisky and picked up the remote control to find a television channel that might just bore him enough to send him into the slumber that he craved. The weariness and tension which had got such a hold on him since his arrival back in Nyddbeck had resulted in sleepless nights during which he had endlessly questioned how his relationship with Andrea could so rapidly have disintegrated. Was the presence of Alex, who ought by now to have departed, the reason for this? Or had Andrea begun to doubt the wisdom of sharing her life and work with *him* while he had been away?

He knew he would have to find the answer to this last question quickly, because while his mind was so chaotic he could not give sufficient concentration to his painting. In fact he could not concentrate on anything except where he had gone wrong with Andrea, and how he could put things right. Nothing else mattered to him. The successful tour of the States organized by Miriam was now only a memory; the forthcoming filming for a TV series featuring his work was something he was dreading, even though it would be likely to stimulate sales of his pictures. His health was beginning to suffer, since he had lost his appetite for food and was finding it easier to settle for a drink and a sandwich rather than a proper meal. Everything seemed to be against him putting things right with Andrea. If it wasn't Alex muscling in where he wasn't wanted, it was Andrea's work. He had been so certain she was about to listen to him tonight, until the sound of her phone ringing had broken in and sent her dashing off somewhere to get involved with someone else's problems rather than with her own Was it always going to be like that?

Yes, the needs of those who came to her churches, and sometimes those who did not, would always come first with Andrea. He had known that when he asked her to marry him, and been prepared to take it on board so long as she would share her life with him. He was still eager to do that. It was just a question of convincing her that he had not changed during the last few weeks; that he still loved her as he had never loved anyone else, and that he wanted to marry her as soon as possible.

He would need to make sure he had her to himself – away from the place where her phones or her doorbell could interrupt them – to convince her of that. There was only one place where he could be certain that Andrea would be alone, and in no danger of being interrupted. It was the place where Andrea went early every morning for a short session of private prayer. She would not refuse to listen to him there.

The decision made, Bill left the remainder of his whisky untouched and went to take a shower.

Julie seemed to have only just fallen asleep when she was woken by the early morning sounds that belonged to Abbot's Fold Farm. She remembered then that Carla was asleep on her sofa in the next room, and that when she woke they would both have to face Dave and explain why his daughter had spent the night here instead of in her own home. Julie was not looking forward to that experience. Dave would be furious with his daughter, and probably with *her* as well. So her last day here would be even worse than she had anticipated. Yet there would be no escaping it. Dave Bramley was an early riser, and Carla would have to catch the school bus as usual. It was time they were getting ready to face the day and all that it would bring.

Carla had also been woken by the sound of Tyke and Brack barking, by the bleating of many sheep and their lambs, and by the crowing of the cockerel. As the sounds penetrated her consciousness, so did recollection of what had happened the night before. She moaned and put her head back under the duvet. There would be the row to beat them all between her and Dad this morning, and she was not ready to face it.

'Time you were up, Carla,' Julie said. 'I've made some tea.'

'I don't want it. I don't want to get up,' Carla groaned.

'You'll have to, because you'll need a shower and some breakfast before you get the school bus. You'll also need to talk to your dad.'

'Do I have to? I can't face it!'

'Yes, you do have to. He'll have been worrying about why you went out so late, and stayed over here with me.'

'I *can't* face him. Please don't make me, Julie,' the girl begged.

Julie sighed. 'I'll come with you if it'll help, but you'll have to hurry because I'm moving out this morning.'

'He'll blow his top.'

'Maybe he has a right to do that when you behaved so irresponsibly. You knew you were not supposed to hitch lifts; that it's a dangerous thing to do.'

'I know now,' Carla said with a shudder.

'You'd better shower and get some clothes on, or your dad will be coming over to look for you,' Julie warned.

Carla sat up. 'Does he know what happened to me? Did you tell him?'

'No, but I'll have to tell him this morning. So – get a move on!'

Julie was already showered and dressed and gulping down a mug of tea when she heard the sharp raps on the front door which heralded the arrival of Dave. She did not at once rush to open the door but emptied the mug first and gave her hair a swift brushing. It occurred to her that if ever there was a time for prayer, this was it. Probably it was too late for prayer to work; Dave would be unlikely to listen to reason. He always was these days. Yet a few weeks ago it had been so different. She had been able to talk to him then, able to share problems with him, able to share love with him. Oh Lord, where did I go wrong? she asked silently. Then she swallowed the huge lump that was swelling in her throat and went to open the door, after Dave had knocked again.

'What's happening then?' he wanted to know.

He looked dreadful. The always thin face was gaunt now and haggard, his shoulders sagged. Julie felt choked at the sight of him. 'She's getting ready for school,' was all she could manage to say. It sounded inadequate.

'Why?' he asked bluntly.

Julie deliberately misunderstood him. 'Because it's almost time for the bus. She won't want to be late.'

'She was out too late last night. Why didn't she come home? Why did she come to you?' Dave demanded. There was a scowl bringing his thick eyebrows close together.

Julie bit hard on her lip. Words were rushing into her mind; words which once uttered could not be taken back. 'Why do you think, Dave?' she said when the silence between them had grown too long.

'I don't know what to think any more.' He shook his head in bewilderment. 'I don't know how to cope any more. I thought I had it all sorted; that things were going to work out for the best, for all of us, and then...'

Her anger with him died and compassion took over. 'And then – what, Dave?' she asked softly.

'Then you decided to leave me; and go with Matt Harper instead.'

'What *are* you talking about, Dave? I'm not leaving you to go to Matt Harper.'

'Why are you leaving me then?'

'Because I'm tired of waiting to find out if you really care for me. Or whether I've just been nice and handy here in Jacob's Cottage for you to spend the odd hour or two with when you've had nothing more important to do.'

'What the hell are you talking about? You know I really care for you. You know I don't want you to go. You know I wanted you to stay and become part of my life, part of my family, but when I told you that, you said you were going to buy a house in Nyddford.'

Julie felt the anger already simmering

inside her begin to reach boiling point. 'You didn't tell me you loved me, Dave Bramley! All you said was that I could have a room in your farmhouse when it was time for the holiday lets to take over this cottage. You made it sound as though I was just another bed-and-breakfast booking. That's why I knew I had to leave here.'

'I didn't! I'm sure I didn't!'

'You did! I made my mind up then that I'd waited long enough for you to commit yourself to me. That's why I'm leaving today. Because if I ever share the whole of my life with anyone, I want it to be with someone who loves me.'

That was the moment when Carla, having waited fearfully inside the cottage for her father to lash her with his tongue yet again, decided to make her escape and head for the farmhouse and her school uniform. Exiting by the back door, she raced across the yard, to the excited barking of Tyke and Brack. Taken by surprise, Dave and Julie stared after her. Julie waited for Dave to set off in pursuit, but he seemed to be rooted to the spot.

'But you know I love you! You must know!' His clenched hands beat against each other as he told her that, then said it all again. 'You must know that I love you, Julie.'

'Why, because you've made love to me sometimes? It doesn't always follow...'

'It does with me. There's been no one else for me since Jill died. I never thought I'd want anyone else, after Jill, until you came to live here.'

Julie laughed shakily. 'Why didn't you say so? Why did you let me go on thinking you were just coming to me because you were lonely?'

'I thought you'd know me better than that, after all these years. You know I'm not one to waste a lot of time on words.'

Now Julie's laughter was ironic. 'I certainly know that about you, Dave! Though you can always find the words when you're angry with people. I expect you came to give Carla some hard words this morning.'

'What do you mean? I knew she was safe when she was over here with you.'

Julie did not comment on that. Instead she waited to hear what he would say next.

'I came because I didn't want you to leave without hearing me ask you to stay.'

Julie took a deep breath. 'Do you mean on a bed-and breakfast basis in the farmhouse, Dave?'

She heard his swift intake of breath and watched the hot colour flood his weather-beaten cheeks.

'No, I don't! I mean moving in with me and marrying me. Sharing everything I shared with Jill. Not that I can offer you the sort of life Matt Harper could offer. There's not much money in farming these days; not enough for luxuries or even holidays. All I have to give you is a home here and two kids who are a bit of a handful.' He stopped then and threw a sudden glance over his shoulder.

'Carla's already gone for the bus,' Julie told him. Her eyes were intent on his face, willing him to go on with what he was proposing.

'It's Jack,' he said. 'I've been up half the night with him. He was crying with bad stomach pain, so I've asked the doctor to call. I'd better go and see if he's any better.'

'I'll come with you, if you want me to?' she offered.

Dave did not answer. All he did was reach out a hand to take her own and hold it tightly while they hurried across the yard and into the house.

Bill watched from the gate of Beckside, peering through the strands of drifting fog as he waited for Andrea to appear. He knew she would walk across the bridge that spanned the beck and skirt round the village green beneath the huge horse chestnut tree, which was now ablaze with candle-shaped flowers. So many times he had watched her do that when he had first come to live in the village. So many times he had strolled as far as the letter box set into the wall with an envelope in his hand simply in order to meet her. So many times he had told himself that he was behaving like a love-sick lad and that Andrea Cameron was not for him.

Now he knew that Andrea *was* for him; that no one else would do, that he wanted to spend his life with her here in this village. To share a home and a family with her. To become involved with her work, and for her to become involved with his. Too much time had been wasted since he came back from America, and now his television filming schedule was about to start. When that came to an end, he wanted to marry Andrea. After he had spoken to her this morning, he would get in touch with Alex and tell him they were to be married soon. Then, if he knew Alex, his cousin would take himself off to some other place and there would be no more talk about him taking photographs of Andrea to raise money for her church. Bill did not want Andrea to be associated with the sort of pictures Alex Ross was famous for producing for the tabloid newspapers. She was a church minister, not a publicity-seeking pop star. Bill had his own ideas about how to raise money for the roof repairs.

There was a blackbird singing sweetly from the roof of the lych gate. There was a brown duck leading her brood of ducklings out of the busily bubbling beck in the hope that Bill had brought bread to feed them. There was mist floating in ribbons over the rising pasture on the other side of the water. There was a tranquillity here which had become precious to Bill. In his studio there was an almost-finished painting which he had been working on as a surprise for Andrea. The picture showed her church, and the green, and the chestnut tree, and a red-setter dog with head uplifted as he listened for the sound of Andrea's footsteps.

Just visible now through the veil of mist Bill could see a woman walking to the bridge, pausing to stare down into the water, then moving on through the deserted village. He could see her bright-red sweater, watch her push back a strand of the black hair which had fallen forward over one of her vivid blue eyes. She had reached the lych gate now and was pushing it open. The key to the church would be in her hand. He waited for her to reach the heavy oak door which she sometimes had difficulty in opening. Then he stepped out of his own gate and began to walk to the church.

Andrea struggled with the weighty key, which felt cold and damp in her hand. At first it would not give. Would nothing go right for her now that she had somehow got at odds with Bill? Her eyes were aching from lack of sleep. It had been almost three o'clock this morning when she got back to the manse and fell into bed, too tired to be able to relax into the sort of rest that she needed. Her mind had still been full of the girl she had visited in Nyddford. She had lain there worrying and wondering whether she had got things right or whether Jane would have lapsed into depression again and taken more tablets. The temptation had been there as she tried vainly to fall asleep to phone Jane, but the thought of waking the two young children stopped her. There was only so much you could do, she decided, and then it was up to God.

Having said yet another prayer for Jane and her children, her thoughts had winged back to Bill and how she could heal the breach between them. Because she had to heal it for both their sakes. She and Bill were meant to be together, of that she was absolutely certain. Bill's friendship had helped her to leave behind the tragedy of her marriage and the loss of her child. Bill's love had made sense of her suffering and brought joy and hope to her life. So, as soon as it was light, she would go to the church for her short time of private prayer and then go to Beckside to see Bill.

Surely, if she told Bill that she had decided not to go ahead with Alexander's idea of having her picture taken by him for a fund-raising calendar, it would convince him that she had not become romantically involved with Alex while he had been away? There had been no chance of her ever forming a relationship with Bill's cousin. She just had to convince Bill of that. Alex was too immature. He lacked the depth of character that Bill possessed in such abundance. As far as she was concerned no man could match up to Bill Wyndham.

It was dim and rather chilly in the little church she had come to love. She shivered as she made her way slowly down the centre aisle. If she got things right with Bill later this morning it would not be long before she walked with her father over this straight stretch of dark-blue carpet to marry Bill Wyndham.

Dear Lord, forgive me for the way I spoke to Bill last night. Help me to get things right with him today, she prayed. You know I could do the job I came here to do so much better with Bill at my side.

She went on then to pray for Jane, her husband, and their children, that they should find a way to get together again. She prayed for Dave Bramley, that he should come to his senses and ask Julie to marry him before it was too late and Matt Harper persuaded her to enter into a relationship with him. Dave, Carla and Jack needed Julie so much. She prayed for Dorothy and Ben Harper, that Ben would continue to recover from his heart attack. She prayed for her parents: for her doctor father, nearing retirement now, and for her mother who worried that his own health was under too great a strain as he fought to do his best for the patients in his care.

There were so many people here in Nyddbeck, and a few miles away in Nyddford, who needed her prayers; so many others in the wider troubled world who needed her thoughts and her prayers. As always at this time of day, Andrea gave total concentration to the needs of those people and ignored the passing of time. So she failed to hear the door of the building open slowly, then close again as Bill entered the church.

Bill slipped into the oak pew which was nearest to the door to wait until Andrea had finished her prayer time. He would not disturb what he knew was an important part of every day for her. She needed to be alone at this time. He would wait for her. She would be worth waiting for. He bent his head and prayed that he would be able to love and care for Andrea as much as she deserved to be loved and cared for. She was an exceptional woman; meeting her had been a kind of miracle for him.

Andrea rose and turned to walk back through the church to the door. She felt calm now and ready for whatever the day might bring. Calm enough to face Bill. As that thought rushed into her mind she caught sight of him as he began to walk down the aisle to meet her.

'Bill! I'm so glad to see you,' she murmured as she held out her hands to him.

'Andrea, my love!' His voice was a caress.

'I was coming to see you...' she began.

'Until I came to see you!' He drew her close and bent his head to kiss her lips. 'I wonder if we were going to say the same things to one another?'

'I was going to say I was sorry for the way I spoke to you last night.'

'I was going to say I was sorry too. I don't know what came over me; except that I was just so put out to find Alex here when I wanted you to myself.'

'I should have told him how it was with us...' she said.

'I should have told him how it *is* with us. What happened between us yesterday has gone now. We need to put it behind us. Can you do that, Andrea?' he said softly.

'I want to do that more than anything in the world. Then I want to talk about what's going to happen between us today, and tomorrow, and all the days to come.'

Bill smiled. 'What is going to happen, my darling?' he asked.

Andrea laughed, and his heart lurched at the joy which lit up the deep blue of her wonderful eyes. 'I'm coming back to Beckside with you right now so we can cook breakfast together. I've been up half the night and am absolutely ravenous now. Then we'll talk about things like wedding music, and honeymoons, if you like.'

Twenty-One

Jack was still in bed, looking pale and washed out, when Dave and Julie hurried into the house and up to his room. His face brightened when he saw Julie. 'I thought you'd gone away and I wouldn't see you again,' he said.

Julie smiled down at him. 'I haven't gone yet; I wouldn't go without coming to see you, Jack.'

'But you *are* going into your new house today, aren't you?'

Dave opened his mouth to answer this question, but Julie turned swiftly to stop him with a hand on his lips. 'Yes, I have to move the things out of Jacob's Cottage that belong to me because some people are coming to have a holiday there next week.'

'So we won't see you then, will we?' Jack's lips quivered. 'I wanted you to stay.'

Again, Dave was ready to rush in and reassure him, but again Julie put a stop to that.

'You will see me,' she said. 'Only I won't be living in the cottage. I'll be keeping in touch with you all, even if I'm not living here, because I'll want to know how you are doing at school, and how you are getting on with training Brack for the sheepdog trials.'

At the mention of Brack's name Jack brightened again. 'Brack's going to be a champion,' he said. 'I always knew she was going to be good right from when I first saw her. Dad said she was too much of a weakling to do any good. She's a great dog,' he finished proudly.

Almost as though the young dog had heard her name, she began to bark from the yard below Jack's window. Then Tyke added his more mature bark as a vehicle came to a halt at the farm gate. It was all Jack needed. 'I told you she was good, Dad,' he boasted. 'She heard the car stop before your Tyke did.'

'I expect that's Dr Grantley come to see you,' Dave said. 'I'll go and let him in.'

'I'll go, you stay here with Jack,' Julie told him. Dave did not argue.

'Who's the patient, Julie?' the middle-aged GP from Nyddford Health Centre asked when she met him at the door.

'Young Jack. He's been complaining of bad stomach pains during the night, Dave says.'

'I thought you were on day off today? Weren't you moving into your new house?' The doctor looked at her curiously as he made that observation.

'Yes, I was. I am.'

'What are you doing here then?' he asked as they reached the staircase.

'Making my mind up,' was her answer. Then she left him to go to his patient.

Carla knew she looked a mess this morning as she waited at the bus stop. Her hair should have been washed, her shoes ought to have been at least dusted over, and her uniform shirt had not been ironed. Josh would think she looked like a slut, because Josh always had that neat almost-too-perfect look that young Americans wore like a badge. It was upsetting that Josh would have to see her looking like this when so soon he would be going back home to the States. A lump swelled inside her throat when she thought about that and it took a huge effort from her not to start crying. Her eyes were already dark-rimmed and swollen from all the crying she had done during the night.

It seemed to her to be a lifetime since she had waited here in the fog for a vehicle to stop and offer her a lift. Yet it was less than ten hours. Less than ten hours since the van had loomed up out of the fog and come to a stop in the layby where she was now standing. Her heart had leapt with excitement because it was all happening as she had planned: her escape from the house with her backpack, undetected by her dad, and after several vehicles shining their headlights on her, one was actually stopping.

She had not been able to catch what the driver said to her as he opened the door of his vehicle. His accent was too thick, but he had smiled and said, 'Hop in.' He had been quite old, nearly as old as her gran's new husband, and he looked friendly. So she had climbed into the front passenger seat and he had moved off. The radio in the cab was belting out pop music, which was a surprise to Carla, with the driver being quite old.

He did not ask her where she wanted to go but since they were heading for the main road that would take them in a few miles on to the A1 that did not worry her. What did bother her was the large, rough hand that moved so close to her that she had to lean against the door to get away from it. That was when she began to have doubts about the man. Doubts turned into anxiety when instead of going left into the by-pass road he went right. They wouldn't reach the A1 that way; they'd get to the moor road instead.

'We're going the wrong way!' she had shouted so he would hear her above the noise of the radio. 'You should have turned left.'

'I know a short cut this way,' he shouted back, almost blasting her ear drums.

'Not this way. We'll get lost in the fog,' she

had argued.

'I wouldn't mind being lost with you, lass. It'll be nice and cosy in here till morning.'

Carla had felt a prickle of fear run down her spine when he said that. All of a sudden she wanted desperately to be out of this van and back home at Abbot's Fold. They were moving very slowly now and there was not a light to be seen because of the solid lumps of grey fog which were all about them on the narrow road. She knew there would be sheep there munching away at the ling and that if the driver was not careful he might hit one of them.

'Bloody sheep!' he growled as a couple of them lurched so close to their headlights that it seemed he would not be able to miss them. 'Better pull over and stop. Make ourselves comfy in the back.'

Now she was frightened in a way she had never been frightened before. Was this driver one of those who kept a mattress in the back of his van? She had heard plenty of jokes at school about battered vans which had mattresses in the back, but she had never seen one. It was not a subject for joking any more, especially as the van was grinding to a halt. She began to feel sick.

'I don't want to stop here,' she said fiercely.

'You do if I'm going to give you a lift to Manchester,' he told her. 'Come on now, you know your way around or you wouldn't be out hitching a lift in the dark.'

'I'm going to be sick,' she gasped as he cut the engine and switched off the lights.

'I've got some drink in the back. You'll be all right when you've had that,' she heard him say in the moment before she thrust open the door and leapt for the ground.

Then she was running, running, running; stumbling into sheep, feeling a fierce stitch in her side and hearing him start the engine again to follow her. That was when she began to pray as she ran. She prayed as she had prayed when she ran for the school in the area sports day. She prayed as she had prayed when her gran had been ill. She prayed as she had prayed when her mum had been killed. Beyond her prayers she was conscious of the van drawing nearer.

'I'm sorry, God. I shouldn't have run away,' she heard herself say out loud. 'I'm sorry! I'm sorry! I'm sorry! Help me! Please help me!'

Her breath was tearing at her lungs. She couldn't go on. She wanted her dad. She just wanted her dad. Then she saw lights shining out ahead of her, moving lights, a vehicle coming towards her very slowly. She turned her head then and looked back to see if the van was following. With a huge surge of relief she saw that it was unable to follow her because it had run off the road and was standing, lop-sided, in a ditch with a huddle of sheep already gathering about it.

So she was safe. Safe! The enormous relief that swept over her added wings to her feet as she ran on to where the moor road joined the main road. Her legs ached and her ribs hurt, but she knew her way home. A few minutes later she was climbing over the drystone wall that enclosed the back garden of Jacob's Cottage. It was then that she longed to share it all with Julie rather than with her dad.

Julie had been so good to her. Julie had let her cry but had not asked too many questions, only the ones that needed to be asked. Julie had made her a hot drink and cleaned her up a bit then let her sleep on her sofa. Julie wouldn't be there to help her though when she got back tonight and had to face her dad...

'Hi, Carla! You're early...' Josh's voice died away when she turned to face him and he saw her tears. 'Hey, what's hit you?'

She shook her head, fighting to hang on to her composure as she rubbed at her eyes. Because any minute now the Nyddford Crawler would grind to a halt here and she would have to get on board with everyone on it seeing the state she was in.

'Was it your dad?' Josh wanted to know. 'Did you get it wrong with him again?'

Again she shook her head. 'It was my own

fault,' she whispered. 'I was the one who got it wrong.'

'How?' Josh asked as the ancient school bus appeared.

'I'll tell you later, after school,' she muttered before she climbed aboard and squashed into a seat next to the window at the front. The vehicle was already half-full but Josh was able to sit beside her as it chugged away to pick up more Nyddford High pupils at the next hamlet.

'Tell me now,' Josh insisted.

'I can't. It's too grotty. It's the pits.'

'You could still tell me. I thought we shared everything?'

'Not this! Not now! I wish I didn't have to go to school. We'll be late anyway because of the fog. I think I'll get off at the stop before school and go to my gran instead.'

'Your gran won't like it. She'll probably make you go anyway,' Josh pointed out as they set off again after picking up more students.

'I'll chance it,' she decided. 'I don't feel well. I feel sick.'

She felt even more unwell as the old bus began to descend the steep hill into Nyddford, taking the hairpin bends cautiously, hampered by the dense fog. Carla was feeling so ill by then that she never saw the ewe with twin lambs following that ambled out into the road on the last tight bend. Josh saw

361

the animals in the moment that the bus driver swerved to miss them. Both he and Carla heard the tortured sound of metal meeting dry-stone wall as he flung his arms round Carla and shielded her with his body as debris flew all about them. Then there was silence.

'What shall we discuss first, wedding music or honeymoons?' Bill murmured to Andrea when they came down to earth at the end of their long, rapturous reunion at Beckside.

'Breakfast!' Andrea said. 'I'm starving.'

'I'll cook,' Bill insisted. 'You sit and catch up on the early news. There's the newspaper or the radio.'

'I'll settle for the radio.'

Andrea felt wonderfully relaxed and blissfully happy as she leaned back on one of the pine chairs in Bill's kitchen and stroked Lucky's ears. Her tiredness was forgotten as she let the background music blend with the spit of grilling bacon. Lucky began to sniff the delicious aroma and lick his lips. It would be like this every day when she and Bill were married, sharing breakfast and the radio before the post or the telephone broke in to disturb their peace. She had no meetings on this morning, and no sick visiting to do, so she would be able to have a leisurely breakfast before going out with Bill and Lucky for some fresh air and exercise. There would be no moorland views today, with the fog still masking the scenery and deadening the birdsong, but it wouldn't matter because she and Bill would be together. That was all that mattered.

'It's not much of a morning for dog-walking, my lad,' Bill said to Lucky when the dog made his way to the back door after they had all finished their hearty breakfasts. 'But I suppose we'll have to go. Would you rather go home and get some rest, darling?' he asked Andrea. 'You must be very tired, since you've been up half the night.'

Andrea did not answer, even though she was already on her feet.

'I said would you rather—'

'Listen!' She turned up the volume on the radio as she spoke.

Bill frowned. 'What is it, love? What's wrong?'

'It's one of the school buses that picks up for Nyddford High. There's been an accident on Nyddford Hill. Some of the children are trapped. I must go there at once!'

As the words were leaving her mouth she was making for the door, grabbing her fleece jacket and her bag as she went.

'I'll come with you,' Bill said. 'We'll go in my car.'

Dr Grantley had departed, leaving a prescription which he had assured them would put Jack right in a couple of days. There was a bug going around, he said, that was very unpleasant but not serious. Jack was asleep now and did not want breakfast, so Julie was cooking for only herself and Dave.

'We'll talk when we've eaten,' Dave said when she put a loaded plate before him.

'We'll talk when I've been to Nyddford to get the prescription,' she told him, quickly cutting into her bacon.

'What about your move?' he wanted to know.

'We'll talk about that later. There isn't time now.'

She was making toast when her mobile sounded. Dave watched her, loving the grace and neatness of her; thinking how right it was that she should be here in his home on this day. So far he had not had the chance to show her how much he loved her, with young Jack needing the doctor, but there would be time later. He would make sure there was.

'Dave,' she was slipping the mobile back in her pocket. The glow had gone from her face. It was white and strained now. 'I have to go. I'm needed. There's been an accident. The school bus. At the top of Nyddford Hill.'

'Oh God! Carla!' His heart seemed to stop, then to belt on furiously. His hands felt clammy.

'They don't know how bad it is yet, but we've been asked to report to the Cottage Hospital. You'll have to stay here with Jack, but I'll ring you when there's more news.'

She was leaving him then, racing out of the kitchen, across the yard, into the cottage and out again at once to jump into her car. Dave leapt to his feet to go and open the yard gates for her. He gave her an intent look and a wave, but all Julie's attention was on the journey ahead of her through the unrelenting fog to Nyddford Cottage Hospital.

Dave closed the gates after her and went back into the house, ignoring the faithful Tyke for once. His shoulders sagged, his chin dropped, he put his head on to his hands and wept as he faced up to what might have happened to his daughter. Shame flooded him as he recalled some of the things he had said to her. He had lost sight of the fact that Carla was only sixteen and had no mother to support her. He had expected too much of her, more than she was able to cope with, and now he might never get the chance to put things right.

'Dear God, give me another chance,' he muttered into the empty room.

Dorothy and Ben were enjoying a leisurely breakfast when the phone rang. Matt had breakfasted earlier and gone to start his work in the farm transport office. They were pleased he was going to stay on and become a partner in the business. Though Dorothy was still feeling uneasy about the attention Matt was paying to Julie. There was something ominous about the fact that Julie was buying this house in Nyddford, and that Matt was talking of moving out of Ford House and into a place of his own. Was he going to move in with Julie, she wondered?

Dave was so morose again these days; so short-tempered with Carla and so unwelcoming to the nice American boy whose father was a teacher at Nyddford High School. Dorothy had tried to talk to him about it, but her son would not listen.

'You'll drive her away from home if you don't give her a bit more freedom to come and go like other young girls do,' she had warned.

'I have to be mother as well as father to her, and I don't seem to have time to do that with things as they are in farming these days,' Dave had argued.

'You should think about getting married again,' his mother had suggested. Then regretted it almost at once when she saw the thunderous look on his face.

'Who'll take me on? A man of forty with a farm that can't pay its way any more. They'd have to be out of their minds!' Dave had protested.

'Farming has been through bad times before and recovered,' she had pointed out. 'In our early days it was my teaching salary that helped your father and me to keep the farm going. Most women are pleased to keep on with their jobs today. Especially if they are in something like teaching or nursing where the hours can fit in with family life...'

'You're wasting your time, Mother,' he had broken in. 'Let's talk about something else...'

She had been thinking back over that conversation while Ben was reading his *Yorkshire Post* and she was finishing her coffee. It was Julie's moving day today and she had invited her to come to Ford House for her evening meal once the removal was over. The sound of the phone ringing out in the hall broke into her musing. She hurried to answer it.

'Can you come over, Ma, right away,' Dave said before she was able to say anything. He sounded as if he had been crying. 'I need someone to be with Jack.'

'What's wrong, is he ill?' Alarm began to flutter in her chest.

'Yes, and there's been an accident to the school bus. Carla's on it. Come as quick as you can, please!' Dave begged.

'I'll come right away,' Dorothy said as she put down the phone.

'What is it, love?' Ben wanted to know. 'It sounds like trouble.'

'It is. The school bus has been in an accident. Carla's on it. Dave wants me to go and be with Jack because he's not well.'

'We'll both go,' Ben said. 'Right away!'

Twenty-Two

Andrea was glad to have Bill doing the driving as they left Nyddbeck behind and began the long, slow ascent of Abbot's Hill. All her earlier elation had evaporated, to be replaced by fear of what they would find when they reached the scene of the accident. They did not speak as Bill's high-powered vehicle crawled through one dense patch of fog after another, with only brief respites when trees, stone wall or road-side cottages suddenly appeared through the gloom.

All Andrea's concentration was given to the silent prayers which mingled with anxiety about the safety of the young people who would not today be reaching Nyddford High School on time. Some of them would be known to her: the sons and daughters of church families, members of the junior church, of the drama group. Young people like Carla, and Josh.

Her heart lurched with fear when imagination carried her thoughts to what would happen at Abbot's Fold Farm if a fresh tragedy engulfed David Bramley. Yet there was nothing she could do about it. The accident had happened. Questions would come later, and answers would not be available for all of them. Andrea knew that from her own personal tragedies. She also knew from her own experience that good things could come as a result of pain and grief, so she must pray that something better would follow here.

All she could do now, as flashes of blue and orange light broke through the gloom to signal the presence of emergency vehicles at the site of the accident, was to give comfort to those who needed it. The first of those, she soon discovered, was Carla. Andrea held out her arms to the girl whose face was streaked with tears and blood and tried to make sense of what she was saying. It was not easy.

'I wanted to go with Josh, but they wouldn't let me. I *have* to see him! I need to tell him...' The rest was lost in sobs.

'Where is he?' Andrea handed a tissue to the girl as she spoke.

'They've taken him away and they would not let me go with him.'

'I expect they needed the space in the ambulance for the others who've been hurt,' Andrea said quietly. 'You'll be able to visit him later.'

Would Carla be able to see Josh later?

How badly had he been hurt? There was no way she could find out yet. At least, though, she could let Dave know that Carla was safe. If he had heard on the radio about the accident he would be frantic. A new thought hit Andrea then. Had Jack also been on the school bus this morning? She must find out at once.

'Carla,' she said urgently. 'What about Jack? Was he on the bus?'

'Jack?' Bewilderment sounded in the girl's voice. 'Why are you worrying about him?'

'Was he on the bus?' Andrea said again, louder this time.

'No. He was still in bed when I left. He said he felt poorly, but it might just have been that he didn't want to go to school.'

'I'm going to ring your dad on my mobile and let him know you're all right,' Andrea told her.

'I'm not all right! I want to see Josh! I want to know if he's all right. He might not be because he put his arms round me and pushed me out of the way when all the glass started falling in on us.' As she said that Carla began to sob again.

'Dave, it's Andrea. I'm calling to let you know that Carla's safe.' As the words were leaving her mouth, Andrea heard his groan of relief.

'Thank God! I was so frightened. Julie told me about the crash when she was called to the hospital. Thanks a lot, Andrea. You'll never know how grateful I am.'

'I'll bring her home as soon as I can,' Andrea broke in. She was anxious to know what else she could do to help the rescue workers.

By now the emergency exit at the rear of the bus had been opened and a stream of children came pouring out. Some were crying, some were silent with shock, some were full of bravado. Some were still neatly dressed in school shirts and ties, some had clothing disarranged during their struggle through the damaged vehicle, some showed grazes or small cuts on faces and hands. Andrea stood by to speak to them while the paramedics dealt with those who had been at the front of the bus. It was an immense relief to her when she was given the information that apart from Josh and the bus driver there were only superficial cuts and bruises to be treated, though all the children would be checked over and treated for shock at the hospital. Another coach was already on the way to transport them there.

'Can I go with you, Andrea?' Carla begged tearfully. 'I want to see Josh before I go home.'

So Andrea sat in the back of Bill's car with her and held her hand as they made the final mile of the journey into the market town. One of the first people they saw there was

Julie, brisk and efficient in her uniform but cheerful too. She was able to lift Carla's spirits when she told her that Josh was conscious and at present being treated for his injuries.

'It looks like a broken arm and some nasty cuts to his head, but nothing too serious. So why don't you let Andrea take you home? You'll only be in the way here, and your dad will be very worried about you,' she said.

'Can't I see Josh, please!'

'Not just now. You'll be able to come in at visiting time this evening. I'll bring you,' Julie promised.

'But you're moving out today,' Carla remembered.

Julie laughed. 'So I am! I'd forgotten about that, with all the excitement of your bus coming to grief. I expect I'll still manage to give you a lift though.'

'I need to thank Josh for shielding me from all the broken glass. He was brilliant.'

Andrea and Julie smiled at one another. 'You can tell him tonight. For now, it's home to your dad. He'll be very pleased to see you,' Andrea told her.

Carla remembered something else then. Her lips wobbled as she spoke of it. 'Dad will be real mad with me, won't he, Julie? For last night, I mean.'

Andrea wondered what mischief Dave's daughter had indulged in then, but was wise enough not to ask. Obviously Julie knew all about it.

Julie looked seriously at the girl, and took her time about answering. 'I think your dad will be so glad to see you safely home that he'll have forgotten about last night. The same doesn't go for me though, Carla. I haven't forgotten, but I will if you promise me there won't be any repeat performances of what you did last night.' She paused, then added, 'Promise?'

Carla nodded. 'Yes. I promise. I'm sorry for all the hassle I gave you.'

'I'll see you later. I've got work to do now.'

With that, Julie hurried away to help with the checking over of the boys and girls who had just arrived on the replacement coach. Andrea tucked her arm into Carla's and led her out to the car park, where Bill was waiting for them.

When Dorothy and Ben reached Abbot's Fold Farm, going the long way round because the shorter way was blocked by the crashed bus and the emergency vehicles, they found Dorothy's son at the open door of the back porch peering anxiously out into the fog.

'Carla's not hurt, just shocked,' he told them as they were getting out of their car. 'Andrea rang to tell me, and to say she'd bring her home as soon as possible.'

374

Dorothy shivered. 'What an awful experience for the poor girl. It can't have been very pleasant for Andrea either,' she added.

Ben agreed. 'It must have brought back memories of when her husband's car came to grief on the day of her ordination. Though of course she wouldn't see that as it took place miles away from here.'

'Come inside and have a hot drink,' Dave said. He remembered Ben's recent serious illness and felt guilty for keeping them out in the chill of the foggy yard. They both looked shattered after hearing news of the accident and having to make the journey from Ford House in such appalling weather conditions.

'I'll go and take a look at Jack,' Dorothy said when they were in the kitchen. She made her way to the hall and then up the stairs of her old home to her grandson's bedroom.

Jack was sitting up in bed, wide-eyed and alert. 'What's happened to our Carla, Gran?' he wanted to know. 'It said on the radio that there was an accident with the bus.'

'Yes, there was, but Carla's not hurt. Julie's going to bring her home soon.'

Jack sighed deeply. 'I wish Julie wasn't leaving. I wanted her to stay here.' His bottom lip quivered as he said that.

Dorothy sighed too. 'She can't stay in the

cottage because there are people coming who've booked it for a holiday.'

'I don't feel well,' Jack said then.

'You'll feel better when you've had some of your medicine, love,' his gran tried to comfort him. 'Shall I go and get you some fruit juice?'

Jack did not answer. She was turning away, heading for the door when he spoke again, and what he said stopped her.

'Why was Dad crying downstairs?' His eyes were large and full of fear.

How could she answer that? Why was David crying? Was it because of the accident? Had he realized at last, when it might have been too late, that he was being too hard on his daughter?

'I don't know, love,' she had to admit, 'but he's fine again now. He's just making us some coffee.'

They were still there in the kitchen when Andrea and Bill brought Carla home. Dorothy, who was preparing vegetables at the sink, found her eyes filling with tears when she saw Carla. This was not the lively, lovely girl who was always ready to challenge the system and fight against the rules. This was a vulnerable young girl who had been through a traumatic experience and had not yet recovered from it. There was no sparkle in the large blue eyes today; they were dull with pain and weariness. The blonde hair was in a tangle about her shoulders and damp from exposure to the fog. Her cheeks still showed evidence of where she had wiped tears away with grimy fingers.

'Sit down and have some coffee, love,' said her gran, as grandmothers do when they can't think of anything else to say that will not set their own emotions into overspill. Carla sat, but did not speak.

Andrea followed her into the room and moved to give Dorothy a quick hug. 'Everything's going to be all right,' she murmured. 'Josh was hurt, so they're keeping him in hospital for a day or two. Julie's going to take Carla in to see him tonight.'

Dorothy frowned. 'I thought she was moving out of the cottage today?'

'She was; perhaps she still is, but when the bus crashed she was called in to the hospital as part of the emergency team in case there were a lot of casualties. Fortunately there were not, so I don't think she'll need to stay there long.'

As she spoke, Bill was greeting Dave, who had belatedly been trying to catch up on his early morning chores about the farm. They came into the house together, Bill to seat himself on the old sofa beside Andrea, Dave to go and look down at his daughter. There was moisture in his eyes as he spoke to her, and a hand reaching out to her shoulder.

'Are you sure you're all right, love? Shall I

give the doctor a ring and ask him to come back?' he asked her.

Carla was in control of herself now, though still subdued. 'No, I don't need the doctor. I just need Josh to get better,' she whispered.

'We should be getting in touch with his mother to see if she needs any help,' Dorothy broke in. 'I'm sure they'll know what's happened by now.'

'Josh's dad would know almost as soon as it happened, with him teaching at Nyddford High,' Andrea said. 'I expect they'll be at the hospital now. They're sure to let you know when there's some news, Carla.'

'If it hadn't been for Josh I'd have been hurt.' Carla shuddered as she recalled the moment when the ominous thud and crunch of metal hitting stone had made the whole front of the bus crumple and brought a shower of debris down on the front-seat pasengers and the driver. 'Josh flung himself over me, and it all hit him.'

Dave, listening to her words, felt shame creeping over him. This was the lad he had forbidden her to see; the lad he had been afraid would harm his daughter. Once again, he had got it wrong!

Dorothy was making tea in a big brown pot. 'You'd best have a drink while you're in here, son,' she said. 'We're going to be a bit late with dinner today.'

Bill got to his feet and drew Andrea up to stand beside him. 'We'll be on our way now, if there's nothing we can do to help you?' He looked round at them all, and saw the relief that was only just beginning to take over from fear and anxiety.

'Won't you stay and have something to eat with us?' Dorothy asked.

Bill smiled. 'No, thanks, Dorothy. We've got a busy day ahead of us, haven't we, darling?' His arm was about Andrea's shoulder as he spoke. 'We have to discuss wedding music and honeymoon trips, don't we?'

This brought Dorothy rushing across the kitchen to embrace them both. It brought Ben to his feet to add his own congratulations. Dave was still gazing at the pair of them as though bemused. Carla was on her feet by then, looking from one to the other of them with a reluctant smile just beginning to lighten her face.

'I'm glad, Andrea,' she said softly. 'Really, really glad. I'm glad it's Bill you're going to marry, because you'll be able to stay here instead of moving away like you would if you married anyone else. People have to get on with their lives, don't they? Even after something really bad has happened to them.'

All of them in the room knew what she meant. Even Dave knew. He was still hearing her words in his mind after Andrea and

Bill had left and his mother was about to put the dinner on the table.

'Don't bother with mine; I'll have it later,' he said as his ears picked up the familiar sound of Julie's car stopping at the farm gate.

The air was full of the collies' barking as he strode out into the yard, peering through the mist that still hung about even though the sun was fighting to overcome it. He met Julie as she got out from the driving seat to open the gate. He opened it for her and waited for her to drive through to park outside the cottage. Then he followed her. As she got out of the car again he spoke, pouring out the words before he could lose his courage.

'Don't go, Julie. Please don't go! I want you to stay here. To marry me, if you like, as soon as you like.'

Julie turned to face him. Her brown eyes were full of sadness; weariness was etched on her face. 'Not now, Dave,' she said. 'It's not the right time.'

'What do you mean?'

She rubbed her eyes. 'I mean we need to talk about it properly, when neither of us is in an emotional state.'

Dave's heart lurched. 'Does that mean you're going today, after all?'

Julie nodded. 'Yes, Dave. I have to go. I've got the house all ready to move in, there are only my few things here to move.'

'Is it because of him? Matt Harper?'

She shook her head. 'No. He doesn't come into it.'

'Then why?'

Julie took a deep breath, knowing that she must make him understand all that was in her mind; all that was worrying her. It had to be said, for both their sakes, even if she didn't want to say it and Dave didn't want to hear it.

'Before I agree to marry you, or to move in with you, Dave, you need to be able to accept that I'll be going on with my nursing. I was reminded, when I was called out this morning to help at the hospital, that you had difficulty in coming to terms with Jill going back to nursing when the children went to school. I feel as Jill did, that my work is as important as yours. You would have to accept that, if I married you.'

Dave frowned. 'But the children are not small now,' he pointed out.

'Carla and Jack are not, but we might have other children and we could have problems then.'

'I thought you loved me...'

'I do, but I love my career too. It's important to me. If you love me, you'll try to accept that.'

'I do love you. I don't want you to go.'

'I'll have to go, the van will be here at one

to move my things, and it's nearly that now.'

'You'll come back?' he pleaded.

'I'll come back tonight. I promised to take Carla to the hospital to see Josh.'

Dave sighed. 'When you bring her back, will you stay and have supper with me, Julie?'

Julie smiled. 'Yes, I will.'

He reached out to take her hands in his own, and try to persuade her to stay on, but the barking of Tyke and Brack when the van came to remove her personal things to the little house in Nyddford cut short his words.

At Beckside, Bill was opening wine, Andrea was taking food from Bill's deep freeze, and Lucky was moving from one to the other of them happily waving his red-gold tail. They had spoken of their plans over the phone to Andrea's parents and arranged to pay them a quick visit before Bill's television filming began. They had decided on a date in early August and a ceremony in the little church at Nyddbeck which had played such a major part in their love story. They would live in the manse, but Bill would continue to have his studio and gallery here at Beckside.

'What do you think to the idea of having a celebration party here, darling?' Andrea asked as Bill poured the wine. 'We could do that at short notice and invite Alexander before he moves on to his next location.'

Bill grinned as he put down the bottle and took her into his arms. 'It could be a good idea,' he said. 'But right now all I want to do is keep you all to myself and make up for all those weeks when we were apart.'

Andrea looked back for only a moment on those long weeks of separation, and the shorter time of misunderstanding which had followed. Yesterday's pain was behind them now. It was time to look forward to tomorrow's promise: the life they would share, the work they would carry on together, the days of joy and the nights of love. Later, her work would claim her, but for now all she wanted was Bill.

She reached up to put her arms about his neck and moved her mouth to meet his.